Hannah

Intrepid Wayúu

Romantic Adventures

AN ILLUSTRATED NOVEL
IN THREE VOLUMES

BALAM ABELLO

VOL. 1

Florida • 2013

Disclaimer: This book is a work of fiction. Names, characters, places and events are either products of the author's imagination or are used fictitiously. Any resemblance to actual events, locales or persons, living or dead, is entirely coincidental.

All trademarks mentioned in the text are the property of their respective owners. This book, its author and its publisher are independent of any product, vendor, company, or person mentioned in this book.

None of the information presented in this book, should be construed as fact: Not medical, legal, financial or any other kind of professional advice.

Published by Balam Abello
Fort Lauderdale, Florida
balamabello.com

FIRST EDITION
FIRST PRINTING: March 2013
PRINT REVISION: 5TH

Library of Congress Control Number: 2012921029
ISBN-13: 978-0-9885806-0-2
ISBN-10: 0988580608

Cover by Kairo & Balam Abello
Illustrations by Balam Abello
Design by Balam Abello

Printed in the United States of America

To my daughter Carmen Isabela and my dear friend Hannah.
They have been a constant source of inspiration.
Always remembering our happy, beautiful
and magical spring day, in Venezuela.

CONTENTS

PREFACE

This book project started many years ago, inspired by Hannah, a dear friend of mine and some of her character traits and experiences. However, after having worked on it for only a couple of months, I shelved the project for many years. About a year ago and influenced by a friend, who had published his own autobiographical work, I picked the project back up again and ran with it till the end. Fortunately, there were good notes and even an outline to guide me through it.

Originally, this novel was intended as an e-book only. Therefore, I used a dialog technique, which departs from modern English usage. Specifically, the use of em-dashes vis-à-vis quotation marks. However, this technique is still widely used today, in continental European languages. It is my believe, it makes it easier to follow on e-readers.

Additionally, I made extensive use of computer technologies, which have proven critical for editing. For example, Text-to-Speech (TTS) has allowed me to edit the material so that, if successful, it sounds almost like the spoken word. The intent being, the use of TTS facilities provided by many of today's e-readers; in essence it should sound like an audio book.

The e-book version and the printed paperback version are identical in almost every respect, except for the illustrations. There are no illustrations on the e-book version. As of this writing and as far as I know, image placement control is not readily available on e-readers, which tend to dynamically format book's contents, thus, altering their layouts. For this reason, I believe that re-sized and misplaced illustrations would detract from the reading enjoyment, on an e-reader.

On the other hand, after doing some research, it seems that illustrations on an adult or "young adult", (YA) printed fiction books, are a welcome bonus, which may enhance the overall reading pleasure. Yes, I understand many people prefer not to have them and to an extent, I do see their point of view. Nevertheless, we live in a world immersed in multimedia imagery, so I asked myself, why not use this resource too?

The novel utilizes an eclectic image-illustration style. But then again, the novel is a bit eclectic, itself. Some images take after cartoons, with their respective speech balloons; some are computer generated composites; and some are digitally retouched and enhanced photographs. Although, we could be tempted to think that because the novel makes use of illustrations, it is a children's book, however, this book is not. It is intended for adult and YA audiences, alike.

This is the first volume of a trilogy in which we witness the development of the main characters, i.e. their family backgrounds, growing up, moving through their teen years and some of their romantic and entangled adventures, which go hand in hand with it. There is, however, a parallel story line which may appear to be unrelated to the main story. Nevertheless, there are in fact many similarities and this shouldn't surprise us because growing up, in general, entails such likenesses. Although there is closure on most salient scenes in the novel, there are definite arcs or bridges left to connect them to future installments.

Lastly, the writing style makes moderate to heavy usage of interjections and onomatopoeia, to give it an informal, light and hopefully, a fun read.

Thank you and enjoy the book!

Balam Abello
Fort Lauderdale, 2012

ACKNOWLEDGEMENTS

I thank the many people who helped directly or indirectly with the book, in areas such as: reviewing the manuscript, checking translations, evaluating the artwork, acting as photography models, affording valuable criticism and above all, providing Open Source, Creative Commons and GPL licensed image sources, as a basis for all derivative work used throughout the book's illustrations: *Please see bibliography.*

In particular, I mention Antonio, Carmen, Hannah, Elyka, Tito, Keith, Kim, Alexandra, Clara, Laura, Anneke, Jeanne, Pierre, Pina, Carlos, Lily, Ana Maria, Asad, Kairo and lastly, to my dear book publicist, Maria Eugenia, amongst many others.

PROLOGUE

—Why did she ruin my life?

—Did she wake up one day and *Poof!* ... said: «*Today I'll find a man, and I'll break his heart just for the hell of it?*»

—Was it ruined? Or was it freed from an otherwise dreadfully monotonous life?

—Looking back to that fateful evening when I saw her at the grocery store, while staring but not seeing, numbed by the strong fluorescent lights and walking like an aimless zombie from isle to isle ... I should have guessed it.

—I mean ... after all, it was prominently displayed all over her attractive yet smartly disguised breasts, which lay bare under an unpretentious dark-military-olive-green long T-shirt, posing as a scanty revealing miniskirt, a thin black snake-leather-belt loosely held over her daring hips, glam bold red lipstick, posh ruby red anklet, stiletto high-heel-shoes and *Bang!* ... announcing in large gold-glittering-letters on her chest ... *TROUBLE!*

WERE WILL YOU TAKE ME NOW, MY WINGED FRIEND???

Hannah

Intrepid Wayúu

CHAPTER 1

HANNAH ENJOYED HER MOMENTS OF SOLITUDE, WHERE THE seashore and the sharp edge cliffs meet, a place faraway from all the noisy tourist traps. She preferred those secluded places where the natural beauty of massive boulders protruding from the black streaks of hot sand, on top of which, she would sometimes stand on, barefooted, with her arms extended like the wings of a seagull, and defying the strong wind blowing her dirty-blonde-hair, ocean surf spraying on her skin and cooling off her tall, gracious, slender and sun-drenched body. A place where she would soak up the bright colours, the wild life, the sounds and energies of massive waves, when they deafeningly came crashing down on the rocks, while at the same time, scouting the endless blue horizon.

It was during these moments of intense inspiration, her wild imagination would fly away riding on Pegasus, the winged horse, heading towards strange and foreign-new-lands and far, far, far away from her native Colombia.

—«*I feel as if I'm flying with my wings stretched out, and barely soaring over the flat and smooth-as-a-mirror, bright, sunny and shiny emerald green seas. My shadow reflects on the ocean's surface, and whilst I look forward accelerating faster and faster and faster and travelling at dizzying speeds, I discover the coasts of Africa and then Europe.*»

Perhaps she felt the angst of the adventurer's blood in her veins, a streak which she probably inherited from her German born father. Or could it simply be she was influenced by the mythical stories, she had so often heard from her stunningly and engaging mother, *Jaséle,* whose name sounds like *Gazelle;* a native princess of great beauty, for whom the years had been so incredibly kind?

Although her father's name was Wolfgang Loewe, she went by her mother's maiden name, Miranda, in accordance with the matriarchal customs of the *Wayúu,* which is pronounced like the words, *"way"* and *"you"*, put together.

The *Wayúu,* are a vibrant Amerindian ethnic called *Arawaks.* They are children of sand, sun and wind; humble craftsmen, fishermen, farmers, traders and brave fighters. Originally, they lived in the Amazon Basin dating back to 500 BC. Currently, they inhabit *La Guajira Peninsula,* which is located on the border between northeastern Colombia, and northwestern Venezuela, on the Caribbean Sea. Today, there is an estimated population of over three hundred thousand inhabitants, organized into about thirty clans. Each of these clans is represented by its own animal totem. They wear beautiful, colourful and embroidered clothes, which they fashion themselves and export as well. The latter contrast the wilderness of the arid, harsh and desolate desert on the northern part of the peninsula; thus, making the *Wayúu,* a race of tough, tenacious, enduring and at times, heroic people.

For the umpteenth time Wolfgang tried to convince Jaséle and said:

—*Hey!* Honey...
—Tell me, my love —said Jaséle.
—How many years have we lived together as husband and wife?
—Nearly ten years, my dear —said Jaséle.
—Don't we have a beautiful daughter ... little Hannah?
—Yes, that's true, my love!
—Jaséle ... don't you think it is high time we get married?
Sighing with an air of sadness, Jaséle replied:
—*Oh, my love!* ... You know that's what I want most, in the whole world.
—Yes, I know.
—But my father protests strenuously ...
—I know that too, because you have told me at least, a dozen times —said Wolfgang.
—... and the last time I discussed it with him he was furious, threatened me and didn't speak to me for months —said Jaséle.
—*Oh boy!* ... He is so stubborn! —said Wolfgang.
—Yes, he is, honey, but ...
—Doesn't he realize the harm he is causing you and the little one? —said Wolfgang visibly exasperated.
—Wolfgang, what can I tell you, my love?
—*Ugh!* ... Why is your father so stubborn?
—*Oh, darling* ... don't get upset, my love —begged Jaséle.
—You know, I try to be understanding but ...
—But perhaps in due time he will change his mind.
—Jaséle, I simply doubt it.
—Besides, what's important is that you and I love each other ... isn't it? —said Jaséle.
—*Good lord!* ... You know darn well my job is dangerous.
—Yes, I know, darling.
—So then ... what gives?
—Wolfgang, I ...

—What would happen to you and Hannah if I were to have an accident? —asked Wolfgang.

—*Oh, honey*, I'm so sorry —said Jasέle.

—Your father's objections seem antiquated and selfish.

Jaséle had tears in her eyes. Feeling a deep anguish in the pit of her stomach, as well as frustration and sorrow, she said:

—I understand, my love, I understand, I understand ... and ... and ... and I'm sorry ... I'm truly sorry....

On many occasions, Wolfgang tried to convince *Jaséle Omüin Miranda* to marry him, so she could enjoy all the benefits she was entitled to, by virtue of his German citizenship. But inevitably, she always rejected his offer. Not because she didn't love him but because her father, an important *Pütchipü,* Chief, or head of a group of *Wayúu* clans located on the northern part of *La Guajira Peninsula,* denied her his consent. On the contrary, indignant, the Chief always reminded her, she should have married one of her own. As far as the *Wayúu's* were concerned, Wolfgang was a non-person, a ghost because he had no relatives. Therefore, Jaséle's union was egregiously injurious to their traditions.

Meanwhile, *Hannah Isabela Miranda* thought her parent's love was kept alive, precisely because of this arrangement. This forged an early impression on her, which played an important role in her many, and somewhat carefree and adventurous entangled love affairs, throughout her life.

The indomitable attraction, vitality and beauty of Hannah were manifested at an early age. She was the product of the potent combination of dominant genes from her father's side, a strong and tall-blond-blue-eyed northern European man, and the recessive ones from her mother's side, who was a native *Wayúu* princess. Jaséle was slender, had exquisite fair-to-light olive skin, shiny and silky long-jet-black-hair, snow-white-perfect-teeth, full sensual lips and delicate facial features, including large almond eyes, which make us think of a Polynesian Venus.

CHAPTER 2

WOLFGANG, A PROFESSIONAL DIVER, CAME TO VENEZUELA, in the early 1980s, seeking fortune working for several oil companies located in Lake Maracaibo. True to the adventurer in him, he quickly befriended the locals and began exploring surrounding regions.

Half a mile south of the great *General Rafael Urdaneta* Bridge, over Lake Maracaibo, on Highway 3, and in the village of Santa Rita, there is a seedy bar called *La Ñapa*. This dive had a few plastic tables and chairs placed on a red-soil dusty concrete floor, overlooking the lake. A rickety electric ceiling fan, which made more noise than the muggy wind it blew, was attached to a steel beam which supported the roof's hot sheets of zinc. An old jukebox was playing depressing Mexican *rancheras'* music with vexation. This side of the lake is extremely hot and humid. But fortunately, a beautiful purple-flower bougainvillea tree, grew alongside this small establishment, cooling it off a bit.

After a hard day's work and in the middle of a hot, damped and suffocating afternoon, Wolfgang and some of his work buddies sat shirtless and sweaty, drinking ice cold beer, smoking and yapping away until well passed sunset. Every so often, Rosa, a salacious, plump and large steamy mulatto waitress who wore a braless Spanish see-through embroidered off-shoulder top, large gold gypsy ear hoops, long sultry curly black hair and no shoes; with a boisterous vulgar laughter, a deep voice and sassy language to keep the boys' hands-off the merchandise, would serve them appetizers: farmer's cheese, sardines in hot sauce, which sometimes were taken out of rusty cans, soda crackers and lots of stale peanuts.

Hermes, a Colombian man from Medellin, called:

—*Hey gringo!*

It was obvious, Wolfgang with his heavy German accent, was not an American; still, they nicknamed him as such, and Hermes yelled:

—Have you heard of *Maicao?*

—*Maicao?* «*Nein!*» No! Why do you ask? —said Wolfgang.

—You don't say.... But tell me, do you like Latin women? —Hermes asked again.

—«*Ja!*» Yes! Sure I like Latinas. They are pretty for sure. —Wolfgang answered, with a gleam in his eyes.

Juan, a Venezuelan man born in Maracaibo, jumped from his seat and *Splat!* he slapped Hermes on his back, interrupted him and shouted:

—*Man, you're so dumb!* Don't you see how big this gringo is? With such huge size, you've got to wonder if he isn't going to kill one of our small women and get into big, big trouble.

Laughing, mocking and teasing the gringo, Hermes continued:

—*Hee-hee!* Well brother, you know, *Maicao* is a small town on the Colombian side, near the Venezuelan border —said Hermes.

—Colombia? —asked Wolfgang.

—Yeah, brother ... and it's chock full of beautiful blonde women —said Hermes.

Juan, irritated at Hermes, again cried out:

—*Baaah!* Don't you pay no attention to him, gringo. In *Maicao,* you'll not see a single blonde woman, *amigo* ... that is, not unless they come out of a hair colouring bottle.

—Then there are no blondes, over there? *Ha-ha-ha!* —said Wolfgang.

—But buddy, if you like small dainty cinnamon-skin Latinas, then, there you'll find aplenty —said Juan.

Wolfgang already realized where the conversation was heading to, so he asked:

—That sounds good, but tell me ... in addition to beautiful women, what else is there in *Maicao?*

—*Gringo,* just about anything you could possibly want. You see, *Maicao* is a duty free zone —said Juan.

—Duty free zone? ... *Wow!* —said Wolfgang.

—There you can buy anything you can think of, such as imported liquor, cigarettes, cameras, electronics, clothing and leather briefcases. In short, a lot of stuff and at really cheap prices too, *amigo* —said Juan.

—*And gringo ...* if you want cocaine, you can buy it there too ... *Bwahaha!* —said Hermes with a huge belly laugh.

As soon as Wolfgang learned there were great opportunities for adventure in this no man's land in the town of *Maicao,* in the nearby *Guajira,* in Colombia, he organized his work schedule so he could spend a whole week vacationing there.

This small border town and free port, is infamous for being home to all sorts of crime and violence, such as: smuggling, drug trafficking, black market, kidnapping, counterfeiting, drunkenness, theft, fights, murders, fast money and even faster women and of course, *Vallenato* music.

Unfortunately, the plight of the *Wayúu* still continues till this day. Even in the 21st Century, the white man is still causing untold hardships to their society, such as poverty, land grabs, force relocations and extreme violence, which relegates the indigenous population to second or third class citizenry and mostly, without any recourse before the law.

However, all these convoluted stories and piecemeal information made it all the more exotic and alluring, in Wolfgang's eyes; hence, this represented a must-see visit. Little did he suspected his life was about to take a sudden leap and a dramatic change in course, when he was completely bewitched, upon encountering Jaséle's otherworldly beauty.

Meanwhile, many years later, Robert would experience similar emotions but with radically different results.

CHAPTER 3

—*Goodness Gracious, Chessie!* —Fred complained to his wife Chelsea.

—What do you want now, Fred?

—How many times have I told you not to discuss politics with Tom?

—Only about a thousand times!

—Don't you see how infuriated he gets when you treat him with contempt? —said Fred.

—*Good grief!* ... Finally ... I thought they'd never leave! —said Chelsea.

—But you and I know that culturally speaking, he is pretty much a nitwit.

—Now tell me something I don't know, will ya? —Chelsea nodded reluctantly.

Being that they had been married for a number of years, by now Fred was accostumed to his wife's temper and at times, poignant conversations and sharp humour. Therefore, he was not going to let his wife's sarcasm distract him, so he carried on:

—And what about Lucy, his wife?

—What about her? —asked Chelsea.

—She sits and sighs not knowing what to do or say ... the poor thing.

—*Aha* ... and why is that my problem? —said Chelsea.

—After all they're our friends and also ...

—And also what, Fred?

—... Tom is one of my best customers!

—*Oh, Fred!* ... Not that again, *pleeease!* —said Chelsea, pretty much annoyed.

—But, Chessie!

—What?

—Next time, could you please try to be nice to them?

—*No!* I cannot, I don't want to, and I won't do it! —cried Chelsea.

—But woman, be reasonable. Just a small change of attitude in you, would be great for my business. Can't you understand something as simple as that? —demanded Fred.

Without trying to hurt his feelings but rather trying to lighten things up a little, Chelsea said:

—*Blah blah blah* ... Calm down my love, or your blood pressure will go through the roof ... *Ha-ha-ha!*

In the eyes of Chelsea Brown, this was yet another excruciating evening with their friends, the Smiths, a simple and uninspiring couple of good manners. However, a somewhat common and dull neighbors, in their small conservative town of Charming Meadows, in the American Midwest. Chelsea thought:

—*«My Goodness! ... Why can't I have a good fight, even if it's only once? Ugh! ... That couple, the Smiths, they are so kind and nice, I think that's about the only thing they are capable of being. They're so friendly, simple and enjoyable that ... I hate them!»*

Fred Brown was perfectly contented to engage in small-talk and inconsequential conversations, sharing the latest town gossip. He disdained controversy, saying it was definitely not good for his business.

With three children, a golden retriever called Mellow, two SUVs, a swimming pool, a huge mortgage, a hardware store, a delivery truck and a strong-headed and stubborn wife to look after, he wasn't about to rock the boat. Although, he did enjoy those finer little-city-folk like things Chelsea would do for him, making him feel comfortable and warm, allover inside. He knew that after such evening's charade was over, she would show up with his slippers, a Cuban cigar and a small glass of fine Portuguese Port wine, so he could relax in their cozy den.

Sometimes, if he was really lucky, she would pull out one of her favorite poetry books and read to him as if he was one of their own children. And for that matter, he was like a child because as he himself admitted, most of these poems he could not even understand. However, Chelsea did not mind that at all.

On this particular autumn evening and after a few cigar puffs, a sip of wine and the rhythmic melodious voice of his wife reading, he quickly fell asleep on his old dark leather chesterfield chair and began to snore. And then the house became exquisitely quiet. With the gentleness of a truly loving wife, Chelsea put out his barely-smoked cigar, for Fred was really not a smoker. She unbuttoned his shirt's collar and since it was a cool evening, she covered him up with a warm deep-red and black Peruvian alpaca blanket. Chelsea told herself:

—*«Bravo! It is a black starry night, tonight; cold and clear as glass. I'll go out for a walk to get some fresh air and perhaps meditate a little. I will bring Mellow along and also, it's a good thing, the children: Robert, Kevin and Kael are spending the night at their cousins'.»*

Fred had met Chelsea, when he went to the East coast, on a business trip to Boston. He was attending a training seminar on a hardware store franchise, he had recently purchased. He met her at a local café and struck it lucky, for although he was a hard working, honest and handsome twenty-eight year old young man from Oklahoma, he was by far, not the most sophisticated lad.

Chelsea was a beautiful young redhead gal with long hair, clear blue eyes, fair skin and freckles. Unlike Fred, she had a feisty, mischievous and mercurial personality. She was sharp, and you could even say somewhat brainy, were it not for her being so passionate, too. She was well educated, artistically inclined and an upper-middle-class Bostonian. She had a Bachelor's degree in Art History and was pursuing a master's degree in Museum Studies, at Tufts University. Although, she was quite aware of the highly competitive nature of such field; nevertheless, she dreamed of becoming a museum curator, somewhere in the Northeastern United States.

Her father, an Anglican vicar, tried to instill in her the love for the arts and the humanities. He introduced her to topics as varied as classical music, literature, plastic arts, opera,

Dinner soirée at Chelsea's parents

history, philosophy, debate and critical thinking amongst many others.

Father, mother and daughter enjoyed the outdoors and boating in particular, especially when sailing in Rhode Island, during the fall. Sometimes these trips took them sailing as far south as Southampton, New York. On one occasion, they attended the Newport Jazz Festival. Chelsea was captivated by the beauty and complexity of these sensual syncopated rhythms of this Afro-American music.

—«*Perhaps someday I will be able to play this kind of music as well!*» —She told herself.

At the precocious age of six, Chelsea seemed to have been cut out to become a concert pianist. She delighted her mother and guests, when father and daughter played light and cheerful piano and violin duets, in their small, intimate and lively dinner soirées or even at formal dinner parties.

Occasionally, her father, full of pride and while boasting a little, would knock on his wine glass with a spoon, *Clink! clink! clink!* announcing to their guests:

—*Ahem, ahem!* ... Your attention, please! And now, we will listen to one of the best and liveliest rendition of *Für Elize,* in all of Boston!

Chelsea, grinning from ear-to-ear from all the attention placed upon her, and poised with the confidence of a professional concert pianist, would perform flawlessly.

One could have never imagined Chelsea and Fred hitting it off so well as to be married within a year, but then, such is love. Before she knew it, at age twenty-five and in the blink of an eye, she was Mrs. Brown and was being carted off to the Midwest, for good.

CHAPTER 4

WOLFGANG COULDN'T HAVE IMAGINED HOW MUCH LOVE he would feel for Hannah, his newly born daughter, who was named after his paternal grandmother. She was a dream baby girl, who was born on the sunny side of the street; namely, with optimism, energy, hope and joy.

Now, we may be wondering how Hannah turned out to look the way that she did. I mean, after all, she didn't much looked like a *Wayúu*. The reason is most likely attributed to her mother, Jaséle, for she was not, strictly speaking, a full blooded *Wayúu,* herself. We can trace her lineage and her maiden name, Miranda, to the northern provinces of the autonomous region of Catalonia, in Spain.

Jaséle, following tradition, was aided by her mother and aunts during the final weeks of her pregnancy. They proved to be indispensable during childbirth, when she gave birth in a squatting position, which they believed prevented tearing. They cut her umbilical cord using a black obsidian rock with an edge as sharp as a razor's edge. Jaséle's mother carefully took the white part of fresh lizard's feces and gently smeared it on the wound to disinfect it.

Jaséle was producing a fair amount of breast milk. However, in order to encourage baby Hannah to latch on and breastfeed, Jaséle's mother wetted her daughter's nipples with brown sugar diluted in water and sure enough, this did the trick. From then on, there was no need for any baby formula.

The first three days after childbirth, Jaséle did not bathe and slept in a *chinchorro,* a kind of mesh-hammock. Jaséle's mother poured fine sand underneath the *chinchorro* to absorb any flows. Throughout the first month, Jaséle was only fed a clear corn *mazamorra,* which is a type of soft corn porridge, and she particularly refrained from eating any meats. During the course of the first two years of her life, Hannah was breastfed, and she slept with her mother, in her *chinchorro,* in accordance with the ways of the *Wayúu.*

Although Wolfgang, the lion, was deeply in love with Jaséle, he just adored his daughter. It was always painful for him to have to leave them for several weeks in a row, to work in the oil fields. But the reward of coming back home to his family, made his anxiety more tolerable.

Wolfgang was humorous, extroverted, fun-loving, outgoing and sociable. He was a physically active man who greatly enjoyed taking Hannah on outdoor expeditions throughout the department of *La Guajira,* with its interesting geography, fauna, flora, and precious and diverse landscapes.

They visited the mountainous region of the *Serranía de Perijá,* which rises nearly 12,000 feet. They backpacked the *Macuira Hills,* which rise to a little over 2,500 feet and are located in the middle of the arid and desert badlands of the northern tip of the peninsula. They enjoyed the view from *Cerro de la Teta,* and *Huesosopo de Rancheria.* Finally, they visited many beaches such as *Manaure,* where there are some ancient salt mines, *Cabo de la Vela,* with its emerald-green beaches, *Bahia Honda, Punta Gallinas, Puerto Estrella, Punta Espada,* and *Castilletes* amongst many others.

On multiple occasions, they spent countless days and nights backpacking, climbing hills, gathering wood to set up campfires, and to prepare hot meals out in the open, riding horses, fishing, sailing, swimming in rivers, lakes, and of course, snorkeling in the sea. Sometimes they slept in the car, at times in tents, or in sleeping bags under the stars. Wolfgang taught Hannah that in order to travel, it was not necessary to spend lots of money. All that was needed was the spirit and a deep desire to do so.

Wolfgang, Jaséle and Hannah went on holiday to the majestic *Sierra Nevada de Santa Marta Mountains,* which reach an altitude of 17,000 feet, and it is located west of *La Guajira Peninsula,* and barely twenty four miles south of the Caribbean coast. Thus, making it the highest coastal mountain region in the world.

It was in the *Sierra Nevada's* where Hannah and Jaséle saw snow for the first time. Although Wolfgang grew up in cold weather, he wasn't a good snow skier. But this didn't stop him, and he tried to teach little Hannah to ski, although, not with much success. On the other hand, Jaséle preferred to watch them while they tumbled downhill on the snow, time and again, from the comfort of their motel-ski-lodge, whilst sipping thick-hot-chocolate, with a little twist of Caribbean rum.

—Hanni, watch me. When you want to stop, place the tips of the skis together as if you were making the letter "V". Let me show you how ... Okay?

—Yes, Daddy ... *Ha-ha-ha!*

—First, I will climb up the slope a little, walking side-by-side like a duck.

—Aha!

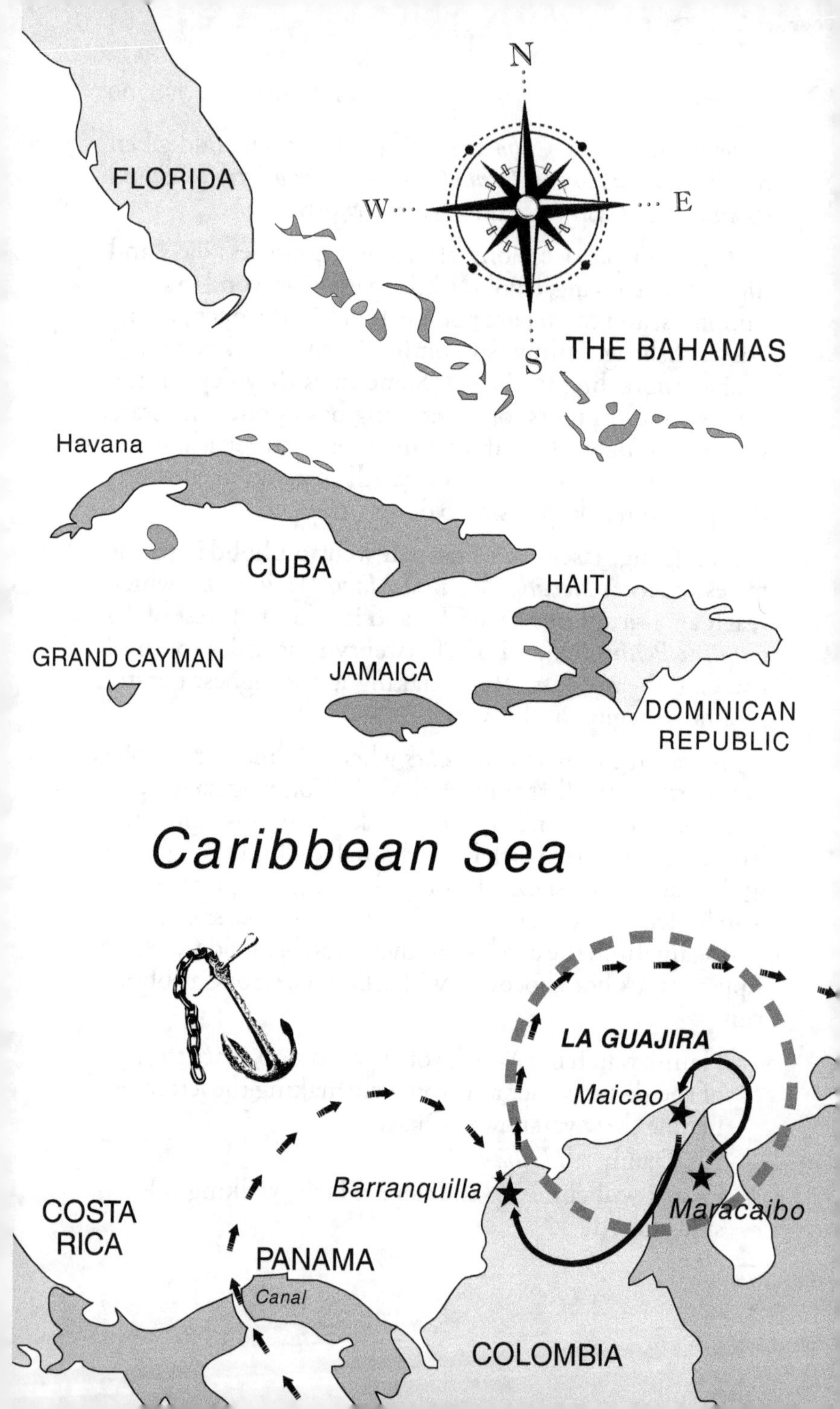

N
W
E
S
FLORIDA
THE BAHAMAS
Havana
CUBA
HAITI
GRAND CAYMAN
JAMAICA
DOMINICAN REPUBLIC
Caribbean Sea
LA GUAJIRA
Maicao
Barranquilla
Maracaibo
COSTA RICA
PANAMA
Canal
COLOMBIA

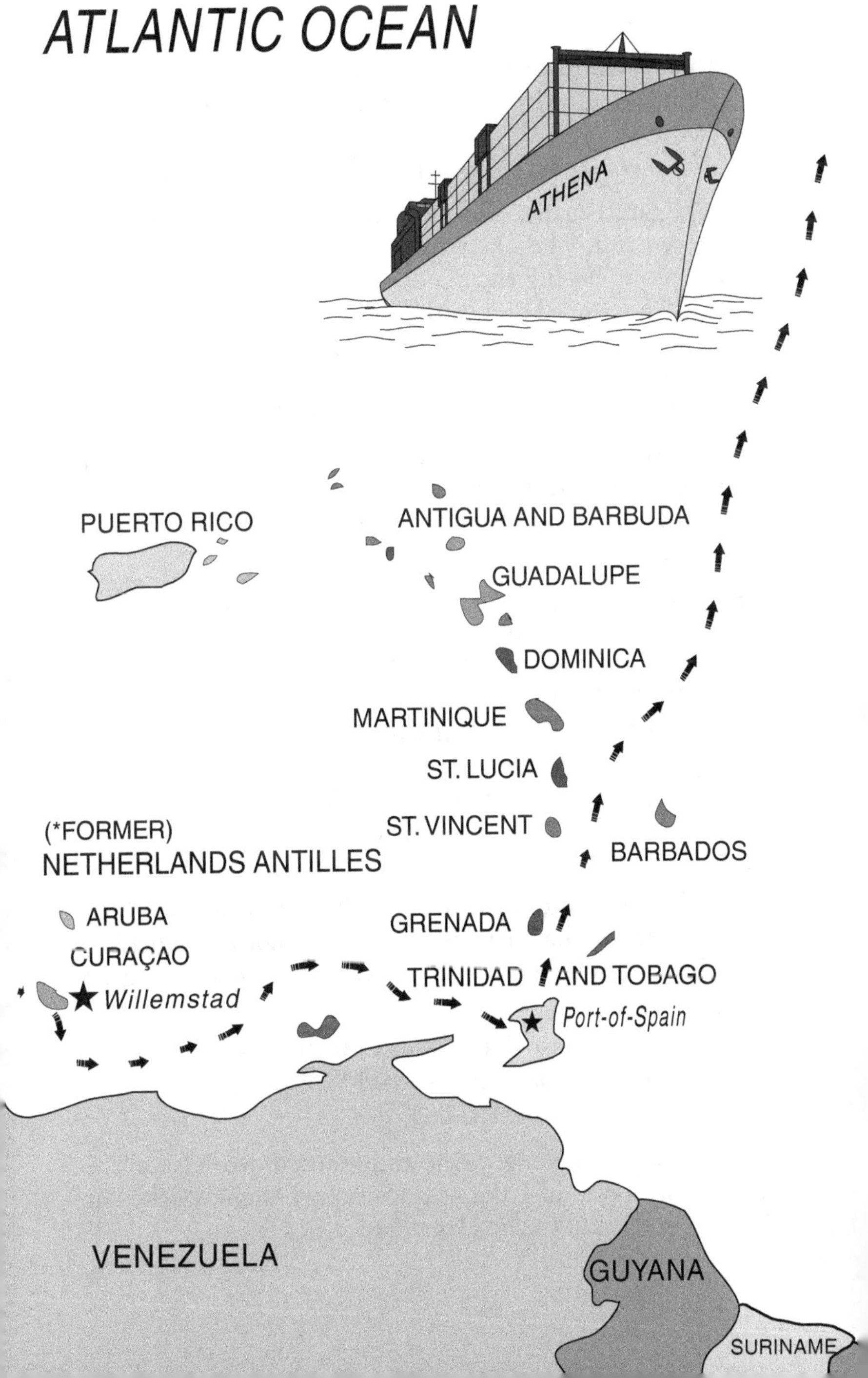

ATLANTIC OCEAN
ATHENA
PUERTO RICO
ANTIGUA AND BARBUDA
GUADALUPE
DOMINICA
MARTINIQUE
ST. LUCIA
ST. VINCENT
BARBADOS
(*FORMER)
NETHERLANDS ANTILLES
ARUBA
CURAÇAO
Willemstad
GRENADA
TRINIDAD AND TOBAGO
Port-of-Spain
VENEZUELA
GUYANA
SURINAME

—Then I will move the ski sideways, like this ... and then I'll follow up with the other ski, as well. Do you see how easy it is?

—*Aha ... Ha-ha-ha!*—said Hannah while having lots of fun.

Wolfgang began to slide downhill. He had barely traveled about ten feet, when he tried to stop using the technique of the plow, closing the tip of the skis. However, his skis jammed, he tripped over, and once again he ended up falling and rolling downhill on the snow. Hannah thought this was all too funny and kept on laughing.

—Daddy, Daddy, Daddy you fell ... *Ha-ha-ha!*

On another occasion, the Loewes were travelling throughout the northern tip of *La Guajira Peninsula,* and when they arrived at the entrance of the *Bay of Portete,* little Hannah asked her dad:

—Daddy, Daddy, Daddy what are those big fans over there? —she said, referring to the *Jepirachi* windmill farm.

—*Aaaah!* ... Those windmills are used to generate electricity —said Wolfgang.

—*Ha-ha-ha! ... Yikes!* And why are they so tall? —asked again the little one.

—Do you remember the sailboat ride we took yesterday in *Cabo de la Vela?*—asked her dad.

—Yeah ...

—Well, these windmills are larger than the sails of the boat, because they have to push an electric motor, a generator, which is way up there. Can you see them? —said Wolfgang.

—Yes, Daddy!

—And look ... just like the sails on the boat, those huge fan-blades are also white —said Wolfgang.

—And why? —asked the little girl.

Recently Wolfgang, Jaséle and Hannah had visited the oil facilities east of Lake Maracaibo, where he worked at. Trying to remind the little one, he asked her:

—Do you remember when I took you to Lake Maracaibo, where your daddy works at?

—*Aha!*—said the girl.

—You asked me why the water was dirty with black oil.

—*Aha* ...

—Well ... The black oil is used to generate electricity too. But it's messy and like you said, the water is awfully dirty —said Wolfgang.

—*Yuck!*—Once again the girl interrupted in disgust.

—Look, my precious one ... these windmills do the same thing, but they do not dirty the water.

—*Ha-ha-ha!* I love those big fans! —Hannah yelled excitedly.

These early experiences formed part of her education; hence, Hannah developed a love of nature to last her a lifetime. Also, this contributed towards making Hannah physically strong and self-reliant; traits which helped her enormously.

On every opportunity he could, Wolfgang spoke to

Hannah in German. But Hannah's pronunciation was not the best, although, it wasn't terrible either. Fortunately, she was still quite young, and if she could be surrounded by people who spoke German all the time, aside from *Frau Moosbrugger,* her private governess, then she would pick it up quickly, become more fluent and speak better German.

Frau Moosbrugger was affiliated to the German School in Barranquilla, which is Colombia's oldest *Deutsche Schule;* founded in 1912. Hannah's grade school education followed the educational methods of *Deutsche Schule.* Thus, it required frequent visits to Barranquilla. This type of education would facilitate the continuity of her *Gymnasium or* high school and college education, back in Germany.

Wolfgang knew that sooner or later, he would have to move with his family to Germany. He thought Hannah would receive a much better education there, and this would definitely prepare her and give her a real fighting chance, to lead a full and abundant life.

CHAPTER 5

MEANWHILE, JASÉLE TRAINED HANNAH WELL. ESPECIALLY when it came to the almost-forgotten customs of the *Wayúu*. She learned to identify plants and herbs for medicinal and therapeutic uses such as *aloe, malambo, tua tua, pringamoza, trupillo* and *dividivi.* She also learned to identify all kinds of wild animals; incidentally, her favorite one's were the brightly coloured exotic birds of the region such as flamingos, toucans, parrots, hummingbirds and macaws amongst many others. Also, little Hannah developed a curiosity for the magical legends of the *Wayúu.*

One day, Hannah came running suddenly, from the gardens in the back of the house. She ran through the hallway, which lead into the kitchen, because her mother was there.

The kitchen was homey, spacious and in the style of the old Spanish colonial homes. The red terra-cotta floors were kept shining, using a mop dampened with diesel or kerosene. The industrial strength stove and oven, were gas-powered.

This kitchen was stocked with all the modern appliances, but these were smartly blended in with the traditional style. In the middle of the room, there stood a large workbench with cabinets underneath. Above it and fastened to the ceiling, was a five foot long black wrought iron rod with hooks; several kinds of pots, pans and cauldrons hung off of it. A large Spanish style window, with a wide sill provided ample light. A long blue Danish patterned-tiles countertop and a glistening white porcelain sink, were located underneath the window. The cabinets for the china, pantries for groceries, spices and a stone oven were on the back wall of this large kitchen, next to the door, which led to the corridor that went into the gardens.

Jaséle was giving instructions to two of her maids about the meals to prepare for the week. Hannah, who was excited, breathless and gasping for air, cried out loud:

—Mommy, Mommy, Mommy ... I cut my finger! *Oh,* Mommy, it really hurts —said Hannah in anguish.

Jaséle, seeing her daughter's anguished face, bent down and quickly examined the wound and saw it was nothing serious, although, it was truly bleeding. She held Hannah's little hand and trying to soothe her, gently said:

—Calm down, honey, and let's see.... Show me that little finger, yes?

The cut was small but somewhat deep and still bleeding. Hannah, rubbing her eyes with her left hand while at the same time, closing the four fingers on her right hand, except her index finger, said:

—*Ouchies!* ... Here, Mommy. Do you see it?

—Yes, my love. Don't you worry because we will heal it, and it'll be fine in a jiffy! —said Jaséle.

Holding Hannah behind her thighs and embracing her, she picked her up and brought her to the kitchen sink. She opened the tap and placed the girl's bleeding finger under the water stream. Blood splattered red, the bottom of the white porcelain sink. Gradually, the water diluted the blood, flowing from red to pink and disappearing into the stainless-steel-chrome-drain-grid. Seeing Hannah absorbed by the way in which the water washed the blood away, Jaséle said:

—And now, let's cure this naughty wound. I want you to pay close attention. Okay, honey?

—Yes, Mommy. Is it going to hurt a lot? —asked the little one, somewhat distressed.

—No, darling, it won't hurt at all. Plus we will cure it in a different manner than what we are used to, and I promise you it'll be fun.

Jaséle took Hannah's thumb, pressed it against her index finger to stop the bleeding, and then she said:

—Now, I want you to squeeze these two little fingers and keep them below the water tap. Could you do that for Mommy? —She asked.

—Yes, Mommy. I can! —said Hannah with pride.

—Sure you can, my sweet daughter! You're so brave, I'll tell your daddy when he comes back home from work.

Turning towards Alma and Yessica, the two young maids who were watching them, she said:

—Alma, please bring me an egg from the refrigerator.

Alma quickly opened the fridge, took a fresh egg and giving it to Jaséle, said:

—Here it is, ma'am.

—Thank you, Alma.

Now turning towards Yessica, Jaséle said:

—Yessica, please go ahead and search through the spice cabinet and bring me a bottle of turmeric or Indian saffron. It's the one containing a fine yellow powder.

Yessica looked in the back of the pantry because there were quite a number of spices and medicinal herbs there. She found a bottle which looked like the one, and showing it to Jaséle from across the kitchen room, she asked:

—Is this it, ma'am?

—Yes, that's the one. Bring it over, please —said Jaséle.

Meanwhile, little Hannah was engrossed with her injury. She watched her fingers under the running water. Her finger was not bleeding anymore. Jaséle turned the tap off, wiped Hannah's finger dry with a clean paper towel, and said:

—My love, this little bottle contains a yellow powder called turmeric. We will put a pinch on your wound. But first, we'll do something fun with the egg ... alright?

—*Yes yes yes, Mommy!* —Hannah replied excitedly because it appeared her mother was going to teach her a new game.

Jaséle sat Hannah on the kitchen countertop. She took the egg and broke it in half and discarded the contents down the drain. She poured water on the eggshells and made sure they were clean. Then she carefully removed the delicate membrane from each of the two shells, while trying not to rip them apart. Now turning towards Hannah, she said:

—Honey, let's put a bit of yellow powder on your little finger's wound, now. Okay?

—Yes, Mommy! —said Hannah.

After applying turmeric powder on the wound, Jaséle took one of the moist membranes, which she had removed from the eggshell, and wrapped the cut on Hannah's finger. She didn't wrap it too tightly because when it got dry, the membrane would shrink and the tightness could cut off blood circulation to the finger. Giving Hannah a kiss on her little finger, Jaséle said:

—*Bravo!* It's finished. What do you think of your new bandage? Do you like it?

—*Ha-ha-ha! Yes!* ... Oh boy ... that was quick, Mommy —said Hannah quite happily, because she felt like she now had a trophy on her little finger.

Finally, seeing Hannah calmed, Jaséle gave her several loud kisses on her cheek, *Mwah! mwah! mwah!* She put her back on the floor, and told her:

—Very well, missy. You can go out and play but try not to dirty your bandage ... Right?

—*Yessss!*—said Hannah while running out of the kitchen, to show off her finger to anyone who came before her.

Many of the things children learn, they learn not at school but at home and this usually happens by imitation. Of course, we have to differentiate between actually really knowing something through and through; in other words, understanding the "*whys*" of something in particular, or simply "getting it", that is, having a general idea of sorts.

Hannah, a precocious girl, understood the importance her mother placed on the responsibilities of running a household. From entertaining, to doing embroidery, to cooking, to caring for the flowers in the garden and to home decoration. Likewise, she was conscious of the importance of the poise and proper way of addressing adults, and in particular the servants, in order to earn their respect. Needless is to say, Hannah enjoyed much more the carefree ways of her father, but never in her recollections did she ever disappoint her mother.

CHAPTER 6

ON THE DAY OF HER BIRTHDAY, WHEN HANNAH TURNED TEN years old, Wolfgang announced he had landed a job on an offshore oil rig, in the North Sea, in Norway. Best of all, it paid exceedingly well. For this reason, he and his family would soon move to the city of Düsseldorf, in Germany. This is where the majority of his relatives lived. It should come as no surprise that Jaséle was quite apprehensive, because they would leave *La Guajira,* her beloved homeland, for the first time in her life. She had no idea what to expect of this complex old world of Europe.

Although Wolfgang had traveled back to Germany, several times over the years since meeting Jaséle, it is not known why she never travelled with him. Jaséle knew that eventually they would have to move to Europe. But she never felt too anxious about it because for some strange reason, she imagined this idea was far, far away into the future. This is the reason why the news took her by surprise, when he said upon his return from his most recent trip, that he had gotten a new job. Furthermore, he had already signed the job agreement. She was even more surprised when he told her he had visited several rental buildings, in search for an apartment, where they could all move to.

As it is to be expected, Jaséle asked Wolfgang a bunch of questions. He tried to reassure her that the move to Germany, would be a good thing for the whole family and especially, for Hannah. But it was the urgency of the trip, which caused her the greatest distress, and she said:

—*Hey, honey!*

—Yes, my dear ... —said Wolfgang.

—I'm worried because of our trip to Germany.

—That's to be expected —said Wolfgang.

—It makes me nervous to think that at least in the beginning, I'll be rather lonely.

—*Oh, my love* ... I can just imagine —said Wolfgang.

—I cannot speak the language, and I have no idea about their customs.

—It is true. Perhaps for a little while that may be so. But we are going to do something about it —said Wolfgang.

—You know I have never lived in cold weather. And besides, I have never, ever, even left *La Guajira*.

—You won't be as alone as you think.

—What do you mean, Wolfgang? —she asked.

—You'll have little Hannah, who speaks German reasonably well.

—That's true.

—She will help you with translations, particularly when you gals go grocery shopping —said Wolfgang.

—I know —she interrupted.

—But more importantly, I already know in which school you'll take German language lessons —he said.

—*Oh yeah?* ... No way!

Wolfgang continued his explanation and said:

—The good news is, I learned there are many Spanish-speaking people taking these courses. You'll be able to talk to them, as well —said Wolfgang.

—Really, honey? You make everything sound so easy. *Oh!* ... But still, I feel so insecure —she insisted.

—*Cheer up!* You know I have many relatives over there.

—Yes I know, honey —said Jaséle.

—They have assured me they'll be watching over you and Hannah; namely, when I am off working in the North Sea —said Wolfgang.

—*Yes!* You had already mentioned them. I'm really dying to meet them; indeed, I would love to meet your whole family!

—*Oh!* ... But getting back to the class thingy ...

—Yes ... what were you saying? —asked Jaséle.

—... I also got the address and phone number of the foreign students' club.

—*Oh,* really?

—Yes, apparently they have a wide variety of interesting activities, including dance parties —said Wolfgang.

Suddenly, Wolfgang changed his facial expression. With melodramatic airs and a serious gesture, because he was about to say something extremely important, and speaking in a deep voice, he said:

—*Aaah, Jaséle* ... there is a serious problem, which I had not spoken to you before.

—*Oh, my God!* You are not serious ... no?

—Well yes, Jaséle ... I'm afraid it's quite serious.

—Darling, you're giving me a fright! —she said.

—What a mess. This is truly awkward ... I don't even know where to begin. *Oh, never mind!* ... Now I will fess up and confess everything to you —said Wolfgang.

Alarmed at Wolfgang's serious conduct, she asked him almost in total panic:

—*Good heavens!* A serious problem, you say ... but what can it be?

—Well you see, Jaséle ... I ... I ... I ...

—*C'mon already!* ... *Oh,* Wolfgang, please don't tell me you have another woman —said Jaséle, visibly distressed.

Polygamy is common amongst the *Wayúu.* And in *La Guajira,* Wolfgang was particularly attractive to local women. On several occasions she had to confront some of her *Wayúu* female friends, who also wanted to be Wolfgang's women. Jaséle could have never imagined he had another woman in Germany.

Wolfgang seeing his wife's anguished face could not contain his laughter any longer. He came up from behind Jaséle, hugged her and while placing his large hands on her breasts, he squeezed them, kissed her neck, and then he whispered in her ear:

—*My gosh, Jaséle!* ... Look here ...

—But tell me once and for all! —she said, forcefully.

—... the grave problem is ... you're just too beautiful!

—What? Are you kidding me? —said Jaséle in disbelief.

—Jaséle, I'm sure you'll have many suitors in Germany. And they will not stop from trying to win your love!

Wolfgang, trying to appeal to Jaséle's sense of compassion, and changing the tone of his voice like that of a pouting child, continued:

—*Tis not fair!* ... And how can I prevent someone from winning you over?

Although Wolfgang was making a joke of it all, he was correct. Once they were living in Germany, their roles would reverse. He would be just another plain bloke while Jaséle's beauty would excel even more. In other words, Wolfgang also felt insecure, and because they were not married, this made him feel even worse.

Jaséle struggled and broke away from his embrace. She turned around and in a roundabout way, tried to console him, and said:

—But have you gone totally mad, my love?

—*No, no, no!* ... I'm saying the plain truth —Wolfgang insisted.

—But I am only, and will always be yours! —said Jaséle.

She raised her fist in a menacing manner and continued:

—And don't you forget it!

—Forget what? —asked Wolfgang.

—You too, are mine, forever! —said Jaséle.

Jaséle grabbed an enormous pair of scissors from her sewing kit. She wielded them onto Wolfgang's face. She winked and smiled at him a little but avoided a hearty laugh, long enough to say:

—And if you forget it, you'll have to deal with these friends of mine ... *Ha-ha-ha!* —she broke out laughing.

We don't know what Wolfgang had in mind with this whole charade but whatever it was, it worked out. Both of them ended up laughing. Jaséle was calmer now, and her previous anguish was gone in some other direction.

The Loewes sold most of their belongings, including *La Esmeralda,* their beautiful and beloved two-story Spanish hacienda-style home. It had whitewashed arches, terra-cotta floors, inward sloped red-tile-roof, and a large open courtyard with a well in the middle, and a rose garden with a birdbath fountain. Lots of terra-cotta pots with lush-red geranium bunches hung over the whitewashed walls, as is typical with many of the homes in Andalucía, Spain. Not only are the lush-red geraniums gorgeous, especially in contrast to the white walls, but they are excellent natural mosquito repellents. One could also see the walkway throughout the wrought-iron veranda railing, along the entire courtyard's second floor.

La Esmeralda, a Spanish hacienda-style home

The furniture was rustic Spanish colonial, made of black stained thick wood and dark cowhide hand-carved-leather chairs, with hammered-in-bronze-nails, revealing their patina and making it look all too manly, but cozy. This was the perfect setting to invite people to take a nap after a heavy meal and sweltering heat. In those occasions they would always serve a good sangria. *La Esmeralda* was located on a small green hill, on the southeast end of the city, by way of Sixteenth Street.

Nevertheless, the Loewes kept a comfortable two-bedroom apartment, modernly furnished, which overlooked Simon Bolivar's Central Park, in *Maicao*. They would use it, when returning to visit Jaséle's family, in her beloved *Guajira*.

Throughout the years, the Loewes had achieved a financially comfortable life style. After completing all the sales, they managed to raise a good sum of money, which would allow them to have a pleasant start, although not necessarily a lavished one, in the old continent.

CHAPTER 7

AS WE WOULD HAVE EXPECTED, ROBERT WAS DESTINED TO follow in his father's footsteps. He had great admiration and respect for the way in which his father had provided a good life for their family, year after year, without complaints nor regrets. Fred had grown somewhat plumb. He now had rosy cheeks, and his hair had turned prematurely silver-gray. He always had a cheerful disposition about him, and this had a calming effect on most people around him, always placing them at ease. However, although we could be tempted to think his beliefs were somewhat simplistic or perhaps even naive; still, they were no less true.

Robert recalled vividly, the lazy days of summer and the customary fly-fishing trips to the lake, and how his father instructed him on the subtleties of being a business owner. Fred seemed to think these were the perfect moments to prepare young Robert, so he would continue running the family business, after he had retired.

On a cool day of clear-blue-skies during the fall, Robert and his father were standing on some rocks, just few feet from one another, fishing at the edge of the lake. Every now and then they would swing their fishing rods like a whip, making a swift and coordinated but gentle arm and wrist movement, *Swish!* releasing the lure again and again on the calm surface of the lake, in search of trout and rock bass.

—Say, Robert —Fred called his son.

—Yes, Dad.

—The other day Mrs. Slim came to visit me at the shop. Do you know who I mean? —asked Fred.

—Yeah, Dad ... I do remember her since I was a kid. I think she has a card gift shop on Wallace Street. Is it not her?

—Exactly. That's her alright.

—And what did she want, Dad?

—She brought me a blender to return it, but unfortunately, it was no longer under warranty.

—Oh, I see.

—Tell me, Robert.

—Yeah?

—Robert, what do you think I should've done?

It took a while for Robert to respond, and then he said:

—I don't know, Dad. What did you do?

—I took it back of course; even though this would produce a small loss.

Fred was silent for a moment, and then he added:

—Do you know why I did it? —Again he asked his son.

—Well ... probably because she is an old friend of the family. Is it not? —said Robert.

—Son, you have a point. But I also did it in order to create goodwill for our business —explained Fred.

—Dad, what do you mean by goodwill?

Fred pulled the line and lure, and then he whipped it back out gently on to the surface of the lake, once more. He remained silent for a few moments, and then he replied:

—Look, son ... the true worth of a business, is not only what it says on the ledger.

—*Aha!*

—The goodwill our customers feel towards our business, make it worth a heck of a lot more —said Fred.

—And thus, a way of gaining goodwill would be to render a good service to our customers ... no? —said Robert.

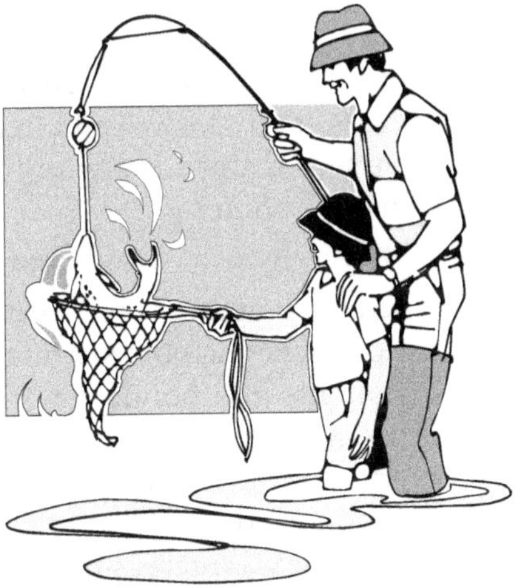

Father and son, fishing

Fred was quite satisfied with Robert's response and said:

—That's right, my son ... that's right.

It had never occurred to Fred that Robert would have liked anything better, than to run their family business. Yet Robert would have ended doing precisely that, were it not for the influence that Chelsea, his mother, exerted on him but from an entirely different angle. Fred emphasized the values of duty, honesty, attention to detail and hard work. Traditional values, which in Fred's mind symbolized the almost immutable and eternal passage of the seasons. Chelsea, on the contrary, insisted on improvisation, art, everything new ... and definitely, on being eclectic and different.

One Saturday afternoon, when there was not much work at his father's hardware store, Robert asked his dad:

—*Hey, Dad* ... I'm curious to know your opinion about something we discussed in history class, in school.

—*Ah,* what is it, Robert? —Fred responded with curiosity because like most teenagers, Robert almost never talked about his school affairs.

—*Aha* ... you see, Dad ... we discussed the difference between success and glory. And after a heated debate; still, I'm not sure if there is any difference at all. Dad, what do you make of it?

—Oh, yes, I see ... —said Fred while stroking his chin.

Fred did not answer immediately. This was not an easy question, so he was going to take a few moments to organize his thoughts and ponder upon them. Suddenly, he had a fleeting idea which made him smile, producing a slight curvature in the corner of his mouth. He didn't know why, but he wondered how Chelsea would have answered the same question. He was pretty sure that whatever her response, this would be emotional, radical and politically incorrect.

Meanwhile, Robert was accustomed to his father's long pauses; although, sometimes this slowness would drive him bananas. But on this day, he had no choice but to wait. Besides, he was in no hurry. Fred coughed to clear up his throat and then he said:

—*Ahem!* Sure ... arguably, the difference between success and glory has to do with the return on investment.

—*Huh?*—cried Robert while getting somewhat exasperated and he continued:

—*Oh c'mon, Dad!* ... I have no idea what you're talking about. Could you explain it to me in plain English, please?

Generally speaking, most people have a frame of reference, a thinking style if you will, which weighs in heavily upon them, influencing their perception of the world around them. Fred was no exception to the rule. And since he had been a businessman all his life, his approach towards problem-solving was, by its very nature, financially driven. Because financial topics tend to be dry and complicated, they usually end up boring us, mere mortals. Without abandoning his entire line of thinking, Fred continued speaking to Robert in terms of investments but from a much lighter perspective, and he said:

—All right then, I have spoken to you about the difference between short-term and long-term investments. Have I not? —asked Fred.

—*C'mon, Dad!* ... You've only repeated it like about a million times —said Robert.

—*Okay*.... Remember I told you that short-term investments are the ones you make when you expect to earn some interest money quickly, usually in less than a year.

—*Aha* ...

—For example, you could lend money to someone, in hopes that he or she, would soon pay the full amount of the loan plus some reasonable interest, which is, your profit.

—*Oh really, Dad?* But what has that got to do with success or glory? —asked Robert again.

Fred, tying up loose ends, said:

—Look, son. Success is like a short-term investment.

—OK ... How's that?

—The person who achieves success enjoys it in his or her own lifetime.

—*Hmmm*.... That sounds logical —said Robert.

—But when the person dies, their success, which is coveted by many, dies with him or her.

—*Ah, I get it.* But what about glory? —Robert interrupted.

—On the other hand, you could say glory is a very, very long term investment and it's almost never achieved during the person's lifetime.

—*Wow!* ... Is that so? —asked Robert.

—Sure it is and unlike success, when the person dies, his or her glory remains. Sometimes this can last for centuries and on rare occasions, for millennia.

Feeling satisfied with his answer, Fred asked:

—Well then, Robert ... what do you think of this?

—I guess if we look at it as such, you could say most people are short-term investors. They're looking to succeed at any cost. Is that right, Dad? —asked Robert.

—That's right. But let me give you a note of caution, son. Don't underestimate how difficult it is to succeed. Could you tell me why this is?

—Could it be because of competition? It seems to me, most people are trying to succeed, all at the same time —said Robert.

—I believe so, Robert. But let me give you a piece of advice.

—*OK* ...

—Look, son. If most people are seeking success then you could conclude that only a handful of them are seeking glory instead, and you'd be right —said Fred.

—*Hmmm* ...

—In other words, the market for glory has less competition —said Fred, pausing.

—*Oh* ... So what you're saying is, there are a lot more opportunities in the market for glory. Isn't it, Dad? —asked Robert.

—Robert, you're right again. But beware.

—Why is that? —asked Robert.

—My son, this is my warning to you —said Fred.

—Dad what is it? —said Robert, most intrigued.

—The path to glory is usually fraught with pain, disappointment and suffering. This is not a path to be chosen and travelled lightly.

—I understand, Dad, I understand ... —said Robert.

—Nevertheless, don't just try to be a man of success. Instead, be a man of value, Robert —concluded Fred.

CHAPTER 8

THE NEWS DID NOT WAIT LONG, AND JASÉLE'S FATHER, THE Chief, learned of his daughter and granddaughter's imminent trip. He had been jealous and quite adamant towards accepting Wolfgang as his son-in-law. However, over the years and after seeing his good nature, the happy-go-lucky attitude and at times boisterous humor, he had a change of heart and eventually grew fond of his unofficial son-in-law. Nonetheless, he was quite steadfast in not showing any kind of approval; lest his reputation as a leader be questioned and tainted by association. The Chief summoned him to a meeting, and asked Wolfgang to come to the northern part of *La Guajira Peninsula,* to discuss a most urgent matter.

—Wolfgang! It would be best if you marry Princess Jaséle, before you all move to Europe.

—Well yes, Chief! —said Wolfgang, completely surprised.

—Therefore, I have decided to give her my consent, and I'll have my people arrange all the wedding preparations at once —said the Chief.

—*Finally and thank God!* It will be a great honor, Chief —replied Wolfgang, extremely elated.

—Alright then ... the wedding will take place during the next full moon.

—*Perfect!* ... What should we do next? —asked Wolfgang.

—I'll see to it that we abide with the ancient traditions of the *Wayúu* and all the requirements demanded by the Colombian authorities —said the Chief.

After a brief pause the Chief continued:

—My son ... it has been a number years since our precious little Hannah was born ...

—That's true, Chief. She just turned ten years old last week.

—... but I need a grandson —said the Chief.

—What is it that you say? ... A grandchild? —said Wolfgang, totally taken aback.

—It is strange for a *Wayúu* princess, to have only one daughter. Would you please think about it?

—And Jaséle, what would she think? —Wolfgang interrupted.

—Jaséle is still of childbearing age.

—Yes, I know that, Chief, but ...

—Now that Hannah is becoming a young lady, Jaséle would benefit from the love and companionship a son could provide her.

—Yes, Chief. I suppose you're right.

—Especially now that the three of you are moving abroad —said the Chief.

Both men knew their women would have an additional level of legal protection, by formalizing Jaséle and Wolfgang's relationship in marriage. Furthermore, in the future, if she chose to, Hannah could apply for her German citizenship.

Nevertheless, although Wolfgang registered Hannah with the German consulate when she was born, and despite the fact she was included in her father's passport so she could travel abroad with him, it was not until years later, while living in Germany, when she finally obtained her German passport and by extension, for the European Union, as well. With it, by not having to deal with visa requirements for most countries, she could easily travel the world over. However, she also carried her Colombian passport, because she never renounced her original citizenship, knowing full well that deep down inside, she would always be a *Wayúu*.

Because the Loewes would be travelling to Europe in just a couple of months, there was not much time left to prepare for the wedding according to tradition.

To the *Wayúu,* there is a sense of reciprocity, which, unlike the beliefs we hold dear in the West, the groom has to pay the future father-in-law a predetermined sum of money, moreover, jewelry and livestock. This is usually done in order to compensate the father-in-law for the many expenses he incurred, throughout the bride's lifetime. These *ápajás* or negotiations may last up to five years, and they are usually conducted by the uncles of the groom, on his behalf.

The *Wayúu* are skilled negotiators, and the Chief, Jaséle's father, was a particularly cunning old fox. Wolfgang had seen him in action, and he knew the Chief was a fearsome opponent and not someone to trifle with. Wolfgang also knew the Chief would drive a hard bargain, and should he be not careful, the Chief would take him to the proverbial cleaners. Therefore, Wolfgang decided to go low in his initial bid, and said:

—Chief, you know I have no relatives here in Colombia.

—Yes, I know that —said the Chief.

—And I have no sheep, goats, cattle or horses either.

—I know that as well —said the Chief.

—At most, all I have is some little emerald stones —said Wolfgang.

—I see ... —said the Chief quite incredulously.

—Well yes, Chief ... they're just a few pebbles, worthless trinkets of no value —said Wolfgang while trying to pull a fast one on the Chief.

The Chief was pacing himself walking up and down the room with his hands clasped behind his back. He was listening to Wolfgang speak while paying a great deal of attention. Seeing that Wolfgang was trying to dupe him, he stopped and asked him point-blank:

—Well then ... what do you propose, Wolfgang?

Wolfgang knew this was the moment of truth. However, he went ahead with his plan and said:

—Chief, would you accept twenty million pesos?

After hearing the offer the Chief stopped cold, turned around and heading towards Wolfgang, waving his arms, yelling and with a melodramatic voice, he shouted:

—Jaséle, your future bride, is a *Wayúu* princess, and your offer does not befit her! ... It is an insult!

—What do you mean? —asked Wolfgang, alarmed.

—*Shame on you!* —said the Chief.

—Chief ... what ... what I meant to say is that ...

—This is totally unacceptable and what's more ...

—*But, Chief ...* —Wolfgang stammered.

—... You offend my ears! —said the Chief furiously.

—*But, Chief* ... I was just —again Wolfgang stammered.

—*Silence!* —Shutting Wolfgang up abruptly and then the Chief continued:

—I know that as a foreigner, you cannot even begin to comprehend the magnificent, sweet, endearing and most precious jewel you're ripping away from my heart!

Pretending a great deal of effort to control his anger, he lowered his voice, approached Wolfgang and grabbing and squeezing his hands tightly, the Chief said:

—Come, come, come now my son. Let me give you a good piece of advice —said the Chief, in a menacing tone.

—Of course, Chief. By all means, please do —said Wolfgang while trying hard to appear genuinely congenial.

—Well then, this is what I propose.

—Yes, Chief. Please ... enlighten me —said Wolfgang.

—I will only accept forty million *pesos*.... Not a penny less, not a penny more!

—*What? Forty million pesos!!!* But, Chief! —cried Wolfgang, crazed at the Chief's extravagant counter offer.

—*Shush!* —Shutting Wolfgang up again and then continuing:

—I will also take possession of those worthless trinkets. I mean your six carat emerald stones. The ones you bought when you visited the *Muzo* mines, in the Province of Boyacá.

—*Oh, well* ... I mean, why not? Would there be anything else, Chief? —said Wolfgang with evident sarcasm.

The Chief simply ignored Wolfgang's comment and said:

—Finally, because you have neither cattle nor horses, I will take your Land Rover too, which will come in handy on the badlands up north —concluded the Chief.

—*Holy smokes, Chief!* —said Wolfgang, beside himself.

—My son, think it over well. That is to say, if you really want to marry Jaséle! —the Chief warned him, sternly.

—*Good heavens, Chief!* ... Is this your final offer?

—That is correct, my future son-in-law. So then, what is your answer? —Once again demanded the Chief, defiantly.

Wolfgang ran a quick mental tally and was astonished, surprised and frazzled to discover that his price ceiling of ten thousand American US dollars, was surpassed by another thirty thousand! And in the midst of all of these surreal negotiations, he thought:

—*«This is insane. For this kind of money, I could buy me ten new wives!»*

But coming back to reality and for all the unimaginable love he had for Jaséle, let alone for Hannah; the countless happy memories; the good life he led amongst the *Wayúu* people; and because he knew he wasn't going to win this one, he chose not to put up a fight any longer and with a handshake, while nodding, he said:

—Very well then ... I agree and so it shall be done. But, Chief... I do have one condition.

—I am listening —said the Chief, without flinching.

—We must hurry because our ship leaves Port Barranquilla, on June 25th.

—*Hmmm* ... June the 25th you say —the Chief muttered.

—This barely gives us six weeks to be ready and only two, to the full moon —said Wolfgang.

—*Aaah, I see ...*

—And this will also be the night of our wedding —said Wolfgang.

—You're correct, my son-in-law.

Wolfgang thought the negotiations were over, but the Chief had one last surprise in hand and said:

—My son, don't you worry about no wedding preparations.

—How is this, Chief?

—My people will take care of everything.

—Thank you, Chief—said Wolfgang, somewhat relieved by what he believed was the Chief's newly found generosity.

—And because we are a humble people, we will make sure the cost of the wedding won't be too expensive or too onerous for you —said the Chief, calmed as if this was just business as usual.

—*No way, Chief!* ... How much more will it cost me? —asked Wolfgang incredulous and visibly livid.

—Calm down, my son!

Wolfgang and Jaséle on their wedding day

—*Chief!* How much more will it cost me? —cried Wolfgang.

—As you can imagine, the wedding of a *Wayúu* princess is not an everyday occurrence ...

—*Aha!* ... and that would be how much? —asked Wolfgang again, sarcastically.

—... so we will have an open house celebration for those who wish to attend —said the Chief.

—An open house, Chief? ... Here in *Maicao?*

—And what exactly do you mean by that, Wolfgang?

—These people are party animals, and they'll drink up a fortune in liquor! —Wolfgang complained angrily.

—My son, don't you worry too much about it.

—What? You ask me not to worry? It is me the one who has to pay for the whole enchilada ... you know!

—We will only invite members of the clans, but as you know, the vast majority of them live too far away, and they are too poor to even own an automobile. So chances are they won't come.

—And is that it, Chief?

—No! ... We will also invite the mayor, his family and perhaps an occasional prominent family or two —said the Chief.

Astounded at the Chief's bargaining prowess, he feared that if he were to stay there any longer, the Chief would leave him out on the streets because of more unexpected expenses to come. He bowed, bid his goodbyes to the Chief and shot out the door back to *Maicao*.

One week before the wedding and following the traditions of the *Wayúu,* Jaséle went into seclusion. They placed her into a room where she could see no one. Not even her mother, father or daughter. At the end of the week and for the wedding day, they cut her hair, dressed her up with a precious white wedding gown but with no makeup, in the *Wayúu* style. Either way, Jaséle looked beautiful, radiant and particularly glorious.

CHAPTER 9

TRUE TO HIS WORD AND AS THE CHIEF HAD PROMISED, NO expenses were spared ... *Ouch!* The wedding was a great success. A write-up about the wedding and subsequent Loewe's party, appeared in the society pages of *La Guajira,* a major newspaper in the city of Riohacha, the capital of the province. The party lasted well into the next morning, with a fairly popular band from the southern city of Valledupar, playing the sensual Vallenato music, drinking lots of liquor, eating gobs of food, wild dancing, joking, boisterous laughter and in short, a good-old-time.

Wolfgang, in a feverish state of happiness, perhaps because he was extremely drunk due to all the rum he had consumed, or simply because it was his wedding night, in all the excitement and trying to overcome the loudness of the band; the inebriated boisterous people who enjoyed themselves eating copious amounts of *chivo asado* in *Friche,* a *Wayúu* dish of roasted goat and beef with bones and offal fried with lots of salt; eating shrimp-rice and beef sticks;

drinking whiskey, rum, *aguardiente* or moonshine, wine, beer and *Ujolu*, which is a fermented corn chicha; and while raising his glass, he shouted to his father-in-law, who was sitting on the far side of the courtyard:

—Here is to you, Chief. And because I am paying for all of this stuff, let's go whole hog and have a blast of a party ... «*¡Que viva la fiesta!*» ... *Ho-ho-ho!*

Jaséle's mother approached Wolfgang, carrying a strong alcoholic chicha.

—Wolfgang, my son ... come here and drink this chicha, which I prepared myself. It'll bring you good luck tonight —she said while smiling sheepishly.

—Sure, mother. Let me try it —said Wolfgang.

—You'll like it, I'm sure. And it will also light the fires of love on your wedding night, and who knows ... maybe we'll get a grandson too? *Heh-heh-heh!*

Although Wolfgang had chicha many times before, this one had a different flavor. It was bitter, highly fermented, and he could detect the taste of cinnamon, hot pepper and a dash of dark chocolate too. He drank this chicha all night. As the night wore on, with the humidity and the hypnotic cadence of the music, things began to look blurry, and he started to hallucinate, until he passed out.

Jaséle would need the help of several men to carry Wolfgang's heavy body upstairs to the second floor, into the bedroom and finally, onto their bed. Amid the drunken stupor, Wolfgang quickly lost consciousness and went into the phantasmagoric world of deep sleep. It took Jaséle time and a lot of effort to undress her husband. And since she could not take off his shirt because it was drenched in sweat, she shredded it with a pair of scissors and laughed out loud when thinking:

—*«If he finds out his brand new shirt would end up as a cleaning rag, after wearing it only once, he will kill me!»*

A learned man's heart, whose learning is deep, seldom sings with joy

—*The Havamal*

The *laapüt* or dreams play an important role in the lives of the *Wayúu*. These form part of the magical world through which they sometimes communicate with their ancestors. The interpretation of dreams is a common activity. But you must tell these dreams to your family, as soon as you wake up and while they are still fresh on your mind.

Hannah was born with the ability to have these vivid dreams, but, in full colour. And this gift would accompany her throughout her life. In many cases, these would play a critical role for her, especially when making important decisions.

However, Wolfgang's dreams were often different from those dreams which were more common amongst the *Wayúu*.

That night Wolfgang had a long string of vivid dreams, two of which he would recall the next day. These dreams were likely influenced by Old Norse sagas, which were told to him by his great-grandmother *Svana,* during childhood.

He dreamt of a beautiful half-naked young woman of fair skin and long-black-hair, riding on a black Arabian thoroughbred while brandishing a long, sharp and shiny sword in her hand. She was galloping about the endless prairies, hills like an ocean of vibrant small-yellow-spring-flowers, which extended as far as the eye could see, under a deep blue sky, such as he had seen many times before, during his trips to the French region of *La Provence.* Flashes of sunlight beamed on her sword when she struck fast and accurate blows, slicing flowering shrubs of different colours, in her path.

Wolfgang also dreamt of an explorer of the mind. A determined young man, not-so-tall but with curly-black-hair and ocean-sun-burnt-and-tanned-skin. He was riding on the prow of an ancient Viking dragon-sailing-longship, gazing at the stars in a moonless night and scanning the horizon while gliding on a deep black sea. And most peculiarly, he could see under the light of the smoking-oil-lamps, piles of thick worn out leather-bound-books, thrown about the deck floors.

CHAPTER 10

BARELY AN HOUR HAD PASSED WHEN WOLFGANG WOKE UP from his dreams, in a feverish stupor. He was sweaty, his eyes squinting, blinking and trying to get his bearings in a room filled with flickering candles, strewn along the walls, and the sensual *cumbia* music playing in the background.

As Jaséle's mother had warned him, he was now on fire, hungry and thirsty for love. He was correct when he noticed the chicha he had been drinking all night was somewhat bitter. What he didn't know is that it was laced with a fair amount of Spanish-fly powder. Jaséle's mother didn't actually collect the insects in order to make the potion. The difference between making an aphrodisiac or a poison is miniscule. Instead, she had gotten it from a local pharmacy, which in turn imported it, of all places, from Germany.

Jaséle, like a trembling gazelle, lay naked on her side and was staring at him with her large-glossy-dark-almond-shaped eyes, just a few inches away from him. The glow of the candle lights behind this demigoddess, cast a perfect silhouette, voiced by the delicate curvature of her hips, revealing the faint reflections of the flames on her silky cinnamon skin, when it rose and fell almost imperceptibly, tuned to the rhythms of her breath, foreshadowing the rapture and magical splendor of her intimate mound of Venus.

—«*¡Mi lobito!*» ... Darling!—she whispered with a seductive voice. She called him *"little wolf"* in their intimacy.

—*Grrr...!* Wouldn't you like to have a baby lion cub?

Wolfgang was still a bit dazed, but he could swear he was being set up. In other words, he was the subject of a family plot: the chicha, the full moon and an exuberant and irresistible woman by his side. But he had no time to entertain these thoughts because as soon as they entered his mind, they escaped and faded away almost instantly, given Jaséle's forceful advances and extreme provocations, which made her even more stunningly attractive, arousing, tempting and especially divine.

—*Aaaaah!* ... My sweet husband.... My *lobito*, do you know what I liked about you the first time I saw you?

—«*Ich weiß nicht, meine Liebe*» I don't know, my love.

—Well ... our men are not quite tall; instead, they are rather short, and you looked like a huge castle towering over all the heads around you, like a giant Viking!

—«*Das war doch klar*» Of course.... *Ha-ha-ha!* —he interrupted.

—*But gee, honey* ... when I quietly caught sight of your eyes up close, I realized, despite your impressive and intimidating figure, you were just another tender, joyful and perhaps playful little boy!

—«*Was Du nicht sagst*» You're joking! —Wolfgang interrupted again.

Jaséle, ignoring all his babbling in German and laughing at him, continued:

Jaséle, like a trembling gazelle, lay naked on her side

—So I asked myself ... Could I conquer and tame this Nordic giant? ... *Ha-ha-ha!*

But being that things are not always what they seem, in bed, Jaséle was not demure, delicate, and the quiet and respectable lady you would have dared say. On the contrary, she was now a wild cat, a panther stalking her prey, and ready to pounce and fight. She was deliberately arousing fierce passions in her new-official-husband, so he would possess her ardently and to give herself in, completely, once more.

She extended her right hand towards Wolfgang's face, and although he thought she was going to caress it, instead, she latched hard on to his left cheek with her thumb and index fingers. She pressed, pulled and inflicted a sharp pain when she pinched him. More surprised by Jaséle's untoward behavior than anything else, Wolfgang shrieked:

—*Ouch! Jaséle ...* You want to fight, don't you? *Grrr...!*

Jaséle was visibly exasperated and while looking defiantly at him, she placed her hands around Wolfgang's mane and ears, seized his head and shook him forcefully. Seconds later, she violently shoved him back onto his pillow and with the back of her delicate hand, she slapped him, *Splat!* and shouted:

—*Oh c'mon, Wolfgang* ... So what? ... Isn't your wife going to get passionately loved on her wedding night?

Adrenaline was now rushing throughout Wolfgang's veins and getting him ready for battle; with saliva overflowing his mouth, heart pumping, pounding heavily and beating like a drum. With his strong arms and large paws, he reached for her waist and took Jaséle and pulled her hard towards him, as if she was as light as a feather and pressed her tightly against his chest. He leaned his head over her neck, almost, as if ready to strike her jugular. His long, tangled and sweaty blonde mane fell on her face. He panted, moaned and babbled while kissing Jaséle's delicate neck, wildly and repeatedly.

Wolfgang entered into action, and while he made love to Jaséle with total abandon, he growled in his native tongue:

—«*Mein Liebling, nichts auf der Welt ist so süß und zauberhaft wie Du es bist!*» My darling, delicious and sweet love!

Jaséle, as if floating on huge ocean waves, reached multiple intense-and-sustained-orgasms, in a row. Blood rushing to her face lighting it fire red, with her eyes closed, tongue-tip caressing and wetting her dry lips, she was bobbing her head gently from side to side while moaning, panting and sighting, too. Her mind entered a deliciously sensual hallucinatory state, *Mmm... mmm... Oooh... Aaah... yesss!* ... Now she felt she was floating on a coloured brightly-lit-sea: oranges, wild reds, yellow chrysanthemums, emerald greens and blue pastels where wave after wave moved rhythmically and rushed towards the shore, crashing loudly on the sand, and quickly spreading its thick-crisp and crackling white foam.

Wolfgang placed his huge paw behind her, holding her under her back, pressing her tightly against him, deeply immersed in pleasure and while feeling the great magic of

Like waves crashing loudly on the beach

the burning passion between the two of them, he could not contain himself any longer and exploded. Once again the lion had conquered and raising his torso over his prey ... *He roared!*

For a brief moment, the wild crowd at the party stopped, stood still and became silent. They all turned their heads and eyes towards the second floor verandah, and looked through the black wrought iron railing, where they could get a glimpse of the Loewe's bedroom door, because they thought they had actually heard the sound of a roar.

Intrigued, they looked at one another. A few seconds later, the crowd erupted in hysterical laughter and the party continued unabated and relentlessly, till well pass daybreak.

Then it was time to give all the guests, the musicians and the help, a good-hearty-breakfast to try to sober them up, before they were emphatically thrown out into the street, to get the hell back home.

They served more *Friche*, coconut rice with shrimp, roasted iguana, fried turtle rice, fish soup, *cruzado,* which is a mixed lamb soup in a coconut *mojito* sauce and minced fish, heavily seasoned with spices. They also served cassava, white corn muffin, fried sweet plantains, pork, cheese, *perico* or scrambled eggs with lots of onion and tomatoes, strong black coffee. And for those diehard-party-animals, *Iguaraya* or cactus fruit wine, and more beer to wash it all down.

CHAPTER 11

CHELSEA ENGAGED HER ELDEST SON ROBERT, WITH A BARRAge of unconventional ideas, including her flaming liberal leanings, stimulating his sense of wonder and adventure. Like her father had done with her in her youth, she took every opportunity she could, to appeal and influence Robert's artistic sensibilities.

She was particularly ecstatic when Robert started to learn to play tenor Sax, which could eventually bring Jazz to the Brown's home.

—Tell me, Robert ...

—Yes, Mom ...

—Did I ever tell you I went to the Newport Jazz Festival once? —asked Chelsea.

—*Oh really, Mom?* ... That's so cool. And did Dad liked it? —asked Robert.

—*Oh, no!* ... That was long before I met your father.

—And who participated in the festival? Was there anyone famous? —asked Robert.

—If I'm not mistaken, I think Miles Davis performed that year.
—That's way so cool, Mom —said Robert.
—It was truly incredible —said Chelsea.
—Yes, Mom. I can imagine.
—And Robert, to think you want to learn to play the saxophone.
—*Ah, Mom ...*
—That's fantastic! —said Chelsea.
—*Whoa, Mom ...* Don't get your hopes up too high.
—And why, Robert, shouldn't I get my hopes up?
—It's because this instrument is difficult to play ...
—Robert, I know you can do it. Have a little faith in yourself!
—... and to be honest, Mom, I don't know how far I'll get with it —said Robert.

But Chelsea was really beyond herself when she learned that Robert was learning to speak Spanish, and that he had enrolled in every single Spanish class he could take in school. Robert was so enthusiastic about it, he even became a member of the Foreign Languages Student Club.

Meanwhile, Fred thought his son's desire to learn a language, which neither he nor his wife spoke, was more attributable to Maria, the beautiful daughter of a Mexican migrant worker, who was also a sophomore at John F. Kennedy's High School, which was Robert's school. Nevertheless, Fred also thought that being able to speak Spanish would allow Robert to communicate with many of his clients, who were migrant farm workers and who came to his hardware store often. And this, was definitely good for business.

Incidentally, this was the topic of conversation between Chelsea and Fred while the two of them were laying comfortably in bed, sitting with their backs resting onto a bunch of down-feather fluffy pillows, against the headboard, at bedtime. Chelsea was reading a novel, while Fred was leafing through the Wall Street Journal.

Chelsea, definitely had something in her mind, so she started the conversation and said:

—Fred, darling ...

—Yes?

—Did you know Robert is taking Spanish lessons in school?

—Yes, dear. I think he made a comment about it, but to be honest, I didn't pay much attention to him —said Fred.

—*Ugh!* ... Why am I not surprised?

—*Oh c'mon, darling* ... I suppose that's a good thing, right?

—What do you mean, Fred?

—Well, after all, many of my customers, only speak Spanish.

—*Oh c'mon, Fred!* You're always talking about your business.

—And what, pray tell, do you suppose I should talk about?

—Did you ever wonder what the real reason is?

—The reason for what, my dear? —asked Fred feigning ignorance.

Chelsea was beginning to lose her patience with Fred and with a voice which showed she was irritated, she said:

—Good heavens, Fred Brown! ... How can you be so clueless? It's your son, you know!

—Which one? You realize we have three, right? —said Fred, mocking her a bit.

—*Argh!* Who do you think we're talking about? —Irritated, complained Chelsea.

—I suppose I don't have a choice, Chessie ...

—What are you talking about?

—... 'cause I know, you'll tell me anyways ... *Ha-ha-ha!*

—*Pshaw, Fred!* ... I'm talking about your son Robert ... Do you understand? Robert, Robert, Robert!

—You see, I told you so.

—*Heavens, Fred!* ... Do you want to kill me?

—Okay, Okay, Okay ... calm down, my love!

Fred stopped reading the newspaper, dropped it on his lap and looking over the edge of his reading glasses, turned to look at Chelsea directly into her eyes. With an air of triumph, because he knew exactly what she was talking about, and with great pomposity, he asked her:

—Maria! ... You mean, Maria del Carmen ... don't you?

Chelsea felt as if she was struck by lightning, *Skratboom!* And immediately she realized her husband was pulling her leg and was teasing her, by pretending not to know a thing. She slammed her book shut, dropped it on the bed and acting like someone who is ready to fight and play around too. She grabbed a pillow and smacked Fred over the head, *Ploff!* while at the same time she scolded him, and said:

—You're a pig, and I will kill you ... Yes, I'm going to ring your neck!

Chelsea jumped all over Fred. She put her hands around his neck to strangle him, but what she did instead was to take her revenge by tickling him, mercilessly.

—Calm, calm, calm down ... *Ha-ha-ha!* —Fred laughed.

—Admit it and say you are guilty!

—I'm guilty, guilty, guilty ... *Ho-ho-ho!*

—Fred, I'll give you what you deserve ... *Hee-hee!*

—Have mercy, woman ... I beg you, have mercy on me, Chessie ... *Ho-ho-ho!*

—There will be no mercy for you ... Take that! —said Chelsea tickling him something fierce.

Fred appeared to want her to stop, but he was really excited and enjoying his wife's fiery *oomph* and playful disposition.

—Do you give up? *Ha-ha-ha!* ... Do you give up, my big Teddy bear? —asked Chelsea.

—Yes, yes, yes ... I surrender, my love. I give up, Chessie ... *Ho-ho-ho!*

—Are you sure?

—Yes, yes, yes ... No more, no more ... Please, Chessie —said Fred, nearly exhausted.

In the midst of all their laughter and bustle, Chelsea began to kiss him again and again, and while she kissed him she muttered, moaned and said:

—*Mwah, mwah, mwah!* ... Come here, my Teddy bear. I feel hot and playful.... I will smother you with my kisses ... *Mwah, mwah ... mwah!*

On any other occasion, Fred would have surrendered to Chelsea's advances but not this time. Although he felt randy, he also felt frisky and was determined to raise the temperature a heck of a lot more. He knew Chelsea was extremely ticklish; this was "*her Achilles' heel*". She could not bear it for more than a second. He began to tickle her and said:

—*Oh, no* ... my dear, Chessie.

—*Oh, no?* What do you mean by that, my Teddy bear?

—Now it's my turn!

—*Freeeeed!* ... What are you thinking about?

—*Muahaha!* ... What's good for the gander is good for the goose too! —said Fred with a devious look and a malicious laughter.

—*Noooo, Fred!* ... If it's what I'm thinking ... don't you dare!

Chelsea, without considering their children were already in bed, gave a shriek and cried out loud:

—*Whoa, Noooo!* ... *Ha-ha-ha!* ... Please my love, don't, not that ... *Noooo!* ... *Ho-ho-ho!* ... *Ouch!* ... *Noooo!*

Chelsea felt jolts of electricity all over her body, caused by Fred's strong fingers tickling her. She managed to slip away and jumped out of bed, ready to run away while laughing uncontrollably. But if she thought for a moment Fred wasn't going to chase after her, she was sorely mistaken because something else was coming to her.

—*«Let's stop this movie for a moment and imagine the aspect of these two raving-mad lunatics!»*

Fred hated pajamas, so he was wearing large red-hearts boxer undies. He was also wearing a white Italian-style sleeveless undershirt, which accentuated his sizable round figure, or should we say, big-fat-belly? Chelsea was wearing a short-white-lace-negligee. In addition, she was also wearing a rather risky and sexy red-hearts bikini panties, which matched Fred's undies.

—*«OK ... let's run the movie again and continue ...»*

Getting out of bed, lifting his arms up like a great bear and growling, Fred yelled at Chelsea:

—*Grrr...!* Woman, I'll catch you ... *Grrr...!*

—*My God!* ... Fred, are you out of your mind? *Ha-ha-ha! Oh, please, no no no!* Look, I'll pee in my panties —shouted Chelsea.

Fred chased after her when she shot out the door, fleeing towards the dining room, laughing and screaming:

—*Help!* A madman and a pervert is chasing after me ... *Help me please! ... Ha-ha-ha! ... Ho-ho-ho! ... ahh-ha-ha! ...*

—Chessie, I will catch you, woman ... *Ha-ha-ha!*

—Not in a million years, my Teddy bear ... *ahh-ha-ha!*

—*Oh, no?* Come here you, you, you ... *Ho-ho-ho!*

Fred chased after her, and they frolicked in the living room. They took several turns from side to side around the dinner table. They ran into the kitchen and tripped into a small bistro table, and then ran back out towards the living room. Mellow, the golden retriever, began barking and joined the party. *Woof! woof! woof!* ... He caught up with Fred and taking a bite at his boxers, he ripped them up leaving him half naked. Fred was trying frantically to escape Mellow's sharp teeth. In the mean time, Chelsea, in view of this hilarious scene and almost losing her breath, was laughing hysterically, unable to contain herself ... *Ahh-ha-ha! ... Ha-ha-ha! ... Ho-ho-ho! ... Bwahaha! ...*

Amid all the ruckus, they noticed their three son's silhouettes: Robert, Kevin and Kael watching them. They stopped short and gasped heavily for air, when trying to regain their composure and their breath, as well. Fred was still struggling with Mellow. With the one hand he was trying to ward off the dog and with the other one, he was holding on to his boxers, as if for dear life. He yelled at the dog and said:

—*Chiss, chiss* Mellow ... *chiss!* ... Stay, you wild dog!

—*Teehee!* ... *Bwahaha!* —Kevin and Kael laughed.

Robert, the eldest of the three siblings, not being able to hold back his curiosity any longer, interrupted and asked:

—*Whoa!* Mom, Dad ... Am I missing something here?

—Oh, children it's nothing. Your father and I were discussing the business —said Chelsea, trying to keep a straight face.

—*Hee-hee-hee!* —Kael and Kevin laughed again.

—Children, off to bed now! —Fred ordered but also trying hard not to laugh.

After the children returned to their bedrooms, Fred, making a gentlemanly gesture, extended the palm of his hand and pointing towards their bedroom and bowing gracefully, he asked Chelsea to go back in, and said:

—After you, milady!

As soon as Chelsea crossed the threshold to their bedroom, Fred pinched her butt ... *Piff!*

—*Ouch, Fred!* ... Behave! ... *Ha-ha-ha!* —cried Chelsea.

—Hey, Chessie ...

—Yes, what is it, my dear?

—You know ...

—Do I know what, my love? —said Chelsea.

—This conversation isn't over yet ... *Okay?*

—Fred, what the devil are you talking about?

—Maria del Carmen! —said Fred.

—*Oh,* alright, honey ... but now ...

—*Yeeeessss...?* —asked Fred with a mischievous anticipation.

—Don't say anything else and make love to me! —Ordered Chelsea, as the two of them crawled back up under the bedsheets.

CHAPTER 12

THE LOEWES MOVED TO THEIR CONDO IN THE CENTER OF *Maicao,* after handing the keys of *La Esmeralda* to their new owners. They would spend four more weeks in Colombia, before sailing for Port Hamburg, in Germany. Fortunately, most of those bulky belongings, which they would be shipping to Europe, such as: furniture, utensils, books, paintings, crafts of the region, clothes, etc., were already packed, stored in a container, and located at the port's facilities with the shipping company, which would transport them to Germany. This container was scheduled to travel on a different date and on a different ship, than the one they would be travelling on, in their journey to Germany.

—Wolfgang, darling, I don't understand why you want to travel to Europe by boat —said Jaséle.

—How so, honey?

—Wouldn't it be easier and cheaper if we travelled by air? —she asked again.

—Honey, you're correct.

—So then, why? —she asked.

—Yes, it would be easier but as you know, I don't have to report for duty until, well into the fall —said Wolfgang.

—Do you think we'll have enough time to get settled in Düsseldorf? —Jasėle asked again.

—Sure we do, honey. Didn't I tell you the last time I was in Düsseldorf, I spent some time looking for a place for us to live?

—Yes, yes indeed, you did tell me.

—Besides, I thought we could use the boat trip as our honeymoon getaway ... *Ha-ha-ha!* —he said.

—My love, as far as I'm concerned, for the last ten years we have been living in a perpetual honeymoon —she said.

—I'm of the same opinion, my darling —said Wolfgang.

—Well, since now I know you not only like to work at sea, but it seems you also like to travel by it, I'm wondering ... why the heck not? —said Jasėle.

—And don't forget this will also be a great adventure for our little Hannah —said Wolfgang.

—I've never traveled by boat before —said Jasėle.

—I know, darling —he said.

—Do you think I'll get seasick during the voyage? —she asked with some trepidation in her voice.

—Cheer up, honey! These container cargo ships are so huge, I'm sure you won't feel a thing. You'll see.

For a few moments, Jasėle remained pensive. She was gathering her thoughts, because she had important news to give to her husband. But as it happens to many women in similar situations, she was not sure how he would take the news. So she decided to tell him in a casual and roundabout manner.

—Hey, honey ... I forgot to tell you. I have a little surprise for you. Do you want to know what it is?

—A surprise? ... Yes, I like surprises. But beware, I don't like surprises from your father because those are way too expensive! ... *Hee-hee-hee!*

Yes, of course ... Wolfgang was thinking about the cost of the wedding, let alone the recent negotiations with his father-in-law. However, he wouldn't have dreamt of telling Jaséle what had transpired between the two of them. Besides, as far as he was concerned, this was already water under the bridge; something he would just have to chalk up to experience.

However, what Wolfgang didn't know, is that Jaséle was well informed as to what had happen, between him and the Chief. Furthermore, she approved of it, wholeheartedly.

You see, the Chief had no particular interest in the monies for himself. He was a man of humble tastes, needs or wants. Instead, as the «*palabrero*» of the tribe, he was responsible for the well being of the clan. Feeding, clothing, educating and providing health care for his people and especially for the children, was of upmost importance, in his mind. Therefore, the Loewe's contributions to the clan would be put to good use.

—*Oh, Wolfgang!* ... Don't be so nasty!

—*Ha-ha-ha!* ... But it's true! ... *Ho-ho-ho!* —said Wolfgang.

—OK, do you want me to tell you, yes or no? —asked Jaséle, a little exasperated with him.

—Well of course I do! Let's see. What is that surprise I have from my wonderful new wife?

—Well alright then ... You know, I have a feeling Germany, will have a new citizen soon —said Jaséle, finally.

—A new citizen? What are you talking about? I don't get it.

It took some moments for Wolfgang to understand what his wife was trying to tell him. And then, with a big smile on his face, he cried out:

—«*Das ist ja wunderbar!*» That's wonderful! ... *Oh*, my sweetheart. Are you sure about this? —asked Wolfgang visibly excited.

—*Duh!* ... What do you think? ... Yes, of course I'm sure I'm pregnant!

—And how can you be so sure? Did you ask your mother?

Wolfgang asked her, thinking maybe they had some ancient *Wayúu* custom, to determine pregnancy.

—Of course not, my nonsensical hubby ... I don't need to ask my mother —said Jaséle.

—So then ... how can you be so sure? —he asked, incredulously.

—*Ah!* ... But you're such a silly boy, «*mi bobito.*» Nowadays it's pretty easy to tell.

—*Aha?* ... And how is that?

—You just go to the drugstore and buy a pregnancy kit.

—Is that all? —asked he, still doubtful.

—Do you see what it says here? *Pregnant!* —she said while showing him the test results.

—«*Das ist ja fantastisch, ich bin so glücklich!*» That's fantastic! ... You make me so truly happy, my darling.

—Honey, you don't know how delighted it makes me see you so ecstatic. And you cannot imagine how thrilled it makes me feel, too —said Jaséle.

—And did you tell Hannah yet?

—No, I haven't told her anything yet. Still, I thought it would be better if we both told her together. What do you think? —asked Jaséle.

—Yes! Absolutely. We'll both tell her. How about if we tell her when we are already settled in Germany?

—*Brilliant!* ... We'll do that, my dear —she said.

The last few weeks before embarking were frantic. Not only had they to attend many family gatherings and farewell parties, but there was a lot of paper work which they needed to take care of, as well. The most important one was to get Jaséle a new Colombian passport with her new married name: Loewe.

Finally, they managed to obtain it. But not without Wolfgang having to "*grease the machinery*", that is, peddling the traffic of influence or simply put: bribery. The translation and

Carnivals in Barranquilla

legalization of all matters pertaining to Hannah's education, with the German consulate, also took them considerable effort.

Two days before leaving on the boat, the Loewes arrived at the large coastal city of Barranquilla. They stayed in a modern and luxurious hotel called *La Sonesta,* taking one of the rooms on the upper floors, overlooking the grandiose Magdalena River, out in the distance.

Barranquilla, the Golden Gate of Colombia, is a river and a seaport-Caribbean-city with roughly over two million inhabitants, within its metropolitan area. It has a modern and busy seaport, which is the third largest in Colombia. It is located at the mouth of the Magdalena River, the most important economic artery in the whole country; so much so that nearly eighty percent of Colombia's population, lives along the path of this river. The Magdalena River, is more than fifteen hundred kilometers or nine hundred and thirty miles long. From the mouth of the river on the Caribbean Sea, called *Bocas de Ceniza,* up to several tens of kilometers up river, there are many shifting sandbars, and these need constant dredging in order to keep the shipping lanes navigable.

Being a vibrant crossroads in which multiple races and cultures that came from Europe, Africa and the Arab countries converged and mixed; it is festive, colourful and musical. Perhaps it is because of this melting pot that Barranquilla, is well known for its beautiful and sensual women. And this is particularly manifested during the famous Carnival of Barranquilla. In short, this city is an exotic tropical paradise.

—Wolfgang, don't you think this hotel is too expensive for us? —asked Jaséle.

—Jaséle, my love. Do you remember you told me the last ten years have been one giant honeymoon, for the two of us?

—Yes, darling, I remember it —said Jaséle.

—Technically we are newlyweds and in addition, we are about to start a brand new life in Europe.

—*Aha!*

—Let's enjoy our last couple of nights in Colombia, in style. What do you say, honey? —said Wolfgang.

—Okay, sweetie. I guess we only live once ... *Ha-ha-ha!* —said Jaséle.

Hannah was exploring the landscape, looking out the balcony of the spacious and luxurious hotel room. Wolfgang called her:

—«*Hannah, mein Püppchen, wo bist du denn?*» Hannah, my little doll, where are you?

—«*Hier, Papi, auf dem Balkon*» Daddy, I'm on the balcony —said Hannah while entering the bedroom and then she added:

—I can see the harbour from here! Do you want to see it too?

—My princess, I have a better idea. I'm starving and I ...

—«*Du hast immer Hunger, Papa*» You're always hungry, Daddy ... *Ha-ha-ha!*

—Why don't we go down to the cafeteria and wolf down two large banana splits? —asked Wolfgang.

—Yes, yes, yes ... I want to, I want to, I do want that! —said Hannah visibly excited.

—And you, my dear.... Would you care to join us?—Wolfgang asked Jaséle.

—Nope ... I don't think so, honey —said Jaséle.

—*Oh, c'mon!* ... You know it'll do wonders for your figure. What do you say, darling? ... *Ha-ha-ha!*

—*Oh, Wolfgang!* You're always kidding but no.... You two go on ahead and have fun —said Jaséle.

—Honey, are you one hundred percent positive you don't want to join us?

—I'm pretty sure. Plus, I will soak in the Jacuzzi and take a long bath. Then I'll unpack a few things. Also, I'll take a little nap because I'm feeling quite sleepy —added Jaséle.

—«*Okay, mein liebes Prinzesschen!*» Well then, my dear princess —said Wolfgang while clutching Hannah's hand.

—I want lots of maraschino cherries on my banana split ... OK, Daddy?

—Sure thing, my baby cakes! Now it's you and me against the world. Let's go out and explore the city —said Wolfgang while they were both leaving the room.

Wolfgang and Hannah were sound asleep after an exciting last day of exploring the city. Jaséle lay awake, next to her husband, trying to imagine what their new life would be like, and thought:

—«*An old Chinese proverb says that a journey of a thousand miles begins with a single step. And if so, then I wonder ... How should our new life begin?*»

Jaséle tried to remember her past life in *La Guajira,* but now everything was blurry and confusing. Perhaps this was the result of accumulated fatigues from the hectic last few months, or perhaps it was the imagination of new adventures and experiences to come, which rushed into her mind. Gradually, feeling heaviness on her eyelids, she fell sound asleep.

CHAPTER 13

FINALLY, THE DAY FOR DEPARTURE ARRIVED. AT FIVE O'CLOCK in the morning, the phone, located on the night-stand next to Wolfgang, rang. He was used to getting up early so he opened his eyes, took the phone and before he could say, *Hello!* and unlike the standard hotel prerecorded computerized wake-up calls, a pleasant human voice, from the receptionist on duty, said:

—*Good morning, Mr. Loewe.* This is your wake-up call. Thank you for staying with us. We wish you a safe and happy journey to you and your family.

—«*Danke schön*» Thank you so much —said Wolfgang.

Wolfgang hung up the phone. Jaséle and Hannah were undaunted and still fast asleep. He sat on the edge of the bed and while stretching his arms, he gave one-big-yawn, *Uoooaaah!* ... He got out of bed, donned his navy blue robe with a white stripe border and headed straight for the bathroom. After taking an invigorating shower, he dressed up quickly; khaki cargo pants, a long-sleeve-v-neck-black-shirt, black Caterpillar work boots, black leather jacket and black Ray-ban Wayfarer sunglasses.

He came back into the room, spread the curtains wide open, letting in the dim lights of dawn, and while clapping, *Clap! clap! clap!* ... he said out loud:

—Good morning my princesses ... *It is time to get up!*

Neither one of the princesses gave any indication of life. Wolfgang would have to be far more convincing than that, to wake them up. Approaching Jaséle, he knelt beside the bed, and leaning his head over her, *Mwah!* he kissed her on the cheek and whispered directly into her ear:

—It's time to wake up, my sleepyhead.

Jaséle extending, and putting her arms around Wolfgang's neck, yawning and kissing him, asked:

—*Oaah, Oaah!* ... Oh, my darling, I'm so tired, *Mwah!* ... Could you please give me five more little minutes?

—All right, my love.

Wolfgang, letting go of Jaséle's embrace, said:

—I'm going to wake up the little princess and then I'll come back for you, my darling.

—*Mmmm ... Aha!*—Jaséle barely muttered.

Hannah was sprawled face down in the middle of the bed with her flowery-cotton-pajamas but with her blanket on the floor. Wolfgang, placing one knee on the mattress and leaning over her, began tickling her playfully and ever-so-gently. Then he said:

—*Grrr...! «Ich kitzele dich bis Du in den Hosen machst»* It's time to tickle you silly, my little princess ... *Grrr...!*

Like a slinky popping up, Hannah woke up immediately; she twisted, turned, started laughing and shouted:

—*Oh, no! ... Ha-ha-ha! ...* Daddy, Daddy ... *Noooooo! ... Ha-ha-ha! ... No, Daddy, no! ... Ha-ha-ha!*

GOOD MORNING, MR. LOEWE.
THIS IS YOUR WAKE-UP CALL.

—«*Zeit zum Aufstehen, raus aus den Feder, mein Schnuckel!*»
It's time to wake up, my little princess. Come, come, come that today we set sail!

At last, Jaséle and Hannah got up and the race was on. While they were rushing and getting ready, Wolfgang called room service and ordered breakfast: omelets with Swiss cheese and chopped parsley, freshly-baked-oven-crisp croissants, butter, jam, tea for Jaséle, hot chocolate for the little one, freshly squeezed orange juice and a fresh fruit salad.

Afterwards, Wolfgang headed down to the front desk to pay the hotel bill and to make a taxi reservation to take them to the port, at seven o'clock sharp. Because he was hungry, and he didn't know at what time they would have lunch on the boat, he decided to eat a heavy, greasy and delicious Barranquilla-style breakfast in the hotel's cafeteria, while his women were busy getting ready upstairs.

A Colombian coastal-style-breakfast is based primarily on fried food in boiling hot lard, *Yum Yum!* ... This gives it, its delicious taste, and this, in spite of complaints from doctors because of excessive cholesterol and the envy of all those poor souls who are dieting.

He started with *patacones,* which are fried slices of green plantains. He ate *carimañolas,* which are similar to fried *empanadas* or dumplings but made of boiled cassava dough and stuffed with seasoned ground beef. He had an egg *arepa* made of precooked white-corn-flour and fried in boiling vegetable cooking oil, with an egg inside. He gobble up several sausages, typical of the region, which reminded him of German Bratwurst; incidentally, the exaggerated town gossip alleged they were made with stray-cat meat. And lastly, he had a large bowl of coffee with milk and sugar.

He grabbed a copy of *El Heraldo,* a regional newspaper with liberal bias, but he only managed to browse a few pages, so he took it with him to read it later on, on the boat. When he got back to their room, mother and daughter were already having breakfast, and he asked them:

—*My princesses* ... Are you girls ready?

—Almost, darling —said Jaséle and addressing Hannah, she said:

—Don't forget to pack your electric toothbrush and make sure the batteries for your video game are fully charged.

—*Yes, Mommy.* I already did it.

—All right then, the taxi will pick us up at seven o'clock. This gives us about twenty minutes to go down to the lobby —said Wolfgang.

—Daddy, don't forget your camera! —Hannah reminded him.

—«*Danke, Schätzchen. Habe ich schon in meine Tasche gesteckt*» Thank you, baby. Yes, I have it in my jacket —said Wolfgang.

With some difficulty, but trying to surprise her husband by speaking in German, Jaséle also reminded him:

—«*Hast du auch die Papiere eingesteckt?*» Got your tickets and passports?

—«*Habe ich auch, danke mein Schatz*» That's quite remarkable, my darling; and indeed, that's not bad at all! And I have them right here in my jacket, too —said Wolfgang, with a large smile.

CHAPTER 14

ONE EVENING, AFTER SCHOOL, STEVE AND ROBERT WERE walking towards the center of town of Charming Meadows. They were in no particular hurry to get back home, so Steve asked Robert:

—*Hey, Robert!* ... Do you mind if we head on over to Big Al's soda fountain and hang out for a while?

—No problem, Steve. To be honest, I don't want to get back home and do homework.

—*That's great, buddy*! ... You see, the thing is I asked Sandy to meet me there, right after school.

—*Oh,* alright, Steve.

—*Hey,* maybe we can grab a bite to eat. What do you say, Robert?

—Yes, Steve. That sounds cool.

—*Oh by-the-way,* Steve ... Do you have any money?

—Yes, twenty-five dollars. Do you?

—*Yeah* ... about thirty bucks —said Robert.

Big Al's was a classic, if not old fashion, American small-town soda fountain. You could almost say it came right out of a Norman Rockwell's painting. It had a long white counter top with fire red siding, a row of shiny-chrome-steel rotating bar-stools with red-vinyl-top, bolted onto the floor and large black and white tiles arranged in a diagonally-placed checkerboard floor. Behind the counter there were the refrigerators, ice box, soda machine dispensers and a small rectangular service window with a counter-top on the wall that led to the kitchen; used for placing and taking out orders. The kitchen's window counter had a service bell and a round metal carousel, where the waitresses would place their ticket orders. On the opposite wall to the counter, across the room, there were half a dozen booths with seats upholstered with the same red vinyl material, like the ones used on the bar-stools. On top of each of the tables and affixed to the wall, there were music jukeboxes, which cost fifty cents per tune. Each table had a bottle of ketchup, mustard, salt and pepper shakers and a roll of absorbent paper towels, which always came in handy, for those who ate messy and spicy-hot Buffalo chicken wings.

Steve and Robert ran lucky that evening because, although the place was already pretty packed, including several students from their school, they were able to sit on the first booth, right smack next to the restaurant's large picture window, overlooking the street. While waiting for Steve's girlfriend, they ordered two tall chocolate malt milkshakes with extra malt.

Robert and his best friend Steve knew each other well, because they grew up together, since childhood. There were no secrets between them. But now that they were teenagers, they became more interested in girls than in most of the games they used to play. Moreover, Steve and his girlfriend Sandy had been dating for a little over five months.

However, Robert was reserved and perhaps somewhat shy. He had not gone out with a girl more than once or twice and when he did go out, this usually only happened when

Big Al's Soda fountain

several friends went out together to the movies. This is not to say Robert didn't have good taste, insofar as the girls he was attracted to, was concerned. And this was precisely one of his biggest problems, because he was usually interested in girls, which he, himself, considered almost impossible to conquer. During his first year in high school, he tried to date two extremely popular girls and was flat-out rejected.

Rebecca, originally from Birmingham, Alabama, was a beautiful and popular school cheerleader who was also, an authentic Southern Belle. He had wanted to take her out to a school dance and had the courage or rather the audacity and the misfortune to ask her out, when she was sitting with a group of friends, having lunch at the school's cafeteria.

—I heard you invited Becky to the school dance. How did it go? —asked Steve.

—*Badaboom!* ... Not good —said Robert.

—How bad?

—*Wham!* ... Got shot down, went into a deadly spin and crashed in flames!

—*Aroooooooo!*—said Steve, howling like a coyote.

—Do you know what she told me, right in front of everybody?

—What? —asked Steve.

—Nothing!

—How is that? She didn't say anything? No way! She must have said something ...

—No, she said nothing. Not a word.... Instead, she just laughed and laughed at me.

—*Yikes, Robert!*

—And then her friends joined in the chorus. As for me, I was embarrassed and had no choice but to pick up my backpack and scram outta there.

—Robert, at least you bit the bullet like a man!

—You think, Steve?

—*Hey amigo* ... Don't you worry, my friend ... you'll get your chance again —said Steve.

—I hear you bro ... and I certainly hope so, but women ... *Ugh!*

Not giving up entirely and right before Christmas break, Robert tried his luck again but with similar results. His classroom had organized a gift exchange party to raise money for the prom. This time, Robert put his hopes up on a beautiful Japanese girl who was highly intelligent, an excellent student, but ironically she spoke with a heavy valley-girl-talk slang. Robert made sure they were not in the middle of a crowd and after leaving math class, he approached and asked *Sumiko Kobayashi:*

—*Hi, Sumiko* ... Got a minute?

—*Like, anyways* ... tell me ... are you not like, Robert?

—Yes, I'm the very same one —said Robert with a big grin on his face, and his hands in his pockets.

—So, like ... how can I help you, Robert?

—Would you like to go to the Christmas party with me?

—*Oh my God!* Like, are you serious? —asked *Sumiko.*

—Yes, I am, *Sumiko.*

—Robert, so like, tell me something.

—Anything you want, *Sumiko.*

—*Yeah!* ... Like, what's my last name? —said *Sumiko,* putting him to a test.

Robert had heard *Sumiko's* name many times before during roll call in class, but he had never paid much attention to it. Not giving up and pulling a vague memory and trying to remember its pronunciation, he chose to apologize before making a blatant mistake, and said:

—*Sumiko,* do you know what?

—No, I don't! ... So like, what do you mean, Robert?

—Look ... I'm terrible, when it comes to foreign languages.

—*Whatever ... Yeah* ... like, am I supposed to be impressed with that? *As if* ... —said *Sumiko,* without being at all convinced and thinking he was being pretty lame at that.

—Well ... let me see.... I think your name is *Sumiko Yoshi* ... is it not?

—*Nah, Robert! ... Duh! ...* Like my last name is *Kobayashi! Oh, my God* ... So like, gag me with a spoon!

—*My gosh, Sumiko!* ... I'm terribly sorry ... Honestly, I mean like, really —said Robert while turning red on the face.

—Anyways ... so like, thanks for asking, but basically I had already promised Jake, from the football team. And you know... well... I have to go with him to the party ... like, totally, you know? ... *Oh, so like, whatever.... See ya!*

During his sophomore year, Robert had not tried dating again. This does not mean he was not interested in girls. On the contrary, since Maria del Carmen had arrived at his school, he was smitten by her, but then again, just-like-about any other bloke was too. He had no idea how to approach her. If Rebecca and Sumiko had rejected him, Maria del Carmen, who was like a goddess to him, would probably send him to be shredded to pieces by the lions in the Roman Coliseum. His friend Steve knew of his love interest. But in vain he had tried to dissuade him from his newly-found obsession.

—Robert, are you still infatuated with Maria?

—Still? Is there any other girl in the whole universe? ... *Ha-ha-ha!*

—Robert, that's precisely your biggest problem!

—Steve, what do you mean?

—Buddy, as far as school girls are concerned, you always aim way too high!

—*Oh c'mon, Steve!* ... Don't exaggerate, my friend.

—I mean ... Maria del Carmen? Robert, are you nuts? Be more realistic, man!

—But Steve, you gotta admit she is beautiful. Isn't she?

—Are you kidding me?

—What do you mean? —asked Robert.

—She is a goddess! ... For heaven's sake man. Even the guys from the senior year, are drooling over her.

—*No way! ... Really?*

—Robert, my friend. Let me burst your bubble. You have no chance ... you hear? ... *Not a fat chance!*

—I know, Steve. Don't worry. I won't try anything stupid.

—Why do I find that, so hard to believe?

—Although, there is no harm in dreaming ... or, is there? —said Robert.

—And if you think that because you're in Spanish class with her, she is gonna look at you ...

—But *bro*, that's exactly the reason.... Don't you get it, Steve?

—Well, think again because the answer is still ... *No!*

—Man, you make it sound as if Maria and I live on two different planets. I mean, it can't be that bad ... or, can it?

—*Dude!* ... You're kidding yourself, aren't you? —said Steve.

—No, not really. I bet she knows I'm in the same class, no?

—*Huh? Oh, man!* She doesn't even know you exist! —said Steve.

—*Ugh!* ... Now tell me something I don't know, will you?

—Listen pal, people like you and Maria are like water and oil ...

—How so, Steve?

—... you guys simply don't mix!

Steve was sitting facing the street and the entrance to the restaurant, and Robert was sitting in front of him with his back to the street. Sandy, Steve's girlfriend, was the first one to enter and following right behind her, it was no more and no less than Maria del Carmen herself. When Steve saw Maria, he managed to whisper:

—*Holy smokes!* ... Robert, may God help you!

—*Bro* ... Steve, what the hell are you talking about? —asked Robert, totally unaware, while sipping his milkshake.

—You'll see! —said Steve with a smirk and coy remark.

Steve got up from his seat to greet Sandy and to let her sit next to him, next to the wall.

—*Hi baby!* —said Steve to Sandy.

—*Oh my God, like, hi honey!* —replied Sandy.

While Sandy was sitting down, she addressed Robert and said:

—*Yay, Robert!*

—What's up, Sandy? —said Robert.

—Robert, so like, I hope you don't mind, but I asked Maria to join us, totally! ... So like, you don't have a problem with that, right? —said Sandy.

Robert was not aware Maria was standing right behind him. Otherwise, he wouldn't have asked Sandy:

—*Huh?* ... Maria? ... Maria who?

—*Oh my God!* ... Like you know, Maria ... from like, school? —said Sandy frowning.

Sandy tried to stop him from committing some indiscretion. She tried to prevent it by beckoning him with her eyes. But Robert, who was the-clueless-type, didn't even noticed her.

—You are not talking about *"My Maria"* ... the school goddess, by any chance? ... *Ha-ha-ha!* —asked Robert.

—*Duh! ... Fer shur, Robert!* ... I mean like, Maria, you know.... Like, the one that is standing right behind you? —said Sandy, quite annoyed at him for being such a ding-bat.

Upon hearing Sandy's last comment, Robert felt as if lightning had struck him dead. He instinctively turned his head and saw Maria del Carmen standing right behind him. It is obvious Maria had heard the entire conversation.

—*«Good heavens! This cannot be. I just screwed it up royally. Please, please earth, swallow me now!»* —Thought Robert.

All the other kids stared at Maria, as if the queen herself had just entered the establishment.

Maria stood right next to Robert. To say Robert had been

stunned to see her, would be a huge understatement. Robert almost choked, turned pale, got flushed, got nervous and did not know what to say. If there is anything, which increases one's self-esteem and sometimes even a love interest in a person, is to see that person blush upon seeing you, and without that person being able to help it. That's exactly what Maria saw in Robert, and she became extremely flattered by the profound effect she had on him. One could even argue that Robert's behavior was pure flirtation on his part ... *«And who knows ... What do you think?»*

—Hi, Robert. Do you mind if I sit next to you? —asked Maria while smiling at him.

Robert thought she had the sexiest voice he had ever heard, including the love goddess, actress Rita Hayworth, in her most famous and best classic *Film-Noir,* called Gilda.

He got up and almost dropped his milkshake but holding it with both hands, he managed to place it on the center of the table and said:

—*Sure, Maria!* ... By all means, please do sit down.

Maria sat down and slid to the side, towards the wall. Then Robert sat down, but leaving a reasonable distance between the two of them.

—So like, tell me, Robert. Do you, like, know Maria? —asked Sandy.

—*Yes, yes, yes!* ... Well yeah, we are in the same Spanish class.

—Sandy and Maria ... What do you guys want to drink? —asked Steve.

—Tell me, Robert.... What are you drinking? —asked Maria.

—*Aaaah!* ... Me, Maria? —Robert stammered, because he was still quite nervous.

—*Ha-ha-ha!* ... Yes, you, Robert! ... Or is there another Robert around here somewhere? —said Maria, trying to calm Robert down with some humor.

—*Uh-huh!* ... Yeah sure, Maria ... it's just a chocolate malt milkshake with extra malt —said Robert.

—OK, I'll have the same thing —said Maria.

—And I ... like, I want a root beer float, *totally!* —said Sandy.

The waitress took the order for the drinks and asked if they were having something to eat, as well.

—How about if we order Buffalo wings with fries, celery and blue cheese? —asked Steve.

—*Oh, gosh yeah!* ... Good idea honey 'cause I'm like, totally famish —said Sandy.

—And should we get them spicy, super spicy or how? —said Robert.

—If it's up to me, you can order them as spicy as you wish. I don't know if you guys know, but in Mexico, we eat a lot of hot and spicy food. So I'm used to it —said Maria.

—Okay then ... we'll have them spicy hot —said Robert to please Maria, despite he couldn't handle the heat.

One of the most important games in football for any school, is the Homecoming game. The one for their school would take place on Friday, that is, in four day's time. Robert was not too much into football and besides, he had no one to go to the game with. So he wasn't planning on attending. On the other hand, Steve and Sandy had indeed made plans to go. But it was Maria the one who brought it up and asked:

—Is anybody going to the football game on Friday?

—Yeah for sure, Steve and I will be, like there, *totally!* —said Sandy.

—Robert, do you plan to go too? —asked Maria.

—Actually, no. I wasn't planning on going —said Robert.

—And what about you, Maria? Are you going? —asked Steve.

—I would love to go but nobody has invited me yet. Therefore, I guess I won't —said Maria.

Maria's comment was not entirely true.... *What the heck are we talking about?* The thing about not having had any invitations to go to the game was a blatant lie. She got half a dozen invitations, including one from the captain of the team himself, which she flat-out rejected without giving it a second thought. It is obvious she was leaving the door wide open for Robert to invite her, but after his previous failures, would he even dare to ask her out to the game?

—*C'mon Robert, cheer up!* Why don't you, like, invite Maria? That would be like, totally awesome —said Sandy, because she was not going to let this great opportunity go to waste. And if that wasn't enough, Maria remarked:

—What do you say, Robert? Shall we go to the game together this Friday?

Robert couldn't believe his good fortune. Maria had just asked him out to the game. And to think she was superior in every possible way to Rebecca and Sumiko. *Unbelievable!*

—*Well, yeah!* ... Maria, I would love to go to the game with you.

Maria scribbled her phone number on a napkin and while handing it to Robert, she said:

—*Fantastic!* Robert, here's my phone number. Call me tonight so we talk about it. Will you?

—Maria, should I call you at 7:30?

—*Perfect!* ... I'll wait for your call —said Maria.

When everyone finished eating, Sandy and Maria left Big Al's together. Steve and Robert paid the bill. Neither Robert, nor Steve knew what to make of what just had happened. So Steve asked him:

—Robert, can you tell me what the heck just happened here?

—Steve, my friend, please pinch me to see if I'm not dreaming... *Ha-ha-ha!*

—*Whoa, dude! ... You nailed it, bro!* —said Steve.

Steve and Robert said their goodbyes and then they headed back home. As expected, Robert had his head brimming with all kinds of ideas. He was now on cloud nine. He tried to imagine what Maria and him would talk about, later on that evening. Robert was afraid to say something that would make her change her mind. Still, Robert could not believe it. He had a pretty good relationship with Chelsea, his mother. She, being more casual than Fred, her husband, had always made Robert feel relaxed and this allowed her to be his confidant. He decided to consult with her before calling on Maria, when he got home.

Chelsea was in the kitchen preparing dinner. Kevin and Kael were busy playing in Kevin's room. Robert came in quietly and sat at the small kitchen bistro table, and said:

—*Hi, Mom!*

Chelsea was startled, because she had her back towards the bistro table, and she had not realized, Robert was sitting there.

—*Oopsie daisy, Robert!* You startled me. I didn't hear you come in —said Chelsea while catching her breath.

—Sorry, Mom. I didn't mean to scare you.

—*Oh,* don't worry about it. I guess the problem is my hearing is not as good as it once used to be.

—Mom, the problem is not your hearing.

—Is it not my hearing? Then, what is it? —asked Chelsea.

—The problem is, you're just getting plain old, Mom. That's all ... *Ha-ha-ha!*

—Robert, that's not very funny. Wait till you get to be my age and then we'll talk ... *Hah!*

—Who? Me? Old? Mother, I cannot even begin to imagine it! ... *Ha-ha-ha!* —said Robert.

—But tell me, Robert. How was school today?

Robert was incredibly excited and told her how beautiful Maria was. He told her she was possibly the most popular girl in school. And he also said he would have never imagined she would go out on a date with him. But he was also curious to know how a girl like Maria, even noticed him. And now that she had, he didn't know how he should behave. Chelsea

asked him several questions trying to get a feeling as to what Maria was like, but other than Robert being deeply in love or deeply infatuated with her, she really couldn't tell much about her.

—I have to call her at half past seven tonight, and I don't want to ruin everything. Mom, what should I do?

—Robert, as I do not know her, I cannot say.

—*But, Mom!*

—Look, Robert. I know this advice is going to sound trite, but the best thing you can do is ... *just be yourself!*

—Be myself? But, Mom! ... I'm not in the least interesting!

—Robert, you're interesting enough for her to want to go to the game with you. And that speaks well of her.

—How's that, Mom?

—It seems Maria is not interested in the flash-in-the-pan sort of thing. Do you understand me? —asked Chelsea.

—More or less, Mom.... No, actually I don't get it, Mom.

—Lookie here, Robert. You said you think you are not interesting enough. Is that right?

—Yeah. That's right —said Robert.

—Also, you think she is far superior to you, right?

—Mom, that's what I said. What are you trying to get at?

—If despite all of that, Maria is still fixed on you, it could only mean two things.

—And those things are? —asked Robert.

—First, there must be something in you she likes.

—*Aha!* Well OK, I suppose so ... and second?

—That she is not swayed by appearances. Otherwise, she would go out with some other guy more popular than you. Do you understand me now?

—*Oh! Wow, Mom!* I'm so dense ... Now, I get it!

While staring at him with a dazed look on her face, Chelsea was pensive for a moment or two, and then she said:

—Robert, I just had a marvelous idea for you.

—OK Mom, let's hear it. What is it?

—Why don't you invite her to have dinner with us? But not this Friday, but next.

—Mother, do you think she'll accept?

—You'll never know until you ask her. Don't you agree?

—All right, Mom. I'll give it a shot!

—Now you're talking, Robert.

—*Thanks, Mom!* ... For everything.

That evening, at seven-thirty sharp, Robert called Maria. Robert was surprised, because he had the impression and perhaps the illusion of speaking with her for a long time, so they'd get to know each other better. However, their conversation was short and to the point. Maria gave him her address, and they agreed he would pick her up on Friday. Afterwards, they'd walk from her place to the game. And that was it.

Robert was starting to get concerned, because Maria had been so business like and so as-a-matter-of-fact. This was nothing like what he had imagined. Waiting for the big date, would prove to be nerve wrecking for Robert, for fear of rejection.

CHAPTER 15

THE TAXI ARRIVED A FEW MINUTES BEFORE SEVEN O'CLOCK in the morning. The driver placed the luggage in the trunk of the small Toyota automobile. It's funny that for such a long journey of about ten days at sea, they didn't carry much luggage as one would have imagined. In addition to the three backpacks to be carried by each one of them, Wolfgang would carry one large sailor's duffel bag. Unlike a voyage on a cruise ship, they would travel on a container-freighter, and this one didn't have all the amenities and luxuries a typical cruise ship provides. Wolfgang expected to find a long and steep gangway to board the ship, and the heavy suitcases, which are commonly used while travelling by aircraft, would not be practical to climb aboard.

Although it was early, it was already pretty hot outside. The humidity was severe but fortunately the air conditioning in the taxi was working fine.

The Sonesta Hotel is located in the northwestern part of the city, near the highway bypass of Beltway Avenue and

Route Forty Six or *Avenida Olaya Herrera.* While en route to the port, Wolfgang started a conversation with the taxi driver, and he asked him:

—Excuse me, sir. How long will it take us to get to the port?

—At this time of day, no more than thirty little minutes —replied the driver.

—Tell me, sir. If I may be so bold. Where are you travelling to, today? —asked the driver.

—We're heading to Germany —said Wolfgang.

—And which cruise line are you travelling with? —asked the driver again.

—It's called *Gesema Shipping, S.A.* Are you familiar with it?

—*Yes, I am!* ... But that's strange. This week I haven't seen any cruise ships at the docks —said the driver.

—That's because ours isn't a cruise ship.

—*Oh! ... no?*

—We're travelling on the container cargo ship called, Athena, of the French line *Livraison Français Cargo* —said Wolfgang.

—Isn't that something. I didn't know cargo ships also carried passengers —said the driver.

They traveled via Route Forty Six, southeast bound for about seven kilometers or about four miles, until they reached Route Forty or *Avenida Boyacá,* and then they headed south. They continued along Route Forty, for another two kilometers until they reached Route Thirty, then turned left and headed east. They travelled two more kilometers, arriving at the port entrance called *Sociedad Portuaria Regional de Barranquilla.* On their left, they could see the three-story blue *Zona Franca* or Free Port building.

Once inside these huge port facilities, to the right they could see a line of small one-story office buildings, warehouses and behind them was a large man-made lake with several docks on it. About half a mile away, in a straight line, there were two huge cargo ships moored on berths one and three, on this huge wharf, along side the Magdalena River. Athena, the larger of the two ships, was moored on berth three.

—«*Guck mal, Papi, dort ist unser Boot*» There is our ship, Daddy! «*Das ist ja riesig!*» It's huge! —said Hannah, tickled pink and quite agitated.

—«*Ja, das ist es wirklich*» Yes, it is huge, my dear —replied Wolfgang.

The Loewes were in luck because they found no traffic jam. It took them less than twenty minutes to arrive at the port. Finally, the taxi stopped at about a quarter of a mile from the wharf, in front of a small mustard coloured building on the right, which belong to the shipping company. From now on and until they boarded the ship, *Gesema* would take care of all the paperwork.

Wolfgang paid the driver and went inside the office building and headed straight for the counter. Meanwhile, Hannah and Jaséle followed the taxi driver, who was carrying their luggage on a dolly.

—Good morning! —said Wolfgang while speaking to the office's agent, a young woman who was behind the counter.

—Good morning, sir ... —she answered, waiting for Wolfgang to tell her his name.

—*Ah, yes!* ... My name is Wolfgang Loewe.

—Let me see ... Yes, indeed, Mr. Loewe. We were expecting you and your family. I just need to see your passports and your tickets, please.

—This is my wife's and this one is mine. My daughter Hannah, who is ten years old, also travels with my passport —said Wolfgang.

—Thank you, Mr. Loewe. Give me a few moments and then I will need you to sign some additional documents. Afterwards, we will drive you to berth three, so you and your family can board the ship.

—Excuse me, Miss. Are we the only passengers?

Port of Barranquilla

—*Oh, no, Mr. Loewe!* You are only the first ones to arrive, but we have another two families, which are also traveling with children.

—*Excellent!* That's good news, indeed.

—The Moore family arrived on the ship from the Port of *El Callao,* on the Pacific Ocean, which is the most important port in Peru. The van Dijk family, of Dutch origin, has not yet arrived —said the agent.

—I see. At least we will have someone to talk to during our long journey —said Wolfgang.

—You know, it is not common to see many children on these long voyages. But oddly enough, in Port of Spain, Trinidad, another family with a child will board the ship, as well.

He was given several documents related to release from liability, which Wolfgang had to sign. He was also given instructions on what they could and couldn't do on the boat. In addition, she gave them a booklet with detailed instructions on safety, disembarking and boarding procedures. The agent stressed to them that it was their sole responsibility, to be aware and constantly monitor, their daughter's whereabouts. She also told them they should read this instruction booklet carefully, and said:

—Mr. and Mrs. Loewe, I know airplane passengers, practically never read the instructions flyer. But in our case, it is extremely important you do read it. Your lives and your daughter's may depend on it.

As a professional diver, Wolfgang understood well, they would be travelling in an industrial environment, possibly dangerous and unlike a cruise ship, in a freighter, it is necessary to take precautions. Moreover, these huge cargo vessels have small skeleton crews because most of the ship's systems are highly automated: not a lot of people to help, on hand.

—Don't worry, Miss. I understand, I agree, and we'll read the instructions manual from cover to cover.

Wolfgang, directing his gaze towards Jasèle, asked her:

—Don't you agree, my dear?

—*Absolutely!* —replied Jasèle.

—*Ha-ha-ha!* ... Okay, your van awaits outside and *el señor Manolo* will drive you to the ship —said the agent.

—All right, Miss —said Wolfgang.

—You will set sail at twelve o'clock noon. Have a safe and fun filled journey! —said the agent with a pleasant smile.

—Goodbye Miss and thank you! —said Wolfgang.

The agent picked up her VHF shortwave radio and hailed Athena's Chief steward and speaking over the static, *Chist! chiss! chiss!* ... said:

—*Click! click!* ... Jürgen, come in please!

You could hear static noise on the agent's radio when someone was trying to communicate with her, by pressing the microphone button, *Chist! chiss! chiss!* ... to speak:

—*Click!* ... This is Jürgen here. Judy, do you copy?

—*Click!* ... Affirmative, Jürgen. Loewe, party of three will be there in ten ... Do you read? Repeat ... Do you read?

—*Chiss! click!* ... Copy that, Judy.... How many bags?

—*Click!* ... Three backpacks and one duffel bag. Over!

—*Chiss! click!* ... Copy that. Jürgen out.

The Loewes were standing at the foot of the gangway of

the huge Athena. On this berth, there was a strong stench of burning diesel fuel or something akin to it, and this, despite the strong breeze blowing in that day. You could see large oil and dust patches on the concrete quay. However, they couldn't smell the scent of the sea because they were upwind and about fifteen miles away from it.

Athena was modern, imposing and possibly the largest container cargo ship to visit the Port of Barranquilla; although, much smaller than the large supertankers, which regularly ply the oceans. It was built within the PanaMax specifications, which regulate the maximum size of ships that pass through the Panama Canal. It was 754 feet in length, 104 feet wide, displacement of 52,000 plus tons and 34,000 horsepower, which were needed to move more than 2,500 containers.

Chief steward Jürgen, a young Dutch man, wore a white uniform with shorts and was accompanied by two sailors. Hurriedly, they came down the gangway to meet and greet Wolfgang and his family. He approached Wolfgang and speaking in perfect German, he said:

—«*Hallo Herr Loewe!*» Hello, Mr. Loewe!

—«*Guten Tag!*» Good morning! —said Wolfgang.

—«*Entschuldigen Sie bitte. Wir haben soviel zu tun*» Please forgive the hurry, but we are rather busy right now.

—«*Ist schon in Ordnung*» No problem —said Wolfgang.

—«*Wir kümmern uns um Ihr Gepäck*» We will carry your luggage.

—«*Danke schön*» Thank you —said Wolfgang while climbing up the gangway and on to the boat.

Jürgen, who had light blue eyes, with a disheveled blonde hair but with a frank smile and stare, greeted Jaséle, Hannah and Wolfgang giving each one of them a firm handshake and said:

—«*Familie Loewe ... Herzlich willkommen an Bord der Athene!*» Mrs., Miss and Mr. Loewe ... Welcome aboard Athena!

CHAPTER 16

ATHENA'S BRIDGE CASTLE WAS LOCATED AFT TOWARDS THE stern or rear of the ship. And the Loewe's cabin was located on one of the highest floors on the bridge castle, only one story below the command bridge itself. They were surprised when they saw how spacious and comfortable it was. With wall-to-wall thick-gray-carpet and recessed ceiling lighting, it was more luxurious than what they had expected for a container cargo ship.

They had to climb four stories to reach their cabin, which was located on the northeast corner to starboard, or right side of the ship. Instead of portholes, it had large rectangular thick glass picture windows with sliding-burgundy-coloured curtains, facing the bow. They had a fantastic view up-ahead where they could see all of the container yard on the main deck, throughout the whole length of the boat. Their cabin also had windows on the starboard side were they could enjoy the vast ocean view.

A fire-red modern sofa for four was evenly placed in the corner. There was a small desk with its respective seat, on the left and next to the entrance door, which matched the sofa. Towards the right side of the sofa, there was an L-shaped six drawer dresser with a huge flat-screen TV on top. One could easily watch it while laying down on the queen-sized-bed, which was attached to the wall and opposite to the starboard portholes. Beside the dresser, there was a small refrigerator. There was a coffee table in the middle of the sofa area. On the back wall of the cabin, opposite to the entrance door, hung a foldaway bunk-bed, which when closed and in an upright position, it displayed a landscape painting of snow-capped-mountains. Hannah would sleep on this bunk bed.

The cabin also had a closet, sink, bathroom and shower, which, although small, they were designed to efficiently cover all the basic needs of hygiene and most importantly, privacy. On the other hand, the crew had to share bathrooms in common areas, throughout the ship.

On top of the coffee table they found a fruit basket, a bottle of wine, a water pitcher and several glasses, cheese, crackers and chocolates. On the desk, there were several fairly recently published European magazines.

The Loewes began to unpack and to get used to what would be their new home, for the next two weeks. They waited for a couple of hours, and no member of the crew had yet come to visit and give them instructions, so Jaséle told her husband:

—How strange. Two hours have gone by, and we have not seen anyone yet.

—Well darling, the Chief steward himself warned us they were extremely busy.

—*Oh!* ... Is that what he said when he met us, when we were coming aboard?

—Well yes, of course. Didn't you hear him? —said Wolfgang.

—Wolfgang, darling. Do you forget I don't speak German?

—*Oh, how silly of me!* Forgive me darling but with all the hustle and bustle, it just slipped my mind.

—What else did the Chief steward say? —asked Jaséle.

—He said they were rather busy preparing to set sail.

—Wolfgang, honey, you're repeating yourself. You said so already.

—*Oh, gee whiz!*

—Is that all? —Again, asked Jaséle.

—*No!* ... He said the captain would welcome all the passengers, when we were out to sea.

—*Ah, I see.* That makes sense —said Jaséle.

—«*Papa, kann ich rausgehen?*» Daddy, can I go out? —said Hannah.

—Hannah, what if we go out together?

—All right, Daddy.

—Tell me Hanni, are you hungry?

—«*Nein Papa, ich bin nicht hungrig*» No Dad, I'm not hungry, at all.

—And you, my love ... are you hungry, Jaséle?

—No, honey. I'm still pretty full from breakfast.

—OK Hanni. Daddy is hungry like a wolf. *Grrr...!* What do you say if we go out to explore and find the galley?

—*Oh, Dad!* ... You're always hungry ... *Ha-ha-ha!*

At twelve o'clock noon, with the moorings released, the containers secured and the powerful ship's horn blasting, *Waaaaaank!* ... Athena was announcing its departure from Port Barranquilla, bound for the ports of Willemstad, on the island of *Curaçao,* in the former Dutch Antilles, Port of Spain, in the islands of Trinidad and Tobago, and finally, Port Hamburg, in northern Germany.

Less than a mile upriver and to the south, they could see the imposing *Pumarejo* fixed-bridge, over the Magdalena River. It is a concrete bridge with a clearance of about fifty feet above the water, which only allows upstream navigation to barges and to lower-height-vessels. This bridge is a major throughway; an artery for road transport and natural gas, because there is a gas pipeline on it, as well. The *Pumarejo* connects Barranquilla, with the country's eastern provinces including *La Guajira Peninsula,* and Venezuela. Great migrations of people, which settled in Barranquilla, passed through this bridge, increasing and diversifying the culture of the city, including among other things, the popular Vallenato music.

Athena was making its way downstream over the river's brackish muddy-waters and heading north, to reach the levees and entrance training-walls, which form the channel at the mouth of the river and the Caribbean Sea, called *Bocas de Ceniza,* or Ash Mouth. From the port and on to the sea, the Magdalena River, describes a wide arc in a general north-northwest direction. When they were seven miles out or about twelve kilometers from port, they reached the northeastern tip of the city and soon, they left her behind. On

their starboard they could see the uninhabited and marshy swamplands called, *Ciénaga la Calestra,* or Calestra Swamps.

At last they crossed the coordinates eleven degrees and six minutes north latitude and seventy-four degrees and fifty-one minutes west longitude (N11°6' W74°51'), passing on their port side a small lighthouse, which is a navigation light tower of metal construction, marking the entrance to the channel, at the extreme tip of the more than three-mile-long seawall.

Athena was now free on the Caribbean Sea. Although the Magdalena River, creates a bit of turbulence in its encounter with the sea, on this huge cargo ship they didn't feel a thing.

From the Loewe's cabin and through the starboard windows, Hannah saw a school of about fifteen dolphins frolicking alongside the ship, possibly giving them a farewell send-off.

—Daddy and Mommy ... come here quick and see! —said Hannah quite excitedly.

—What is it, Hanni? —asked Wolfgang.

—*Dolphins, dolphins, dolphins! ... Ha-ha-ha! ...* How cute!

—They are wonderful, Wolfgang.... Yes, I see them too —said Jasèle, in amazement.

—And Daddy, look how fast they swim!

Wolfgang approached the window and said:

—Yes, sweetheart, you're right. I see them. Also, did you know dolphins can swim at speeds of nearly fifty-five miles per hour?

—That's amazing! —said Jasèle.

—Sailors believe a dolphins' send-off is an omen for a safe trip —said Wolfgang.

Although happy to be on their way, Jasèle wondered about the voyage and thought to herself:

—*«Now that I'm pregnant, I wonder if this trip will make me dizzy, more easily. I don't remember any morning sickness when I was pregnant with Hannah. But you never know. I have to speak to Wolfgang, so we talk to the ship's doctor and keep him abreast of our situation. But I wonder, do they even have a physician on board?»*

Athena's crew consisted of a complement of thirty people, and this is minuscule when we compare it with the crews of some super cruise-ships, which have crews of nearly two thousand people. That is why this huge ship appeared to be deserted, most of the time. Only in the dining room, at meal-times, was there any human activity to speak of. The rest of the time the sailors were carrying out their duties and responsibilities, in their respective shifts.

Nevertheless, Athena's crew was truly friendly, and they were always eager to engage in conversation with the passengers, or doing tours of the boat, to break up the monotony during these long journeys. The crew was mostly quite young, exclusively male and made up of: Filipino, German, Indian, Dutch, Italian and the captain, from Denmark.

Traveling by freighter is generally more expensive than air travel and in many cases, even more so than taking a cruise.

This is because cargo crossings generally take a greater number of days. Fares range from sixty-five to over two hundred U.S. dollars per person per day, plus insurance and fees, and this depends on the type of cargo ship, too. This includes lodging, meals and stops at multiple ports of call, along the way.

Many of their own needs had to be met by the passengers themselves. Garbage was collected daily but the bedding and towels were changed every week. Athena didn't have elevators so passengers got their daily dose of cardio, going up and down the stairs all the time. In a couple of days, the adults grew accustomed to this routine. But for the children this wasn't an issue, for they enjoyed racing up and down the stairs, certainly, much faster than their parents.

Although the captain is the highest authority on board, for the passengers the most important person for them is the cook. And the passengers and crew of Athena lucked out in a big way, because *Alessandro Pallazzini,* from Modena, Italy, was their Chief cook.

The city of Modena, is well known for its car engine manufacturing industry because several famous automobile manufacturers such as *Ferrari, Lamborghini and De Tomaso* assemble their engines there. The food from Modena, is rich and diverse. And Alessandro was truly a master of the culinary arts.

However, outside the hours of breakfast, lunch and dinner, if someone wanted to eat something, they had to go down to the galley or kitchen and prepare a snack for themselves. It was always a good idea to store cold drinks and sandwiches in the cabin's refrigerator, to avoid having to go down several floors to the galley, in the middle of the night. Wolfgang learned this lesson quickly and always kept snacks and ice cream for Hanni, in their fridge.

Suddenly, they heard a loud but short duration bell ring to draw attention, and then they heard a powerful announcement echoing throughout the loudspeakers, placed all around the boat and throughout the intercoms in their cabins, too.

—*Attention! Attention! Attention!* Now hear this! —said the Chief Officer.

Moments later they heard:

—Good afternoon, ladies and gentlemen! This is your Captain speaking. My name is *Olaf Sørensen*. Today we have the pleasant company of three families who will accompany us to Port Hamburg, in Germany.

Captain Sorensen spoke fluent English and continued:

—Ladies and gentlemen ... passengers, welcome aboard! Please join us for a small toast and dinner, in the dining room located on the main deck, at 1900 hours. Thank you.

The Chief Officer took the microphone again and with a strong Nordic accent, said:

—Good afternoon. This is Chief Officer *Axel Østergård,* speaking. Currently, we are travelling at twenty-one knots. Our next port of destination is Willemstad, on the beautiful island of *Curaçao,* north of the Venezuelan coast. Willemstad, is located at four hundred twenty-five nautical miles, so we should be docking tomorrow morning at eleven o'clock. We expect to have good weather along the way. Thank you.

At six-thirty in the afternoon, Jaséle, Hannah and Wolfgang were getting ready to come down to the ship's mess, when Jaséle said:

—Wolfgang, please don't forget to ask the captain if they have a physician on board.

—Mommy, a physician for what?

—*Oh,* it's nothing, sweetie. It's just a precaution —said Jaséle.

—*Ah,* Jaséle. That's precisely what I wanted to talk to you about —said Wolfgang.

—Is there something wrong, dear?

Wolfgang approached Jaséle to talk to her up close and prevent Hannah from hearing their conversation.

—Look, our contract specifies that none of the passengers should be ... well you know —said Wolfgang while making eye gestures and looking at her womb.

—*Really?* And then, what do we do?

—Anyways, I'll ask Captain Olaf to see if they have a physician on board, just in case. Fortunately, it is still quite early, right? —said Wolfgang, referring to Jaséle's pregnancy.

—Yes, it is.

—Early for what, Mommy? —asked Hannah.

—*Grrr...!* Early to go to bed, but it's never too early to tickle Hanni! —said Wolfgang, tickling Hannah to divert her attention.

—*Oh, no!* ... Daddy, Daddy, *noooo tickles! ... Ha-ha-ha! ... No no no! ...* —cried Hannah trying to escape her father.

International maritime law does not require cargo ships to have a physician on board, if they do not carry more than twelve passengers. For this reason it is extremely rare for cargo operators to exceed this number and Athena was no exception. However, officers do have first aid and to some extent, emergency medical training. They can tend to certain types of trauma, suture wounds, administer medications, give an injection and deal with certain types of fractures. But major medical problems, could pose a serious risk at sea. Especially, if these occur far away from helicopter access for an emergency medical evacuation, or airlift.

Although he did not want to alarm his wife, Wolfgang was somewhat worried and thought:

—*«Could it be I'm putting my family under an unnecessary risk by travelling on this boat? Not only Jaséle, who is pregnant but also the little one? I'll have to stay alert with these two. Hopefully, nothing bad will happen during our voyage.»*

To be fair to Wolfgang, he did not find out about his wife's pregnancy, until a couple of weeks before they were due to embark and after having purchased the tickets. Because he was aware, carriers will not accept passengers under five-years-old, more than seventy-nine years of age and of course, pregnant women. Moreover, passengers age sixty-five years or older, must show a medical certificate ensuring their good health at boarding time. If you think that in most cases these vessels do not have elevators, all passengers must go up and down multiple stairs all the time, and should they have health issues, these exercises could aggravate their conditions. For all other passengers, these forced exercises represent a welcomed bonus, helping them to get fit.

Athena had two galleys, one for the crew and the other one for officers and passengers. While neither one was large, both were practical and cozy. The passenger's galley had six rectangular Formica-white-tables bolted to the floor, which seated six people each. These tables had a wooden lip around them to prevent dishes and utensils from falling off because of the boat's sudden movements. There was also a round table which seated eight people.

Captain *Olaf Sørensen* was an old-sea-dog who was born in the village of *Grenå,* which is located on the east coast of the northern Jutland Peninsula, over the *Kattegat Straits,* in Denmark. He began his naval career at an early age working with ferries, which serviced the route from *Grenå,* to the island of *Anholt,* and to the town of *Varberg,* in Sweden. He continued his training at the Royal Danish Naval Academy, graduating with honors as a civilian licensed marine Chief Officer. Tall, slightly overweight, about sixty-eight years of age, white hair, good humor and a well-trimmed George V type beard. He had a jovial disposition, which exuded professionalism and confidence to staff, crew and passengers alike.

The Loewes were the last ones to arrive to the dining room. One could hear Johann Strauss' waltzes playing in the background. Everybody was well dressed, including Captain Olaf, Chief officer Axel, Chief steward Jürgen and Chef Alessandro. They all wore their impeccable white uniforms and long trousers. They were busy talking with the other two families, when Captain Olaf saw Wolfgang and his family arrive. He addressed them effusively, and said:

—«*Hallo, Herr Loewe*» Hello, Mr. Loewe.

—«*Guten Tag, Herr Kapitän*» Good day, Captain! —said Wolfgang shaking hands.

—«*Herzlich willkommen!*» Welcome! And tell me ... how are you doing? —said the captain.

—«*Und wen haben wir denn hier?*» So what have we got here? —asked the captain referring to little Hannah.

—This is my daughter Hanni, Captain.

—«*Nein, Papa! Mein Name ist Hannah!*» No Daddy. My name is Hannah!

—«*Fräulein Hannah also*» Then it is Mademoiselle Hannah, so I see.

—And this is my wife Jaséle —said Wolfgang.

—*Aha!* ... Mrs. Loewe, at last —said the captain.

—It is nice to meet you, Captain Olaf—said Jaséle, smiling and giving him her hand.

—«*Enchanté, tout le plaisir est pour moi*» I am delighted and I guarantee you the pleasure is all mine! —said the captain while kissing her hand and flirting with her.

—I have to tell you, Mr. Loewe, the rumor which reached my ears about your wife, is dead wrong! —said the captain.

Jaséle and Wolfgang looked at each other surprised, and with fear and trepidation. The two of them thought, somehow the captain had found out she was pregnant.

—«*Unbelievable! There is no way. Even Hannah doesn't know it! How could he have found out about this?*»

Thought Wolfgang, with a feeling of guilt because in truth, they had brought a four week old stowaway aboard.

—Chief steward Jürgen ... I have to say you were quite wrong! —said the captain, turning towards the Chief steward and raising his voice.

Jürgen was talking with the Moore family and when he heard the captain's comment, he blushed. He apologized and when he approached the Loewes and the captain, he asked the captain in French:

—«*Qu'entendez-vous par là, mon capitaine?*» What are you referring to, Captain?

—Chief steward Jürgen, Mrs. Loewe is not attractive as you said. «*Elle est tout simplement magnifique Monsieur Jürgen!*» She is simply magnificent, Mr. Jürgen ... *Ho-ho-ho!*

Wolfgang and Jaséle looked at each other again. They breathed an air of relief because it wasn't what they had imagined. The captain put his arm around Wolfgang's shoulder and comforting him, he said:

—«*Keine Sorge, Wolfgang*» Do not worry, Mr. Loewe. In our small community there are not many rumors, which don't reach the captain's ears.

Captain Olaf was in good spirits and hitting his champagne glass with a spoon quickly and repeatedly, *Clink! clink! clink!* to draw everyone's attention and make a toast, said:

—«*Mesdames, mesdemoiselles, messieurs, trinquons à un bon voyage!*» Ladies and gentlemen ... here's to a great trip!

—CHEERS AND HURRAY FOR THE CAPTAIN! —They all said in unison while raising their champagne glasses.

Throughout the evening they had spoken in several languages and Alessandro, like a good Italian, was not to be outdone and remain silent. With a booming opera voice, he said:

—«*Applausi per un grande viaggio!*» A big round of applause for a great trip!

—*Hear, hear!* To our trip and Godspeed! —cried the Moores, a British family.

The van Dijk family, of Dutch origin, although a bit reserved, also joined in the chorus and said:

—«*We heffen ook het glas op een geslaagde reis!*» We also lift our glasses to a good trip!

Captain Olaf, addressing Chef Alessandro because it was high time he became the center of attention, asked:

—«*Alessandro, Cosa mangeremo stasera?*» Alessandro, what will we have tonight?

—«*Il mangiare, come fare l'amore, deve essere fatto con gusto!*» Eating, like making love, must be done with gusto!

—*Ha-ha-ha! ... Ho-ho-ho! ...* —several passengers laughed at Alessandro's comment.

—«*Stasera avremo una cena tutta italiana!*» Tonight we will have a traditional Italian dinner!

—«*L'antipasto*» will be «*insalata Capresa fatta di mozzarella, pomodori, basilico, olive nere, olio d'oliva e peppe*» a salad with mozzarella, tomatoes, basil, black olives, olive oil and black pepper.

—«*Il primo, pasta Capellini*» Our first course, angel hair pasta with spicy Napoli sauce on a bed of tender asparagus.

—«*Il secondo, Cotechino di Modena*» The second course is a typical dish from my hometown. A sausage made with ground pork rinds, well cooked and served in slices, accompanied with mashed potatoes and lentils.

—«*Il contorno, insalata di Fusilli*» Accompanying the main course we will have a short pasta salad with zucchini, tomatoes, mushrooms, carrots, onions, peas «*Parmigiano-Reggiano*» and lots of grated Parmesan cheese.

—«*Il dolce, Torta Nera*» For dessert, black cake, which is also another favorite dish from my hometown and it is made with coffee, chocolate and various nuts.

—«*Il digestivo, liquore di carciofi*» For our digestif, artichokes liqueur, «*formaggio e frutti varie*» several cheeses and assorted fruits.

—«*E, quello più importante, da bere*» And most importantly, to drink «*Il vino bianchi, rosso e lo spumante*» white, red and sparkling wines. «*Col dolce, caffè ed acqua gasata*» With dessert, we will serve coffee and mineral water.

After Alessandro had finished reciting the menu for the evening, everybody was hungry. Especially, those passengers which had not eaten anything, since climbing aboard. Anybody with a good ear could probably hear some rumbling stomach noises. And frankly, many had their mouths water, just thinking about the food. Captain Olaf took the floor again and said:

—«*Bravo! Un applauso per il nostro chef!*» *Bravo!* ... A big round of applause for our great Chef Alessandro!

Everyone applauded, *Clap! clap! clap!* ...

Alessandro, a waiter and two assistants served dinner. Dinner lasted a couple of hours, between introductions, getting to know one another and the food itself. The banquet was a total success. At about ten o'clock, the passengers were happy, well fed and some of them feeling a little tipsy because of one-drink-too-many, retired to their cabins, to sleep.

CHAPTER 17

MARIA TOOK ROBERT'S HAND INTO HER OWN AND SLIDING her soft, delicate and warm fingers into his, she pulled him closer to her and laid both hands on her lap. Trembling but determined, with a seductive voice and wearing her long-and-shiny-black-hair parted to one side, à la Veronica Lake, she glanced at him sidewise, and asked:

—Tell me, Robert.... Is it true what they say about you in school?

—Maria, what do you mean? What do they say?

—They say that ...

Maria stopped in mid-sentence and completed it in Spanish to cause a greater effect on him and said:

—*«¿Que tú me quieres?»* That you love me?

Robert couldn't help it and blushed. He noticed how soft Maria's hands were. His mind was racing. He knew he was sailing uncharted waters and this made him feel uneasy. Throughout the evening he had been polite and gentlemanly like and yet ... *Yes!* ... There was nothing he wanted more in the whole-wide-world than to be with her, but Maria's audacity took him by surprise. And now, with his heart pounding, he was at a loss for words not knowing what to do or say. Maybe he was too shy. Or maybe Maria was more experienced. He just didn't know, and this made him feel totally self conscious and embarrassed. He too was trembling, but he hoped she wouldn't notice, because he was wearing his school's letter-leather-jacket. This was the moment he had been waiting for; still, here he was, and he didn't know what to do. With his mouth completely dry, he managed to babble something and said:

—*Oh, Maria* ... I ... I ... I ... don't know what you mean!

No sooner had he completed his sentence, than furious with himself, he thought:

—*«Oh, my God! Did I say that? What a stupid thing to say. C'mon, get a grip on yourself and say or do something! ... Talk, talk, talk ... now!»*

It was Friday and a gorgeous Midwest summer day. A warm-and-soft-balmy-breeze was blowing, in the late afternoon. There was a pale-blue-sky towards the south and over the horizon, one could see huge streaks of bright orange lit clouds. To the north one could already detect the stars appearing in the twilight, as dusk was settling in.

They had managed to find seats towards the top center section of the aluminum bleachers, which were jammed pack with noisy and energetic fans, for the Homecoming game. The cheerleaders were jumping, singing and shouting while the school band played on, as the football game entered half-time.

However, Robert could just as well have been in an isolated monastery, totally silent, and everything would have been indifferent to him, because he was tuned in, imbued and completely soaked in by Maria's seductive and tantalizing beauty. Maria knew that for the moment, she had the upper hand. Aware of her situation, she thought:

—«If you don't play your cards right you will lose him.... Just like an African bushman loses his prey by being careless.»

Maria was quite popular in school. How could she not be? By all accounts, she was a stunning Latin beauty. Shy she was not. She had to fend for herself against the gossip from mean-spirited and jealous competitors. But Maria was not the football team groupie either. Perhaps she was the way she was, because she had attended so many different schools, due to the nature of her parent's humble trade, who were Mexican migrant farm workers, which frequently travelled from one state to another, depending on the types of crops being harvested and work availability. Maybe this is why she was forced to grow up a little faster and to develop a stronger and certainly, a more alert and assertive personality.

Robert met Maria in Spanish class, which she was taking in order to prop up her grade-point-average because as you would have expected, she spoke Spanish fluently. As for him, Maria thought that Robert's tortuous and strange pronunciation was kind of sweet, and his stuttering, most charming. On one occasion, Sandy, her best friend, said:

—Hey, Maria!

—Yes, Sandy, tell me.
—Like, I bet you can't guess what-big-gossip I heard today? I mean, like totally!
—*Gossip!* ... You know I don't like gossip ... *Ha-ha-ha!*—said Maria mockingly.
—*OK then, suit yourself!* ... In that case, I won't tell you a thing! —said Sandy, annoyed at Maria for being such a killjoy.
—*Nooooo girl!* ... Are you crazy? I was just kidding. Please tell me ... pretty please, Sandy?
—Well like ... alright then.
—Go ahead, Sandy.... For you, I'm all ears —said Maria.
—So like, the thing is I've heard rumors Robert, is like, head-over-heels for you ... totally! —said Sandy.
—*What?* You must be joking, right? Is this for real?
—*Fer shur, girl!* ... Yeah, of course it is, Maria.
—But he's so serious.... I can hardly believe it —said Maria somewhat incredulous, but still, curious.
—*Oh, you fool!* ... What? So like, are you blind too? —said Sandy.
—But, but, but ...
—*Lookie here, girl* ... I've seen him myself going like, totally gaga over you!
—*Hmmm!* ...
—But honestly, like I don't think he's your type —said Sandy.
—*Wait a minute, Sandy* ... You say he isn't my type?
—*Oh my gosh, well yeah!* ... that's like, exactly what I said. Why do you ask?
—But even, I, don't know which guy *"is"* my type.
—Are you serious? I mean like ... *Duh!*
—*But, Sandy* ...
—*Hello!* ... Planet earth calling Maria ... *Hello, Hello* ... is anybody home?
—Sandy, how do you know that? I mean, really. How can you be so sure?

—Because he's like, so shy ... and you ... I mean, c'mon ... the most popular girl in school? That's just impossible! —said Sandy completely flustered.

—Well, who knows? —said Maria, shrugging her shoulders.

—*Oh, my God!* I cannot like believe my ears.... Are you gonna, like tell me you actually like Robert? *As if*...

—*Ha-ha-ha!* ... And tell me, Sandy ... what else do you know about him?

—*OK fine, whatever!* ... Have it your way. Anyways, like I think on weekends he works at his dad's hardware store. *Oh!* ... and actually, it's not like, too far from here.

—*Oh really? Wow!* ... Well at least he isn't afraid of work. *Hee-hee-hee!*

—*Oh, yes!* ... I believe he is like, also learning to play the saxophone. It seems like, he is into Jazz. He's kind of like, totally weird.... Is he not? —added Sandy.

—*Hmmm!* ... He likes Jazz? —said Maria.

—*Yup!*

—Sandy, my friend.... Could you do me a big favor?

—*Fer shur, yeah!* ... So what is it, Maria?

—Could you find out which hardware store he works at? ... I mean, the name?

—*Oh, is that it? No sweat!* ... My boyfriend Steve and Robert are buddies ... so like, they know each other well. I'll check with him and like, I'll give you a call tonight ... Okay? —said Sandy.

—That's wonderful, Sandy!

—*Hey,* I'll fill you in on all the gory details ... *Ha-ha-ha!*

—Thank you, Sandy ... I owe you a big one, girl!

—It's like, totally awesome! ... *Yay!* ... *You go girl!*

Maria began to pay close attention to see if these rumors were true. After her friend Sandy told her the name and address of the hardware store where Robert worked at, she tried, casually, to bring the topic up in conversation and while having supper with her parents, she asked her dad:

—Papa, there is this boy in school who I believe works at Brown's Hardware Store, on Will Rogers Street. His name is Robert. Have you ever heard of him?

Her father took a moment to think about it. He was familiar with the hardware store, which he visited often to buy supplies during harvest season. Suddenly, his face lit up and said:

—«*¡Sí, sí, sí!... ¡Roberto, yo le conozco!*» Yes, yes, yes! Robert, I know him. He works for el señor Fred, at the hardware store. Roberto «*es un buen chico, buen chico*» he is a good boy, good boy!

—Really? What can you tell me about him? How is he? What's he like? —asked Maria anxiously.

It was quite obvious, she was extremely interested in Robert, and she wasn't conscious, her mother was paying close attention to what she was saying.

—Roberto is a nice guy, a very nice guy, indeed. A little quiet but hardworking —added her father.

Her mother, upon seeing Maria's strong interest in Robert, felt enormously curious, herself. She looked straight into Maria's eyes, over her reading glasses, and asked:

—Tell me, Maria ... How do you know this boy?

Maria realized she had been careless while expressing her emotions. She pretended she did not attach much importance to the issue and said:

—*Oh,* he's just a guy from class. That's all.

Her mother, not satisfied with her daughter's reply, said:

—*Oh, is that so? Wow!* ... You sure kept it a secret long enough. That's pretty slick, Maria.

—*Oh, Mom ... Pleeease!!!*

Her father smiled and teasing Maria, said:

—*Bingo!* You see, I think our little *niña* is falling in love with Robertico... *Ha-ha-ha!*

Nodding his head, he repeated himself:

—Robertico, yes, yes, yes he is a good *chico, buen chico!*

CHAPTER 18

ATHENA'S COURSE WOULD TAKE THEM ALONG THE COLOMbian coastline in a north-northeast heading and then, eastbound towards *Curaçao*. First, they sailed around Port Santa Marta and Peninsula. Then they passed close to the coastal town called *Riohacha*, which is the capital of the province of *La Guajira*. Continuing on course, they went around the lighthouse of *Cabo de La Vela,* which is on the western tip of *La Guajira Peninsula*. Then they sailed a few miles offshore from *Punta Gallinas,* positioned in the northernmost part of the peninsula and the South American continent.

This route was a couple dozen miles south from where the Canadian SS John A. Holloway cargo ship was sunk by the German U-164 Kriegsmarine U-boat, in September of 1942. One crew was lost from a total complement of twentyfour.[1]

Far in the distance, one could detect a lighthouse but as it was dark, one could not see the wreckage of an old cargo ship, which also ran aground on the beaches of *Punta Gallinas.*

Nevertheless, Athena sailed far away enough from the coast, to suffer the same fate. From the moment they crossed *Punta Gallinas,* Athena changed its course and its new heading was now one-zero-zero degrees (100°) eastward. A couple of hours later they passed north of the lighthouse on the islands of *Los Monjes* or Monks archipelago, which are a group of three small islands of rock formation, at the entrance of the Gulf of Venezuela.

Following this course they sailed north of the *Paraguana* Peninsula, in the state of *Falcón,* in Venezuela. When you look at a satellite photograph of this Peninsula, you could easily see why geologists say that in ancient times this must have been was a huge barren island. It appears that throughout eons, a narrow corridor of rock and sand was formed, which today, connects it to the mainland. *Amuay,* the largest oil refinery in the world, is located on this peninsula. North of *Paraguaná,* and less than twenty miles away, is the island of Aruba. An immensely popular holiday island for both, Americans and Europeans, which like the island of *Curaçao,* was also a member of the former Netherlands Antilles. Finally, this course led them directly into Port Willemstad, in *Curaçao.*

Onboard Athena, meals were served every day at the same time, on time. Passengers did not take long to get used to this schedule. Breakfast was served from 0700 to 0900 hours, lunch from 1200 to 1330 hours and dinner from 1800 to 2000 hours. Of course, if anyone did not arrive on time, he or she could prepare themselves a snack and wait until the next meal.

After the wonderful dinner party from the night before, the van Dijk family didn't make it for breakfast. The Loewes and Moores did arrive on time, and they sat down to have breakfast together at one of the rectangular tables for six. Mrs. Elizabeth Rose Moore and eleven-year-old Andrew were sitting side-by-side. Jaséle and Hannah sat in front of them. Mr. William Moore and Wolfgang sat at opposite ends of the table, facing each other.

Elizabeth Rose was a British citizen. She was tall, slender, of fair skin, light brown glam medium-wavy-layered wild hair with streaks of blond, light gray eyes, long neck, good complexion, delicate features and genuine aristocratic airs, which made her look stylish, somewhat pretentious and perhaps arrogant; in other words, a bona fide English snob.

Meanwhile, William Moore was burly with a thick mustache and tangled and fairly short brown hair. He was a good Old Chap and a landlubber, who would probably be more comfortable in a Fox Hunt, than aboard a ship on the high seas. Young Mr. Andrew was the same height as Hannah. Black hair, light eyes and fair skin, which was now red from being exposed to the intense sunlight of the tropics. Interestingly, Andrew had no resemblance to Elizabeth; although, only a little to William Moore, who was his father. In any case, he didn't much look like either one of them.

The night before, during the welcome dinner party, Elizabeth had been watching Jaséle throughout much of the evening. She resented Jaséle's captivating and exotic beauty, which seemed to attract every man on the boat, particularly if these were Caucasian, and this, annoyed her to no end. Afterwards, when the Moores retired to their cabin, she told William:

—How is it possible that Mr. Loewe, so fair and handsome, married her? That is simply scandalous!

—Who do you mean, Elizabeth? —asked William.

—I speak of Mrs. Loewe. I understand she is a native from *La Guajira Peninsula,* in Colombia.

—*Ah!* ... Jaséle. Is this who you mean?

—*Yes, precisely!* ... The very same one.

—*By George, Elizabeth!* Be reasonable, my dear. Today mixed-race marriages are most common. Don't you agree, Lizzie?

—*Sir!* ... That is absolutely beside the point! The fact it occurs does not mean, I, have to like it!

The Loewes and Moores spoke about the weather, about Germany and Britain, about why Wolfgang and his family were moving to Germany, and about the Moore's trip throughout South America.

The Moores boarded Athena in Peru. They said they were vacationing and touring some of the popular archaeological sites such as Machu Picchu, Cuzco, the magnificent and gigantic ruins of Sacsayhuaman. They also visited the plains in the valley of Nazca, with their strange and giant drawings, which can only be fully appreciated from an airplane. They mentioned, with some pride, they had made a train trip across Lake Titicaca, on the Peruvian Railways, which is affiliated with the Orient Express; consequently, making it remarkably comfortable, luxurious and as Elizabeth had said, civilized. But the jewel of their journey, so far, had been crossing the Panama Canal. Up until that moment, William had not spoken much about their holidays in Peru. But when they mentioned the trip across the Canal, he took charge of the conversation and narrated with enthusiasm, many of the technical engineering details, which he thought were simply marvelous.

While the adults were engaged in conversation, Andrew and Hannah did not pay any attention to them. Children, being children, they were simply too busy sizing each other up. If Andrew mocked her by making faces, Hannah would not let him wait and responded in kind, immediately. Andrew took advantage because the adults were distracted and he pinched Hannah, to annoy her. Although Hannah felt pain, she said nothing. Instead, she kicked him in the shin, below the table and a loud cry, immediately followed:

—*Ouch!* ... Dad, she kicked me —cried Andrew.

It's funny how the child complained to his father and not to his mother, which is usually the norm. But before William could utter a single word, Elizabeth jumped-in at the opportunity to attack, scold and discredit Jaséle.

—Mrs. Loewe ... I suppose in your country, they do not teach table manners to your children. Isn't it a pity?

—Please accept our apologies, Lady Elizabeth —said Wolfgang.

—*Oh!* ... Don't you worry, my dear Wolfgang. It is only children's stuff —said William.

—*«Hanni, bitte entschuldige dich bei Andrew!»* Hanni, please apologize to Andrew, now! —said Wolfgang.

—I'm sorry, Andrew. Did it hurt a lot? —Hannah asked him with a mischievous grin and enjoying every minute of it.

Andrew replied with another smirk, and Hannah returned the compliment by sticking her tongue out at him. It's funny how often human beings, when initially acquainted, begin as antagonists and after the first few skirmishes, they windup best of friends.

Athena made better time than expected in its overnight journey. They arrived at the entrance of Port Willemstad, at ten o'clock, instead of eleven, as planned. Suddenly, they heard the sound of a short-bell-ringing to draw attention and immediately, the respective announcement ensued:

—This is your captain speaking. We will be arriving to *Curaçao,* an hour before scheduled. I invite our passengers to enjoy the view to the entrance to the channel and port arrival, from the bridge, at 0945 hours. Please check with the Chief steward. Thank you!

It was almost nine o'clock when the van Dijk family came rushing into the dining room. They greeted the Loewes and the Moores. While Lars and Laura van Dijk poured themselves a cup of coffee to have with their donuts, Klaus, their son, helped himself to a glass of ice cold chocolate milk. Jürgen came into the dining room from the galley, approached them and asked everyone:

—You heard the captain. Who wants to come to the command bridge with me?

As expected, they all wanted to come to the bridge.

—Well then, meet me here at nine-thirty sharp —said Jürgen while heading back to the galley.

The original inhabitants of *Curaçao,* were Arawaks, the same ones which currently inhabit *La Guajira Peninsula,* in other words, Jaséle's people. The Spanish arrived to *Curaçao,* on an expedition led by Alonso de Ojeda, in 1499. They captured and deported most of the natives as laborers, bound for other colonies. The Dutch occupied the island in 1634, and because it had a great natural harbor, it soon became a strategic port for trade. Such was the case with the massive slave trade across the Atlantic, which was managed by the Dutch West India Company. The island also lent itself to piracy, amongst many other things. Throughout its history, it changed hands several times between England, France, and Holland. When one of the largest oil fields in the world was discovered in Lake Maracaibo, in Venezuela, the Royal Dutch Shell Company built a huge oil refinery and port facilities in *Curaçao,* which allows, till this day, major traffic for large tankers and freighters alike.

As they entered the bay of Santa Ana, they saw the beautiful tourist spectacle of the opening of the Queen Emma Pontoon Bridge. It was built in the nineteenth century and the people of Curaçao affectionately call it, *"The swinging old lady"*.[2] Athena was about two hundred yards away while the bridge, like a hinged door, folded to one side of the canal to allow boat traffic in and out. Once inside the channel, they went underneath the large and tall steel-fixed-bridge called, Queen Juliana.

All along Willemstad Bay, they observed the Dutch architecture with its multitude of small buildings in vibrant colours. These vistas were an open invitation to explore the city, its shops and its varied culture. But before the passengers went gallivanting around the island, Chief steward Jürgen gave them some instructions and advice, as to which places to visit in Curaçao. He warned everyone, Athena was leaving in twenty four hours, with or without them, and said:

—Ladies and gentlemen welcome to the island of *Curaçao.* The crew will be busy with port duties. Therefore, I ask you. Please don't interrupt the staff unless it is absolutely necessary. And especially, I beg you not to disturb the commanding officers.

Although the van Dijks were Dutch citizens, they had never before visited *Curaçao*. But because it seems they had done quite a bit of research on the island, they automatically became the default tour guides. Everyone was excited and when they had already come down the gangway and were standing on the quay, young Andrew, impulsively grabbed Hannah's hand and whispered softly to her ear:

—I'm coming with you ... right?

—*Ha-ha-ha!* ... OK, Andrew —said Hannah, thinking he was being funny.

Klaus van Dijk was fifteen years old, and he was oblivious to Andrew and Hannah's plan. To him they were just two snotty children, because he already felt like a grown-up. He

INDUSTRIAL DE VENEZUELA
OLD

AUDEMARS PIGUET
DAVID YURMAN
JEWELRY
WILLEMSTAD BAY.
DUTCH ARCHITECTURE
OF VIBRANT COLORS

deplored the fact there was no one closer to his age, but then, so be it. For the time being, he would stick to the company of his parents and other adults.

Athena's passengers would not be able to visit and do all those things they'd wished to, for there was simply not enough time. The island of *Curaçao,* has many tourist attractions such as bike tours, canoe trips, fabulous beaches, fishing, horseback riding, jeep safaris, windsurfing, visiting the Venezuelan fishermen's floating market, casinos, or simply strolling around the city, perusing museums, shops, restaurants and much, much more.

They rented bicycles and rode together. However, sometimes families were separated to follow their own routes, in order to explore on their own but agreeing to meet at a predetermined time, in some central location in the city. The one thing they all visited together, was the opening of the Queen Emma pontoon bridge, a must-see tourist site. In fact, they were just a few of the many tourists wandering around town, because three large American cruise ships, had also docked on the island on the same day.

The van Dijk family returned to the ship at about seven o'clock in the evening. They managed to arrive on time to have dinner on board. The Moores and Loewes arrived later, at around nine o'clock, because they had decided to dine out in Willemstad and try the local Creole cuisine.

The loading and unloading of containers using the port's large automated cranes, continued throughout the night and well until dawn.

The day they were due to depart, the passengers tired but happy and hungry, came down to the mess hall early, around seven in the morning.

Athena departed for Port of Spain, at eleven o'clock in the morning. When they left the bay of Santa Ana, Chief Officer *Axel Østergård* made another announcement and said:

—Ladies and gentlemen, this is Chief Officer Axel speaking. Our next destination is Port of Spain, in Trinidad and Tobago. We will travel about 460 nautical miles and expect to dock in twenty four hours. Thank you!

The distance of about 450 plus miles from *Curaçao,* to the island of Trinidad, was somewhat similar to the distance between Barranquilla, and *Curaçao.* Most of this trip's leg, would take place in and around Venezuelan territorial waters.

Maintaining a course of zero-niner-five degrees (095°) eastward, two hours after having left the Santa Ana Harbor, they navigated south of the island of Bonaire, which also belonged to the former Netherlands Antilles. Then they sailed far south of the small island of *Las Aves* or Birds' Islands, and two hours later they crossed south of Venezuela's beautiful archipelago of *Los Roques.* This last group of about 350 islands, cays and islets are similar in composition to the islands of the Bahamas. Namely, semiarid, of marine limestone rock formation with beautiful sugar-white-coral-sand-beaches and hosting a wide variety of aquatic, and of course, bird life. Late that night, they sailed south of the islands of *La Orchila, La Blanquilla,* and north of the famous tourist island of Margarita, in Venezuela.

The next day Athena arrived to the peninsula in the *Gulf of Paria* or Whale Gulf, christened the "Land of Grace" by Christopher Columbus, during his third expedition to the Americas.

Venezuela, and the island of Trinidad, are separated by the Strait of *Paria,* or as Columbus called it, the Mouth of the Dragon. And it is only six miles apart at its narrowest point. They changed course to one-eight-seven degrees (187°) and crossed the straits, entering the huge Gulf of *Paria,* on which the Orinoco River, one of the largest rivers in the South American continent, flows into the sea. Upon entering the Gulf, Athena resumed its eastbound course, arriving and docking at Port of Spain, within a couple of hours.

Port of Spain, is a modern city with several skyscrapers overlooking the water's edge, and it is the largest and most developed city in the country. It has a population of over half a million inhabitants. Also, it has the largest port facilities in the island, and this one has become an important center of maritime transport, in the Caribbean. Especially, with the large number of goods imported, and the huge amount of minerals exported from Venezuela, throughout the Gulf of *Paria*.

If the passengers had no time to visit all the places they had wanted to visit in Willemstad, they would have less of an opportunity to explore the many activities offered by this modern city. Chief steward Jürgen suggested them, to opt for a guided tour. Being nine passengers in total, they followed his advice and contacted a tour company, which picked them up on a twelve passenger minibus.

Meanwhile, Athena's port activities were quite frenzy. Not only loading and unloading containers but also, taking in the necessary fuel to cross the Atlantic, on their journey to Port Hamburg. Chief cook Alessandro Pallazzini and Chief steward Jürgen were busy stockpiling the galley. After all, they would have to feed forty-two people during the journey's estimated ten days at sea. Any delays, such as those caused by the weather, could make the duration of their trip even longer, so they had to anticipate any contingencies.

At one o'clock in the afternoon, the Loewes chose to separate themselves from the group and told the Moores and van Dijks they wanted to explore the city on their own, for a couple of hours. They agreed to meet them at Trinidad's Hyatt Regency Hotel, which is located on the waterfront and only a few blocks away from the city's central business district. When they left the hotel, the Loewes took a taxi, which brought them to Port of Spain's General Hospital, located a few miles north on Charlotte Street. They managed to find a obstetrician to examine Jaséle, at a moment's notice.

Up until then, Jaséle had not suffered any dizziness. But they wanted to make sure everything was alright, and they thought that getting her a physical, would not be such a bad idea.

While Jaséle was undergoing her physical examination, Wolfgang took Hannah to have ice cream, near-by. Hannah did not know why they were at the hospital and asked:

—Daddy, why are we here at the hospital?

—Your mom is getting a medical exam to see if everything is alright.

—Daddy, why wouldn't she be OK?

—*Oh sweetheart,* she feels quite well. But because she has never been on such a long journey by boat before, we just wanted to make sure she was OK. Do you understand, Hanni?

—*Ah, I see.* And what about us?

—Tell me something, Hanni. Do you feel good on the boat?

—*Yeeessss!*

—Me too ... So you see? ...

—What, Daddy?

—We don't need to get a checkup ... *Ha-ha-ha!*

—*Ha-ha-ha!* —Hannah laughed too.

—Hanni, can I ask a big favor of you, sweetie?

—*Aha!*

—Please don't tell anyone we came here today, alright?

—Yes, Daddy!

—Thank you, sweetheart ... I love you, baby!

—I love you too, Daddy!

When she left the doctor's office, Jaséle was feeling quite happy and lively. Later on that evening she would tell Wolfgang that her pregnancy was going well. She told him the doctor had made some recommendations on her diet, which she should try to stick to, in order to prevent problems with morning sickness. For example, she should avoid eating fatty foods and never eat too much in a single meal. It was better to eat six small meals a day. Also, the doctor said the meals should be rich in complex carbohydrates such as whole grain and whole wheat breads and pasta, potatoes, legumes, brown rice, oats, nuts and more. Before going to bed she should eat something rich in protein. And if she happened to feel queasy, a few sips of Ginger ale would help calm her stomach. Drinking ginger or peppermint tea in the mornings, could also prevent further unpleasantries.

The doctor emphasized she should supplement her daily diet with vitamins, so she gave her a bottle of multivitamins and folic acid. She also recommended her to eat cantaloupes, which apparently helps with the baby's brain development.

The Singh family, of Indian descent, boarded Athena at three in the afternoon, when the other passengers were busy sightseeing around the city. Mr. Ernest, Mrs. Lucy and their fifteen-year-old daughter, Tilly, would travel to Holland, via Port Hamburg. Most people of Indian origin in Trinidad and Tobago, don't speak Hindi. Many take Christian first names and they usually dress in western style. This was precisely the case with the Singhs. Young Klaus would have in Tilly, someone of his own age to play with. And the adults could easily organize two tables for playing cards by way of entertainment, during their long journey.

All the passengers returned to Athena at seven in the evening. Some went straight to the dining room for supper. As the crew was busy with preparations for the voyage, dinner was not as varied as usual, but of course, they did have pasta.

Around ten o'clock the next morning, the crew of Athena initiated all the activities to leave Port of Spain, bound for Europe.

CHAPTER 19

THE FOOTBALL GAME RESUMED, BUT NEITHER ROBERT NOR Maria, were interested in it. In fact, both of them were trying to guess what the other one was thinking. Robert didn't much care where he was sitting, as long as it was next to Maria. Meanwhile, all the noise around them, bothered her a lot. She wanted to talk to Robert and on the bleachers, it was just about impossible to hear him speak. Maria wanted to get to know Robert, and to do so, there was nothing better than to have a quiet conversation with him, anywhere but there. Ten minutes had passed, and Maria was pretty much fed up, so she shouted at him:

—Robert, I can't stand it any longer ... would you like to go out for a walk?

—*Yesss!* ... Excellent idea, Maria. *C'mon, let's go!* —said Robert while nodding his head.

They were off, forcing their way down steep steps, tripping on spectators, *CAREFUL!* ... and stepping on toes, *SORRY!* Finally, they reached the pavement. Now they walked slowly and silently while strolling out of the football field and leaving it behind.

Robert, mustering all the courage he could get, but without dwelling on it for too long, gently but firmly, took Maria's hand again. Maria did not reject him. It took them a few seconds to interlace their fingers, once more. Robert's hand was not much bigger than Maria's. She was pleased with his grip and smiled ever so gently to herself.

—*«Bravo, Robert! ... Maybe you are not as painfully shy as you'd led me to believe.»*

He was trying to pace himself and make time so they wouldn't reach the school building too quickly. He wanted to prolong the feeling of walking hand in hand with Maria, as long as possible. Lost in thought, he told himself:

—*«What a joy! ... Maria is even more beautiful than what I thought. I'd never imagined she would go out with me, let alone hold hands together. If my mother could see me now, I think she would be mighty proud!»*

After a glorious summer afternoon, there was a dark and cloudless sky but fortunately there wasn't too much humidity. And this made it a perfect night for stargazing. Despite the romantic atmosphere, neither one of them looked up at the stars, not even once that evening.

—Robert, would you rather have me call you Bob? —asked Maria.

—Actually, Maria, I prefer to be called by my first name... you know, Robert.

—*Good!* The nickname *"Bob"* seems so boring to me too.

—*Heh-Heh!* ... Maria, I'm glad you think so —said Robert.

—Its use is so common. But I thought perhaps this is what other people called you —said Maria.

—How about you, Maria? Do you have nickname too?

She laughed.

—*Ha-ha-ha! ... Oh, Good Heavens No!*

—Maria, is that truly so?

—*Ha-ha-ha!* ... Well, actually I do have one —said Maria.
—*Aha, I new it!* ... You must tell me. What is it, please?
—Look, at home they call me Maricarmen. But in school nobody knows that —said Maria.
Robert tried to pronounce her nickname.
—Marri ... Carmen ... What does it mean?
—My full name is Maria del Carmen Garcia Aragón. But my friends and family simply call me, Maricarmen.
—*Oh, Wow!* ... Now that's a pretty long name.
—But watch out, Robert!
—Maria, what do you mean by *"watch out?"*
—In School they called me Maria and that's the way I like it!
—*Ah!* Yes of course ... I understand, Maria —said Robert.
—Don't tell anyone ... OK, Robert? —Maria warned him.
—Tell me, Maria ... your last name, Aragón ...
—*Aha!* ...
—Does it have anything to do with the province of Aragón, in Spain, which we recently studied in class?
—*Yes!* ... I've been told our family tree goes back several centuries to that region of Spain.
—*Incredible!* ... Tell me more —asked Robert.
—I think the tree was burnt, or maybe someone chopped it down, because we don't know of any distant relative, who still lives there.... *Ha-ha-ha!* —said Maria.
Distracted, but thinking out loud, Maria continued:
—Someday, I would love to visit Spain and rediscover my family's history —said Maria, staring and lost in thought.
—I don't see why not! —said Robert.
—How's that?
—Maria, you know it's quite common for many Americans to travel to England, in search of their roots —said Robert.
—They say Spaniards have always been good at record keeping —said Maria.
—I wasn't aware of it —said Robert.
—*Oh gosh!* ... But what am I talking about? —sighed Maria, thinking this was just an impossible dream.

Getting back from her momentary lapse, Maria placed all her attention back on Robert again, and asked him:

—Tell me Robert, would you like to call me Maricarmen, too?

Robert tried to pronounce it, but stammered. Maria stopped walking and turned towards him. She extended both of her arms, took his face into her hands and squeezed his cheeks playfully. Robert, petrified and without moving a single muscle, was staring back at her. She nudged him and teasing him, she said:

—*C'mon, Robert!* ... I know you can do it!

—But Maria, that's kind of difficult for me. You've heard my lousy pronunciation before....

—*Oh,* but it's not hard, Robert. Or could it be you just don't want to be my friend? *Ha-ha-ha!*

—*Oh, Maria,* how could you even think that of me?

—*C'mon, Robert!* ... Let's do it together!

—*Whaaat?* —said Robert, revealing a sneaky thought he had, caused by Maria's seemingly innocent remark.

—Robert? ... What are you thinking about, you naughty boy?

—Maria ... I ... I ... I ...

—*Ahh-ha-ha!* ... Repeat after me ... Ma-ri-car-men. See how easy it is? —said Maria.

Robert stuttered again but managed to pronounce it, more or less, and then he smiled. But this time, Maria didn't smile.

She still had her beautiful and delicate hands holding Robert's face. Maria stared at him, intently into his eyes. Robert, like her, was staring back at her, without blinking. It almost seemed as if they were both trying to penetrate into each other's soul. They spent a few moments, motionless and enthralled with one another.

To say time had stopped for the both of them, fails to describe what they both felt. More appropriate would be to say Robert and Maria had now crossed into a parallel universe, which belonged, only to them both. Both knew or at least

suspected what their next step should be. But like the notes in a sublime music score, which can only be played at their precise moment, they needed to bide their time.

Maria and Robert slowly and gently approached each other. Although their hearts were beating fast, it appeared as if they weren't breathing at all. She tilted her head slightly to one side and like the reflection on a mirror with an opposite movement, he leaned to the other side until their lips met. And lo and behold, a strange thing happened. At the precise instant their lips touched, both felt, simultaneously, a small but unmistakable explosion in their heads. They heard it and felt it, like the dry sound of a powerful gunshot being fired ... *Spaaak!*

The impact was such, Maria lost consciousness and collapsed. But Robert was agile and just at that crucial moment when it was critical for him to be heroic, bold and brave, he took her by the waist and held her against his chest.

Robert also felt slightly weak at the knees, but while embracing her and for a split second, he leaned on her too. However, he knew his legs would fail him soon, and before they both fell to the ground, he held her by the waist and head, and gently placed Maria on the grass. He kneeled next to her, and using his hand as her pillow, he simply lay there staring and admiring her, and then he thought:

—*«Maria, however ridiculous and corny this may sound, you look as if you are Sleeping Beauty, sound asleep. Could it be that if I kiss you ... you will awake again, my sweet princess?»*

Robert kissed her and she opened her eyes and smiled. Maria was barely recovering from this incident, when she spoke to Robert, as if she had known him all of her life. Perhaps they were legendary and mythical soul mates.

—My love ... did you feel that? —asked Maria.

—Yes, yes I felt it ... and like you, I almost fainted too.

—I believe you, Robert.

—Maria, are you all right?

—Yes, Robert.... Although I'm a little dizzy. Yes, I believe I am alright.

—Maria, may I help you get back up on your feet?

—Yes, Robert ... thank you —said Maria, holding on to his neck and pulling hard in order to get back up, while Robert was helping her, as well.

Maria slowly got up and stood next to Robert. With her right hand she seized Robert's left hand and then they laced their fingers together, one more time. She took her left hand and placed it around Robert's left arm. Then Maria gently bent her head and laid it on Robert's shoulder. They continued walking without uttering another word.

CHAPTER 20

GETTING A LARGE CONTAINER SHIP READY FOR CAST OFF, IS a fairly complex operation requiring the coordination of a lot of people, including dock personnel, tugboats and local pilots. Depending on the port's wind, tide and currents' conditions, a ship may choose one departing procedure over another.

On the day they were due to depart Port of Spain, weather conditions were excellent. Athena was getting ready to cast off. Two tugboats were on stand-by, all mooring lines were released, and the powerful bow and stern thrusters began to turn, gradually separating this huge ship from the dock while at the same time Athena's powerful aft engine pushed the boat forward, gently and slowly.

Aboard modern vessels, it is sometimes possible to have pre programmed onboard computers carry out these maneuvers. However, all relevant personnel must have a careful watch and be ready to act quickly because a small mistake could cause a catastrophic accident: as has happened many times in the past.

Except for the Singh family, all the other passengers were on the balcony, outside the command bridge, enjoying the view, as they departed Port of Spain. Thirty minutes after leaving port, Chief steward Jürgen led the passengers to the dining room because it was lunchtime, and the Singhs joined them there. The adults sat at the round table, and the children shared a table for four, with Hannah and Robert sitting side by side. This was a good time to swap stories in order to get to know one another, better.

Once Athena crossed the narrow Mouth of the Dragon, it set a north-northeast heading of zero-three-zero degrees (030°), which would take them towards the English Channel, almost in a straight line and covering a distance of four thousand seven hundred nautical miles, or about 5,500 miles, or 8,700 kilometers. Depending on the weather, the trip would take between nine and ten days of sailing on the high seas to reach Port Hamburg, in Germany.

This course would take them along the Windward Islands. First they sailed pass Tobago, on their starboard or right-hand side, then Grenada, and St. Vincent, to port or their left-hand side. They continued on to Barbados, on starboard and finally, Santa Lucia, Martinique, Guadeloupe, and Barbuda, to port. At that point Athena left the warm waters of the Caribbean Sea, and entered the Atlantic Ocean. Three quarters of their way to Europe, if all went according to plan, Athena should sail pass north of the Azores islands.

The navigation course chosen by Captain Olaf and his officers was a less-traveled-sea-lane. Many captains prefer to sail their ships eastward, intercepting the Cape Verde Islands, which are four hundred nautical miles off the coast of Senegal, in West Africa, before heading north towards Europe.

Captain Olaf was somewhat concerned because they would cross the Tropic of Cancer, at the beginning of hurricane season and although rare, it could pose some risks.

That is why he asked his Chief officer Axel to keep him well informed with daily satellite weather reports.

—Mr. Axel, what do you think of our navigation plan? —said the captain.

—Captain, the boatswain and I worked together making sure the cargo is well located and secured. In addition, Athena is designed to withstand any storm —said Axel.

—Thank you, Officer Axel. I am sure you have done a thorough job, but ...

—But is there something troubling you, Captain?

—I was thinking about the passengers. We have twelve of them between men, women and children.

—*Ah!* I understand, Captain. Of course, we can adjust the course according to weather conditions —said Axel.

—That's precisely the problem, Mr. Axel.

—What do you mean, Captain Olaf?

—If we deviate too much from our planned route, we will burn more fuel and what's worse, we could end up delaying our arrival and that's costly. You are aware we're spending over fifty thousand dollars per day... Are you not?

—Well yes, Captain. But we could try to anticipate bad weather and make small course adjustments in advance —said Axel.

—Sure, sure we can, Mr. Axel.

—Also, we have a margin of four knots to increase or decrease our speed —said Chief officer Axel.

—Good point, Mr. Axel. What is our current speed?

—We're moving briskly, averaging twenty-one knots, Captain.

—Excellent, Mr. Axel. Thank you and that will be all for now —concluded Captain Olaf.

At their present speed of twenty-one knots, which is one knot above their planned "*slow steaming speed*", which is used for optimal fuel consumption, Athena was covering about five hundred nautical miles a day. By noon, on the second day of their voyage, they had already left the Caribbean Sea.

The first few days of the journey were pleasant, sunny and with almost cloudless skies. The passengers made several tours throughout different sections of the ship. One of their favorites was the aft engine room, below the bridge castle. Unlike cruise ships, which typically have two propellers for propulsion, a freighter only has one propeller but this one is huge.

They toured the boat in groups of two to four people but taking care not to distract the crew. Before entering the engine room it was essential to put on industrial-strength ear muffs because the noise was enormous. The engine room and the ship in general were extremely clean, freshly painted, and it had signs highlighting all the areas of the ship, especially those which could pose some danger. They also noted the ship produced huge quantities of drinking water, using seawater.

The passengers enjoyed walking the length of the boat to reach the forecastle, at the bow or forward end of the boat. Not only was it good exercise but this section of the boat was quieter. They could lie down and soak up the sun, read a book, or feel the sea breeze caressing their skin. Plus the view of the horizon during sunsets, was spectacular.

Soon, all the passengers got used to a daily routine. They ate, they walked, they exercised throughout the ship, they played cards and they read because there was certainly much time to read. On a boat, when you have no other reference to anything but the vast ocean and sky; when the sounds of the city vanish; when there are no phone calls; and when you watch almost no TV; time seems to stretch making the days appear to be much longer. But what for adults may be a wonderful time for rest and relaxation, for children, it could be a torture of boredom.

Fortunately, Hannah, Andrew, Tilly and Klaus could play all day long and sometimes well into the night. They went up and down the stairs, endlessly and tirelessly. Their parents had to warn them repeatedly, over and over again, not to run because of the potential hazards throughout the ship.

On the third day they had a barbecue on the main deck, behind the bridge castle, where a small swimming pool and half-a-basketball court were located. The officers, passengers and nearly half the crew shared in on this feast. The young crew, some of whom were not much older than Tilly and Klaus, had fun telling the children exaggerated sea-adventure-stories.

It was precisely one of the young crew members who suggested playing hide and seek, to the children. The boat was full of ideal places to hide, besides being enormous. The rules, however, said they could only play in the midsection of the ship and on the main deck. But in no way should they venture into other decks, under penalty of being thrown in the brig, for the rest of the journey. Fortunately, this resonated with the children, and they took heed of the warning and did not break the rules. Otherwise, they would have exposed themselves to risks, which may have well been lethal.

Every day the children played hide and seek and often played it several times a day. Andrew, in confidence, told Hannah he had a favorite hiding place, which was impenetrable and right amid ship.

—Hannah, do you want to see my hiding place? —asked Andrew.

—*Yeeessss!*

—Hannah, I'll show it to you but on two conditions.

—What conditions, Andrew?

—First, don't tell Tilly.

—And what's the second condition, Andrew?

—That especially, you don't tell that cocky Klaus.

—All right, Andrew. Where is your hiding place?

—You have to promise me, Hannah! You cannot tell anyone, Okay? —Andrew insisted.

—*Ugh!...* Yes, Andrew, I promise —said Hannah annoyed.

—Well, follow me, but try not to attract attention.

HJCU
1322 54 0
45G1
HANJIN
SHIPPING
CO LTD

ANDREW, HOW CAN YOU BE SURE THIS IS YOUR HIDING THE PLACE?
HANNAH, CAN YOU SEE THE UNION JACK RIGHT OVER THERE?

Hannah and Andrew ran down the roof-covered passageway, on the starboard side, arriving at the center of the ship. They climbed a vertical and tight hatch-access-ladder with a metal safety cage, which put them on the main deck; a place which was jam-packed with containers. They walked about fifty feet through a thin passageway in between containers. The containers were placed up to six units stacked, one on top of the other, above deck. Andrew and Hannah had to walk sideways to get through. Certainly, an adult could not enter this deep into the middle of the main deck.

—Hannah, this is it —said Andrew.

—Andrew, it's extremely dark in here.

—*Oh,* it's not so bad.

—How can you be sure this is the place? —asked Hannah.

—Look at the colour of the container. It is navy blue.

—But Andrew, there are lots of blue containers. And with all kinds of different colours too! —said Hannah.

Andrew raised his hand and turning his head sideways, pointed and said:

—Hannah, can you see the Union Jack right over there?

—What is it, Andrew? I don't understand.

—It's my country's flag ... *the United Kingdom!*

—*Wow, Andrew!* No one could find you here. Are you not afraid?

—No, Hannah. My dad says men have to be brave.

—Andrew, I don't like it here. Please, let's go ...

—Hannah, don't be afraid. I'll protect you. Follow me!

The antagonism Elizabeth Rose had towards Jaséle was increasing. This became more evident when Elizabeth, Laura, Lucy and Jaséle played cards in the dining room, during their usual game at three o'clock in the afternoon. Although Elizabeth's snide remarks seemed to have racist overtones, Jaséle suspected there was more to it than that. She couldn't put her finger on it, but it seemed to her Mrs. Moore had a truly deep pain, which had nothing to do with her.

Unfortunately for Jaséle, she wound up being the lightning rod for Elizabeth's frustration, anger and fury. The obvious contradiction was that at a first glance, one could easily see Elizabeth was a lady of good upbringing and possibly, on other occasions, refined manners.

It was curious that on the fourth day of travel, as Elizabeth became bitter and impertinent, not only with Jaséle but with Laura and Lucy too, the weather began to change relatively quickly, as well. The sky was filled with ominous dark clouds, and the horizon turned gray. The wind was blowing a little harder than usual but nothing to cause alarm. The waves exceeded eight feet, and this made Athena oscillate a little. Occasionally, a rain shower would fall but this would only last a short while. Instinctively, the children decided to watch movies on TV, first in the Moore's cabin and then, in the Loewe's.

On the fifth day, the sky was completely overcast. The wind was blowing hard, with frequent rain showers. The waves were already over twelve feet tall, but the wave troughs or distance between the crests, was long enough as to allow time for Athena to rock itself back up, gently; therefore, avoiding an awkward wobble. Now the passengers had to be careful when climbing or coming down the stairs and especially when using the head, i.e. the toilet, and the shower.

Athena would cross the Tropic of Cancer in twelve hours, but they had already been sailing in hurricane prone waters for a while. These hurricanes sometimes develop on the northern coast of Africa, over the Sahara desert. At 0600 hours, early in the morning, Chief Officer Axel appeared at captain's Olaf cabin. He woke up the captain and brought him the latest Atlantic Ocean's marine weather fax.

—Good morning, Captain. Sorry to bother you, but I have information about sudden weather changes —said Chief officer Axel.

—Do we have satellite data in real-time?

—Affirmative Captain, all systems are functioning normally.

—Okay. I'll see you on the bridge in fifteen minutes, and then we'll go over these reports.

—All right, Captain. Is there anything else? —asked Axel.

—Yes. Tell Chief steward Jürgen to bring me coffee and donuts to the bridge.

—Immediately, Captain!

—Who else is on the bridge?

—The third officer, the boatswain, the helmsman and I, Captain —said Axel.

—Let's have coffee and donuts for everyone!

—Thank you, Captain!

—One more thing, Mr. Axel. Talk to the Rotterdam office and ask them for instructions.

As the Chief Officer turned to go back to the command bridge, the captain shouted:

—Mr. Axel, make sure not to alarm the passengers!

—*Aye aye,* Captain! —said Chief Axel.

Although the captain is the ultimate authority on a ship, and it is he who makes the final decisions, some headquarters for major shipping companies have large logistics and navigational resources, which represent a huge help for the captain. Today, modern and sophisticated freighters are always connected to the computer networks of their home offices, which may constantly monitor a number of on-board automated systems.

Jaséle had followed the advice of the physician to the letter and this helped her immensely. It was ironic that Mr. and Mrs. Singh became seasick and she did not. Wolfgang had a hunch that Athena was about to encounter bad weather. What he didn't know was, how bad it was going to be. Wolfgang and Jaséle lay awake in bed and then she asked him:

—Honey, you seem preoccupied. What's troubling you?

—Although they haven't said anything yet, I think we'll encounter bad weather.

—Are we in any danger?

—*No!* But I worry that with the boat's movement you'll become seasick. Well ... in reality just about anybody could get sick, including the crew.

—What about little Hannah? —asked Jaséle.

—I think she'll be fine.

—Wolfgang, how can you be so sure?

—Hannah has never been seasick when we sailed before or during our long car trips. But I guess it's a matter of luck.

—*God willing, she won't!* —said Jaséle.

After a few moments in bed without saying a word, Wolfgang then asked:

—Honey, how are you getting along with Elizabeth Rose?

—*Ugh!* ... It's really bad. I think the poor woman has a lot of problems.

—It's a shame because her brother William, is such a good fellow —said Wolfgang.

—What did you say? Did you say, her brother? I thought they were married.

—No, obviously they're not.

—So, Andrew is not her son? —asked Jaséle.

—Andrew is William's son.

—And where is Andrew's mother?

—William told me she was killed in a car accident, in London, scarcely two years ago —said Wolfgang.

—*Oh, what a shame!* And to think Hannah has taken quite a liking to Andrew.

—Yes, that's true —said Wolfgang.

—And Elizabeth, what role has she got in all of this?

—Elizabeth tried to assume the role of Andrew's mother.

—*Aha!*

—At first all went well, but after losing her baby, things quickly went from bad to worse.

—*What? She lost a baby?*

Wolfgang explained that Elizabeth Rose was engaged to marry a British nobleman. Apparently she had become pregnant, after having announced her intentions. But after losing her baby, she went into a state of deep depression and decided to call off the engagement. The gentleman, who she was to marry, insisted the wedding take place, but she did not budge. Her fiancé said he would wait for her, as long as necessary. This is why they decided to go on an adventure trip, to try to leave all those sad memories behind them.

—Wolfgang, my darling… now I understand why she behaves the way she does towards me. Thank you.

It was about seven o'clock and the weather was getting worse. Jaséle got up to prepare a mint tea. Wolfgang also got out of bed, put on his bathrobe, went into the bathroom and afterwards, he sat on the couch next to Jaséle. She leaned over his shoulder. Hannah slept peacefully on her bunk bed. Jaséle took a sip of tea, put the cup on the table and rhetorically, as if talking to herself out loud, said:

—I'd like to do something for the Moores.

—But Jaséle, what can you do?

—I don't know, but I'll think of something.

Captain Olaf had reached the command bridge and just right then and there, Chief steward Jürgen arrived with coffee and donuts for everyone.

—Mr. Jürgen, could you come here please? —said the captain.

—How may I help you, Captain? —asked the Chief steward.

—Tell me, Chief… How are the passengers faring, so far?

—They all seem well, Captain. Mr. and Mrs. Singh got seasick, but I gave them some medication and now they are feeling much better.

—*Aha!* ... I see —said the captain.

—Captain, are you worried about the passengers? —asked Jürgen.

—It's likely we will encounter bad weather, and I want you to be my liaison to the passengers —said the captain.

—Understood, Captain. Would there be anything else, Captain?

—Yes, Chief ... Try to keep the passengers calmed. And restrict their movements to the bridge castle, until further notice.

—As you wish, Captain!

—*Ah!* ... And Chief Jürgen, under no circumstances they should be allowed on the command bridge.

—*Aye aye,* Captain! —said Chief steward Jürgen while leaving the bridge.

The third officer had finished his shift and the second officer arrived to replace him. Now the captain, the Chief Officer, the second mate and the boatswain were meeting to discuss the strategy for the bad weather that was upon them.

Chief Officer Axel's report said the barometer had fallen during the night. It was now registering an atmospheric pressure of 980 millibars and it was continuing to drop. On the coast, this could indicate a severe storm but not quite a category-one-hurricane on the *Saffir-Simpson* scale. But on the high seas, it would be a Force 10 storm on the Beaufort scale. The storm followed a course of two-seven-seven degrees (277°), and it was moving on a westerly course, at ten knots.

Headquarters advised them to alter their course to zero-three-eight degrees (038°); subsequently, intercepting the storm on its eastern flank. If the severe storm did not change its course, they would only have to endure between twelve to eighteen hours of foul weather.

Following this new heading, Athena would still sail pass north of the Azores as planned. Although they could suffer a delay of one day, because they would have to slow down to maintain the safety of the passengers, crew, cargo and ship. Captain Olaf agreed with headquarters' recommendations and ordered a change in course.

—*Helmsman!* —called the captain.

—*Aye,* Captain —said the helmsman.

—Set heading to zero-three-niner degrees (039°).

—New heading zero-three-niner degrees (039°), Captain —replied the helmsman.

—Mr. Boatswain, is the cargo secured? —asked the captain.

—Yes, Captain. The Chief Officer and I performed a visual inspection yesterday, at 1300 hours —replied the boatswain.

—Mr. Boatswain, I want you to take a group of five men and take a fresh look at the containers' lashing systems. Check ties, fasteners, wire rope, rigid rods, chains, turnbuckles ... you know, the works. Do it from bow to stern, again!

—*Aye aye,* Captain!

—Please report with the Chief Officer when you're finished.

—*Aye aye,* Captain! —said the boatswain, turning around and briskly leaving the command bridge.

—Second mate ... —called the captain.

—At your service, Captain.

—Meet with the Chief Engineer, review contingency plans and prepare a report on the current status. Please report with the Chief Officer when finished.

—*Aye aye,* Captain! —replied the second officer, on his way to the engine room.

—Captain! —called Chief officer Axel.

—Tell me, Mr. Axel.

—Why did you ordered a course of zero-three-niner degrees (039°) instead of zero-three-eight degrees (038°) as recommended by headquarters? —asked Axel.

—Call it insurance, Mr. Axel.... It's only insurance. I don't want to risk a sudden change in the storm's heading.

CHAPTER 21

ON THE SIXTH DAY, ATHENA HAD ALREADY CROSSED THE Tropic of Cancer and was sailing on the eastern front of a severe Force 10 storm, on the Beaufort scale. The barometer dropped to 965 millibars. They were already experiencing 40-plus-foot-waves. The water surface was covered with white foam, created by the spray of breaking waves. The wind howled at over sixty-five miles per hour. The sky was overcast; it rained continuously, there was lightning and haze obstructing visibility. Every now and then, Athena's bow would dig into a huge wave and despite being so high, the spray from the violent collisions would splash the container yard amidship and up to the height of the main deck. In spite of these severe storm conditions, at no time was Athena in danger of sinking and thanks to the savvy of the helmsman, rolling movements from side to side, which are the most dangerous for the boat and the worst for motion sickness for crew and passengers alike, were kept to a maximum angle of fifteen degrees (15°).

ATHENA

Chief steward Jürgen distributed seasickness pills. Luckily none of the children got sick. And now the four of them played in the Loewe's cabin, which had large picture windows, allowing them to enjoy the magnificent view of the container yard, and also, the huge ocean waves of an angered sea to starboard.

Of all the adult passengers, only Mr. Ernest Singh and Mrs. Laura van Dijk got severely seasick, having to run several times to the toilet to vomit. They managed to calm their nausea by eating crackers and sipping warm soda.

It was three o'clock in the afternoon and all the adults were in the dining room playing cards. William, with his peculiar phlegmatic English humor, said:

—We cannot let bad weather ruin our regular game!

Elizabeth Rose was drinking Scotch whisky neat and water back. Perhaps because of the alcohol or maybe due to the storm, but she was in a truly foul mood. Lucy Singh, like her husband, was of Indian descent. She had a lively, friendly and agreeable sort of face. She wore thick short and shiny black hair, had a tan skin and although English was her native language back in Trinidad, she spoke it with a tinge of an accent, characteristic of Hindus. When Elizabeth got tired of assaulting Jaséle, she took it against Lucy. Suddenly, Elizabeth misread a play by Lucy and hysterically, she shouted:

—*Cheater!* ... Is it that you cannot play without resorting to those imbecile ways from your backward country?

—*Calm down, Elizabeth!* It's just a game —said Laura.

—This trip to South America has been horrible! —said Elizabeth.

—What do you mean, Mrs. Moore? —Inquired Lucy.

—*Ugh!* Everything I've seen on this trip has been filth, stench, ugliness, extreme poverty, sweltering heat and humidity, disease, noise, flies and mosquitoes!

—Elizabeth, don't you think you're exaggerating? Nothing could be unquestionably that bad —said Laura.

—*Yuck!* These people make me sick! —cried Elizabeth.

—Don't you worry, Elizabeth. In just a few days we'll be back in Europe —said Laura while trying to calm her down.

—*Bravo!* Finally, we will get back to civilization!

—Mrs. Moore, did I hear you say civilization? —asked Lucy, ironically.

—And ... do you know what's worse? —said Elizabeth.

—No, I don't know. What is it, Elizabeth? —asked Laura.

—I'm quite certain the rabble, those half-breeds ... they have no feelings —lambasted Elizabeth.

—Elizabeth, do not say such things —said Laura.

—And why ever not, Laura? —said Elizabeth.

—Tis not nice to say things you will later regret —said Laura.

—*No, no, no ... I got it! ...* —cried Elizabeth.

—What? What is it, Elizabeth? —asked Laura.

—Those people have no souls. Yes, yes that's it. *They have no souls!* —cried Elizabeth.

Although she was quite drunk and exhausted, Elizabeth took another swig of scotch. At times the storm seemed to get worse. Lucy, tired of all the insults she was enduring from Elizabeth, with an ice-cold voice, a sharp-tongue and with the intent to injure or at least to ridicule, said:

—*"If you prick us, do we not bleed?*
If you tickle us, do we not laugh?
If you poison us, do we not die?
And if you wrong us, shall we not revenge?"

—What are those stupid things you're saying? —cried Elizabeth.

—Those words were written, over four hundred years ago, by one of your own countryman —said Lucy undaunted.

—*That's a pack of lies!* Who said that? —asked Elizabeth.

—William Shakespeare. Tis a passage from The Merchant of Venice, Act Three, Scene One —said Lucy.

Elizabeth, who was now extremely irritable, upon hearing Lucy's explanation became enraged and pounded the table with her glass, spilling her whiskey. Then she shouted and demanded:

—*Arrggh!* ... How can an ignorant, such as yourself, quote the most important author in the whole universe?

This was precisely the opportunity Lucy had been waiting for. Calmly, in control, with coldness, with all the serenity she could muster, and salivating at the prospect she was about to taste a sweet revenge against Elizabeth's racist comments, which had been leveled against her, she said:

—I ... an ignorant half-breed, as you so aptly put it, graduated with honors from St. Catherine's College, at *"your"* Oxford University!

It was clear Elizabeth was suffering from a dangerous mental breakdown, a hurricane of emotions equivalent to the violent storm, which raged outside. When Lucy's words penetrated Elizabeth's ears, she completely lost it. In her mind, this was outright preposterous! She slapped the glass of whiskey violently, crashing it onto the floor and shattering it into a thousand pieces. And before her fury was dissipated into a state of desperation, despair and desolation, she screamed:

—*Noooooooo...!!!*

Athena pitched deeply, slamming its nose down hard while at the same time, it rolled heavily to one side. Immediately, they felt the blow of a huge wave crashing loudly against the hull, throwing tons of blueish cold water and foam across all decks, as if determined to break her into two pieces, like a helpless matchstick. Athena jerked violently forcing cabinet doors to slam wide open in the galley. China, pots, pans, cans, cutlery and bottles fell off the shelves and tables, crashing onto the floor and making great noise in its wake. This must have been the largest wave they had faced, so far.

Elizabeth couldn't take it any longer, and burying her face in her hands and with a deep sense of grief, sadness and despair, she burst into tears and began weeping out loud with an extreme sense of anguish and total abandon. Lucy, like everyone else, was surprised and alarmed at Elizabeth's reaction. In the middle of this appalling scene, Laura was speechless. Jaséle jumped up and hugged her, trying to comfort her. William too, jumped up from his seat to come to the aid of his sister and do the same. He clutched the table, held his sister and tried to maintain balance while he apologized to everyone in the room, in an effort to take her back to their cabin.

—Please, Mr. Moore ... let me accompany you —begged Jaséle.

—I am afraid that's not a good idea, Mrs. Loewe. Thank you anyways —said William.

—I am sorry, Mr. Moore, but I must insist! As a woman I can assure you, I fully understand Elizabeth's problems. Please let me help her, William —forcefully, implored Jaséle.

—All right, Mrs. Loewe. You are most kind and I am grateful for it. Please come with us!

Elizabeth was crying and sobbing incessantly. With one arm holding onto Jaséle's shoulder and the other one onto William's, the three climbed up the stairs, holding on to the railing tightly. Trying to maintain their balance and amid the ship's severe swaying, they headed towards the Moore's cabin.

The children, at times, watched cartoons on television. Sometimes, they entertained themselves with video games, and other times they simply got up to watch the storm with their noses pasted on to the picture-window's cold glass. Klaus was constantly trying to prevail and lead the small group, but Andrew, despite being four years younger than him, would not allow it. Tilly didn't see Hannah eye-to-eye either. She couldn't understand why Hannah was not interested in talking about fashion, the boys on her favorite rock 'n' roll band or even playing with her doll collection.

Meanwhile, Hannah felt bored with the ongoing feud between them. She was more interested in knowing what her parents were up to. She missed her home in *La Guajira,* and missed the sun, too. And she just couldn't understand, why her beloved sea was so angry.

Klaus and Andrew were arguing because they couldn't agree on what to watch on TV. But in reality, it was mostly a continuous rivalry and jockeying for power, amongst the two of them. Tilly tried to mediate between the two but that didn't work. Hannah, like Tilly, couldn't do much either. Klaus was furious, but Andrew wouldn't budge.

—Andrew ... you behave like a sissy! —said Klaus.

—No! I'm not a sissy! —said Andrew.

—Yes, you are too! ... *Naaa ... na na na na ... naaa! ... Sissy, sissy, sissy-girl! ... Ha-ha-ha!*

—I'm not a sissy and you're an idiot! —said Andrew.

—*Whaaat?* You dare call me an idiot? Shut up, or I'll break your face! —said Klaus trying to intimidate him.

—I'm not afraid of you! —said Andrew sounding a bit defensive.

—*Guys, guys, guys!* —complained Tilly.

—Mind your own business, Missy! *Ha-ha-ha!* —said Klaus.

—*Klaus, leave him alone!* He is a lot younger than you —cried Tilly, trying to defend Andrew.

—I know you're afraid. You're so afraid you have to hide behind a girl's skirt! —Klaus egged him on.

—*No!* It is not true! I have no fear! —said Andrew.

—Yes ... you're too afraid, and I'll prove it!

—How? —Unfortunately for Andrew, he asked the wrong question while trying to show his valor.

—I dare you go down to the main deck, now! —Klaus challenged him.

—*Oh no!* Don't listen to him, Andrew! That's just too dangerous —said Hannah disturbed and quite agitated.

—You see, I was right. You're terrified. *Chicken!* —Klaus challenged him again.

—Klaus, get out of here! I will tell my father! —said Hannah angrily.

—Alright, I'll go to my room, but Andrew is a coward!

—*No, no, no!* ... I'm not a coward ... not a coward! —said Andrew while feeling livid.

—*Cluck, cluck, cluck!* ... *Chicken!* ... *Bwahaha!* —Klaus jeered him on something awful and then, he left the cabin.

You never know which emotional strings, such that, when pulled, will effect an unpredictable behavior in a person and more so, in a child. Andrew had recently suffered the loss of his mother. Then his aunt suffered a nervous breakdown, turning her into a madman. His father tried to instill self reliance in him and to develop a strong character. He was emphatic about Andrew always behaving like a man, that is to say, being brave. In the midst of all of this, he felt he had to be proving his manhood to all the kids on the block, but unfortunately for him, on this trip that kid was Klaus.

—Captain Olaf, we have good news —said Chief Axel.

—Let's hear it. What is it, Mr. Axel? —asked the captain.

—Sir, the storm changed course. The new course is two-six-zero degrees (260°). This means it is moving away faster than we first thought.

—Chief Axel, what is the weather forecast for the next twelve hours?

—Currently, at 1730 hours the storm is still Force 10. In six hours it will be Force 5. And in twelve hours we will have light breezes at Force 2.

—Excellent, Mr. Axel. Please alert Chief steward Jürgen to notify the passengers —ordered the captain.

—*Aye,* Captain! —replied the Chief Officer.

—Helmsman! —called the captain.

—At your service, Captain —replied the helmsman.

—When we reach Force 4, resume zero-three-zero degrees (030°) and twenty-one knots again —ordered the captain.

—Twenty-one knots ... *Aye,* Captain! —said the helmsman.

—Chief Axel, tomorrow at 1400 hours, phone headquarters and tell them we will arrive on time.

—*Aye,* Captain! —said the Chief Officer.

—*Oh* ... and Mr. Axel, inform Chief steward Jürgen and Chief Cook Alessandro that tomorrow we will have a gala dinner, at 1930 hours —again ordered the captain.

—*Aye aye,* Captain! ... Great idea, sir —said Chief officer Axel, quite pleased with the captain's orders.

It was six o'clock. The storm had not abated but even the passengers realized the weather was improving. Still, they had large waves breaking against Athena's bow, throwing spray over the deck and containers, but these were becoming less frequent.

The Loewes were in their cabin debating whether to come down to dinner that evening. Jaséle, as usual, had little appetite. Following the physician's recommendations closely, she decided to remain in her cabin. Father and daughter did plan to come down to the mess hall for dinner. All of the sudden there was a knock on the door, *knock-knock!* ... Wolfgang opened it and found William and then, he said:

—Hello, William! How is your sister?

—She's doing much better, thank you. We gave her a strong sedative and she is sound asleep —said William.

—Excellent! That's excellent! —said Wolfgang.

—By the way, Jaséle ... I cannot thank you enough for all your help with Elizabeth this afternoon —said William.

—You're most welcome, William. Tomorrow I wish to spend the day with her, if it is not a problem? —said Jaséle.

—Jaséle, that is a capital idea! —said William.

—And I shall spend the whole day with Andrew ... *Ha-ha-ha!* —added Hannah.

—That is precisely the reason why I am here. I came looking for Andrew. I thought he was with you —said William.

—«*Hanni, wann hast Du Andrew zuletzt gesehen?*» Hanni, at what time did Andrew leave? —asked Wolfgang.

—«*Ich weiß nicht, Papa!*» I don't remember, Daddy!

—I suppose he is with the other kids. I'll look for him there... *Cheerio!* —said William while leaving the cabin.

—Good night, William —said Jasèle while bidding him goodbye.

Within forty-five minutes, the usual strong bell ring reverberated throughout the ship to draw attention. Then they all heard the captain's voice with an urgent announcement:

—*Attention! Attention! Attention!* This is Captain Olaf speaking.

With a no-nonsense demeanor, Captain Olaf continued:

—*This is an emergency!* We are having difficulty locating one of our children. Come down to the galley immediately, for further instructions! —The captain ordered sharply.

Soon thereafter, all the passengers began to arrive at the dining room, as the captain had ordered; except for Elizabeth, of course, because she was still fast asleep due to the strong medication she had taken earlier.

Athena was still in the midst of the storm but it was subsiding rapidly. The ship was no longer rocking so violently, but it was raining heavily and the wind was still raging outside.

William looked severely distressed, with a slight twitching of his upper lip. Nevertheless, his temper was composed. Chief Officer Axel informed them, young Andrew was missing, and they needed to find him most urgently and quickly. Nobody said it, but the horror of thinking Andrew had fallen overboard in the middle of the storm, went through everyone's mind. The adults formed a circle around the children. No one knew his whereabouts, but Axel did not waste any time, and he questioned the children severely. Klaus was pale, white as a sheet of paper and terrified at the prospect he was the reason for Andrew's disappearance and frankly, both Hannah and Tilly, thought so too.

—Tell me, young Klaus. What do you know about Andrew's disappearance?
—*Me?* ... I ... I ... I ... know nothing! —Klaus hesitated.
—When was the last time you saw him? —asked Axel.
—I went to my cabin and left him with these two —said Klaus pointing towards Hannah and Tilly.
—Miss Tilly, is what Mr. Klaus said true?
—Yes, it is, officer! —said Tilly.
—When was the last time you saw Andrew?
—When we both went to our cabins. He followed me and I entered my cabin —said Tilly.
—And Andrew, did you see him enter his cabin?
—*No!* I did not see him.
—How come you didn't see him? —asked Axel.
—His cabin is down the hall and around the corner from mine. So I went into mine before he went into his —said Tilly.
—«*Sagen Sie mir mal, Fräulein Hannah*» Tell me, Miss Hannah, Is it true what Miss Tilly is saying? —the Chief Officer asked.
—*Yes, it is true!* —said Hannah, leaving no room for any doubt.

Chief officer Axel suspected the secret of the puzzle lay with the children. So he didn't question a single adult. The children were terrified. Axel, in an effort to contain his anxiety and concern about the whereabouts of young Andrew, and with his usual professional voice, warned the three children:

—The life of young Andrew is in your hands. Think before you speak. Do any of you know why your friend Andrew disappeared?

There was only silence. None of the children ventured to utter a single word. Wolfgang, appealing to the excellent relationship he had with his daughter, asked her:

—«*Hanni, was ist passiert?*» Hanni, what happened?

—«*Klaus und Andrew haben sich mit ihrem Vater gestritten, Paps!*» Klaus and Andrew had a fight, Daddy!

—*Lies, lies, lies!* That's not true. Those are lies from a foolish little girl! —cried Klaus scared and trying to save his skin.

—Hannah is telling the truth. I saw it too. *Klaus and Andrew had a fight!* —said Tilly while rediscovering her courage in Hannah's response.

Axel didn't want to waste any more time arguing about who was to blame. But his intuition told him Hannah might have the answer to this problem. He crouched in front of Hannah. And with a gentle smile, so as not to frighten the girl even more, he asked her:

—«*Mein hübsches Prinzesschen*» My beautiful princess ... Do you know where Prince Andrew is?

Hannah moved her head up and down and nodded. Calmly, Chief officer Axel asked her again:

—«*Hannah, wo ist Andrew?*» Hannah, where is Andrew?

Hannah raised her right hand and pointed with her finger into the container yard on the main deck. Nobody said anything. The only sound you could hear was the rain pattering on the windowpane and the wind howling. Chief officer Axel, who was still crouched, asked her once more:

—«*Hannah, kannst du uns hinbringen?*» Hannah, could you take us there?

Hannah turned towards her father seeking approval in his eyes. Jaséle was in shock but said nothing. Chief officer Axel was conducting a life or death investigation. This was no time to give in to fears. It took a lot of strength, but neither Wolfgang, nor Jaséle showed much emotion. You could say young Hannah was being tested by fate. She would have to make this vital decision alone. It is possible that if she told them where to find the boy, the crew could eventually find the whereabouts of young Andrew. But this could easily take a long time; therefore, increasing the risk the rescue mission would fail. Everybody waited anxiously for the little girl's answer. She turned and saw Chief officer Axel straight into his eyes and said:

—«*Kommt schnell her, ich zeige euch, wo er sich versteckt haben könnte!*» Yes! Come quickly, I will take you there.

—«*Vielen Dank mein tapferes Prinzesschen*» Thank you, my brave little princess! —said Chief officer Axel.

Chief Officer Axel grabbed his VHF radio transceiver and hailed Captain Olaf who was on the command bridge. He pressed the microphone button, *Click!* to speak but there was a lot of static, *Chist! Chiss! Chiss!* and yelling out loud, he said:

—Captain Olaf, Captain Olaf, come in please.

—*Chist! chiss! chisss!* This is the Captain speaking, over.

—*Click!* ... Found boy's whereabouts. Total container yard lighting requested. Also, message to boy. Rescue underway. Over.

—*Chist! chiss! chisss!* ... Understood. Captain Olaf, out.

The boatswain was in the dining room with them. Chief officer Axel called him:

—Attention, Mr. Boatswain!

—At your orders, Sir!

—Young Hannah, her father Wolfgang, Mr. Moore, you and I need full-rescue gear at once —ordered Axel.

—*Aye Aye,* Chief! —said the boatswain and then he left the room quickly, with an extreme sense of urgency.

A few minutes later the boatswain returned with two sailors, carrying the rescue gear. It was already night and dark, it rained heavily, it was cold, the wind blew hard, the decks were slippery and occasionally the spray from the waves crashed madly on the container yard.

They all donned their marine-foul-weather-gear, which is a United States Coast Guard approved anti-exposure-work-suit. Fortunately, Hannah was tall-for-her-age, so she was able to wear a young sailor's gear. These suits were bright orange colour with lots of refractive material strips. This gear is designed to self inflate if falling overboard into the ocean, to float and to protect them against hypothermia. It has a strobe light, whistle, mirror, electronic transponder, which serves as a personal GPS locator beacon, adhesive thermal gloves and boots, lots of pockets with zippers, knife and a black hood with an elastic to seal it around the face. Lastly, they fastened their harnesses and safety lines with snap-on hooks.

They were told they would all be bound by their harnesses and safety-lines, one behind one another, just as mountain climbers do. They were also instructed to engage and disengage their safety-lines with the snap-on-hooks at all times before walking, to avoid accidentally falling overboard. They put a pair of bright yellow goggles with an elastic safety cord on Hannah, so she could see clearly and to protect her from the salt water spray.

Poseidon, the god of the sea, would test innocent little Hannah's mettle, because precisely when they were getting ready to go out, the storm regained its strength, raging on with great force, rain, deafening noise, *Yoooooo!* ... howling wind, thunder and lightning.

The strobe lights on their suits were lit and they exited in single file: Chief officer Axel, Hannah, Wolfgang, Mr. Moore and finally, the boatswain. All of them but Hannah, had flashlights strapped to their heads. The container yard was lit. The strong wind and rain hit them hard. Athena was pitching vigorously once more and what's worse, rolling from side to side.

All the passengers and especially Jasèle, who was scared out of her wits, saw them leave one by one and then disappear down the ladder, which led to the passageway or platform, on Athena's starboard side. They clung tightly to the metal railings and Wolfgang kept close to his daughter, to protect her against any danger. Engaging and disengaging their safety-lines, like they were told, they began to walk slowly against the fury of the elements and towards the ship's bow.

INE
NE

YOUNG MR. ANDREW, ...
THIS IS CAPTAIN OLAF.
WE KNOW WHERE YOU ARE!!!

Chief officer Axel was visibly worried and thought:

—*«What in the world is this boy doing on deck in the middle of this storm? I hope young Hannah is correct. I cannot even imagine all the problems we'll have with the authorities if we don't find him, let alone all sorts of inquiries, insurance, lawsuits ... Oh, gosh!»*

From the bridge castle, the captain could see the strobe lights flashing brightly, resembling the lights of police cars and ambulances at a car crash site, in the middle of the night. Every so often, the captain sent a message through the loudspeakers to give young Andrew some encouragement.

—Young Mr. Andrew ... This is Captain Olaf speaking. We know where you are. Be patient please. Don't move from your current location. Your father, your friend Hannah and her dad are coming for you.

When they were halfway there, a huge wave exploded against Athena's side and the spray fell on the passageway, throwing thousands of gallons of green water rushing quickly on deck and sweeping them all, as if they were bowling pins. They fell and were submerged in cold sea water and the impact dragged them along the passageway, but Wolfgang grabbed hold of his daughter. Luckily all their harnesses, safety lines and snap-on hooks were all latched on, and they withstood the wave's brutal onslaught. Like a wild river or a flash flood, the torrent of water rushed all the way back to the stern and fell back into the sea. Everyone was shook up. Hannah swallowed some water and coughed. Wolfgang patted her on the back to clear up her lungs, and her cough did relent. Chief officer Axel shouted:

—*IS EVERYONE, ALRIGHT?*

Everyone nodded. Wolfgang spoke directly into Hannah's ear and asked:

—Hanni, my sweetheart. Are you alright?

—Yes, Daddy! —Hannah yelled.

—*What?* —Wolfgang asked again because the noise was unbearable.

Hannah nodded and Wolfgang, who had her embraced, kissed her and yelled into her ear, he was proud of her for being so courageous. Then Wolfgang gestured Chief Axel, giving him a thumbs-up indicating everything was fine, and they should continue on.

—*HANNAH, WHERE?*—Axel yelled again.

Hannah pointed forward and they all resumed walking. When they reached the vertical and tight-hatch access ladder amidship, Hannah pulled hard on Chief Axel's harness. Then she pointed up the ladder. They climbed the tight ladder with great difficulty because their heavy gear was rubbing against the metal-safety-cage. Once on the main deck, they could only advance about eight feet into the tight passageway, in between the containers, because it was way too narrow. The boatswain was standing dangerously close to the edge of the deck or gunwale, while perilously holding on to the ladder.

Hannah was the only one who could travel the distance to the middle of the deck, which was the hideout place Andrew had shown her a few days before. Faced with sudden ship's movements, the heavy containers creaked from rubbing metal on metal, producing a terrifying noise. They would have to hurry because there was a real danger, these containers could move or worse yet, break loose and crush them to death.

Chief Officer Axel asked Wolfgang and Hannah for their consent and explained she would have to walk roughly fifty feet deep, by herself, in order to find Andrew. Wolfgang and his daughter agreed. Axel attached another small harness onto Hannah's and gave it to her to take it to Andrew. She was also tied to her father's harness. Axel lit the way for Hannah, and she started walking sideways, but slowly.

When she reached the middle of the main deck, she saw Andrew crouched, soaked, pale and *Brrrr!* trembling cold, but holding fast to the blue container. It was critical to get him out of there as soon as possible. Otherwise, Andrew could suffer from severe hypothermia, go into shock and this could cause him a certain death. Hannah shouted as loud as she could:

—ANDREW! ... What are you doing here?

—WHAT? —Andrew cried out loud because he could not hear her.

—WHAT ARE YOU DOING HERE? —Hannah yelled again.

—I AM NOT A CHICKEN! —replied Andrew, *Brrrr!* shivering with cold.

—ANDREW, YOU'RE CRAZY! ... *HA-HA-HA!*

—YES I AM! ... *HA-HA-HA!*

—ANDREW, CAN YOU PUT THIS HARNESS ON?

—NO, HANNAH, I CANNOT MOVE! —yelled Andrew, for there was no room to move, even for a child. The place was just too narrow.

—UNDERSTOOD! ... TAKE MY HAND AND LET'S GO, NOW!

—OK HANNAH, LET'S GO!

Before Hannah and Andrew could finish walking back fifty feet, another huge wave exploded, flooding the passageway. The force of the water swept them back out towards Chief Axel. Nevertheless, Axel managed to grab hold of the both of them, right at the edge of the stairway. Both were coughing because they had swallowed water. The wave's impact threw the boatswain off the ladder, hitting his head on the metal-safety-cage and knocking him unconscious. His safety line snapped off, and he was now hanging on the outside of the gunwale and pulling hard on the line attached to Mr. Moore, and swaying dangerously. William had all the boatswain's dead-weight pulling on him. In turn, William's safety line was dragging strongly against Wolfgang's harness. Amid all this chaos, Chief officer Axel thought:

—*«Good Heavens! That's all we needed, a wounded boatswain. Careful! ... What in the world is Mr. Moore doing? If they are not careful they could lose him overboard!»*

With great awkwardness, William, Wolfgang and Axel pulled the boatswain back up and on to the ladder. The boatswain was bleeding on his forehead, and his clothes were stained with blood. William managed to hook the boatswain's snap-on hook safety line back on. Having secured the boatswain, William hugged his son. They didn't say anything because the noise was deafening, but no doubt they were both extremely happy and excited about being reunited once more.

Axel fastened a harness on Andrew. He took an emergency protein bar out of his pocket and ordered Andrew to eat it. Meanwhile, Axel grabbed his VHF radio again and hailed Captain Olaf. He informed him they had found young Andrew, the boatswain was semiconscious and bleeding on the forehead, and they would begin their journey back to the command castle, immediately.

—*«Uh-Oh! We'd better get out of here before we have another accident!»* —Thought Chief Officer Axel.

Chief Axel ordered everyone to return.

—Wolfgang and William help the boatswain! Children, stay alert and close to me. *Let's go!*

Slowly and with great difficulty, they lowered the boatswain's semiconscious dead-weight body, down the hatch-access-ladder and continued on, down the passageway: first, the boatswain, then Mr. Moore, Wolfgang, Andrew, Hannah and lastly, Chief Axel. Their way back was a struggle because they had to help the boatswain along, holding him under both arms. And from time to time, they were still being hit by the spray of waves, which pounded heavily against Athena's hull.

At last, it seems Poseidon was satisfied because, when they climbed the stairs, which would put them back on deck in front of the entrance to the bridge castle, the storm slacken up somewhat.

As they entered the dining room, everyone clapped and shouted. There was a clamor and everyone was jubilant. But when they realized the boatswain was bleeding, and Andrew was pale, dangerously cold and trembling, all their enthusiasm dissipated quickly.

Axel applied first aid help to the boatswain. William and Wolfgang took care of Andrew and Jaséle of Hannah. They removed Andrew's harness, clothes down to his undies, shoes and socks. Then they rubbed a wet and steaming hot towel all over his body. They dried him up, clothed him, wrapped him in a thick wool blanket and put on dry wool socks and slippers, from his dad. Also, they monitored his pulse and his breathing. Fortunately, there was no need to administer CPR.

Chief cook Alessandro, Jürgen and an assistant handed out cups of hot chocolate for everyone. They put three cups on the table: one for Andrew, one for Hannah and one for the boatswain. Jaséle gave hot chocolate to Hannah while William helped Andrew with his chocolate. Andrew slowly began to show signs of coming around.

Captain Olaf entered the room and walked straight towards Chief officer Axel. The Chief gave him his report on what had happened and its current status. After hearing it, the captain said:

—Chief Officer Axel, I'm proud and truly grateful with your performance in this crisis. I will make an entry in my log, and I will make a strong recommendation for a promotion.

—Thank you, Captain. I was just doing my job, sir —said Axel.

Klaus was especially happy and relieved because Andrew was alive. He approached him and embracing him said:

—Andrew, you're a brave man! Please forgive me.

—*Ha-ha-ha!... Ha-ha-ha!...* —Andrew laughed in a tone of approval.

Andrew and Hannah were sitting side-by-side. And it didn't escape him he was sitting there drinking hot chocolate, because of how gutsy Hannah had been. Overwhelmed by his feelings of gratitude, he put his arms around Hannah and gave her a hug and a kiss on the cheek and said:

—*Oh, Hannah,* I think you're the best and I ... *I think I love you!*

—*Oh c'mon, Andrew.* You're acting goofy. Go ahead and drink some more chocolate! —said Hannah while sticking her tongue out at him, flirting and mocking him too.

—*Ha-ha-ha! ... Heh-heh-heh! ... Ho-ho-ho! ...* —they both laughed hysterically.

Alessandro congratulated young Andrew.

—«*Bravo giovane Andrea, Bravissimo!*» Bravo, young Andrew, bravo!

Turning towards Hannah, he asked everyone to toast for her and shouted:

—«*Cin Cin per Hannah, la nostra eroina!*» Here's to Hannah, our heroine!

—*Hip Hip!* —cried William.

—*Hooray!* —They all shouted.

—*Hip Hip!* —cried William, again.

—*Hooray!* —They all shouted, again.

—*Hip Hip!* —cried William one last time.

—*Hooray!* —They all shouted enthusiastically.

The next day the storm had disappeared and the sun shone bright. Jaséle and Elizabeth walked arm in arm while heading towards Athena's bow. Like the storm, Elizabeth's mood had changed completely. They had a few more days left in their journey, so she would have ample time to apologize, make amends and repair the damage her conduct might have caused with Jaséle, Laura and especially, Lucy. Throughout the rest of the journey, Jaséle and Elizabeth spent a lot of time together. They developed a friendship that would grow beyond the confines of the majestic Athena. Elizabeth told her about the events with her fiancé and the loss of her pregnancy back in England; the main reason for her unhappiness and her bitterness, too. After a long conversation, Jaséle said:

—Elizabeth, I think he is still waiting for you. Is he not?

—Yes, Jaséle, I think you're right.

—So ... why don't you go to him and start a new life together? —asked Jaséle.

—You know, Jaséle, I was so afraid.

—Afraid of what, Elizabeth?

—I feared I was inadequate for him.

—How so? ... I don't understand —said Jaséle.

—I thought I had failed him and my life with him, was pretty much over with —said Elizabeth.

—Elizabeth, love is something wonderful and at times, strange and complicated.

—Yes I know, Jaséle ... but ...

—When you see it don't let it escape. But beware, there should be no strings attached! —said Jaséle.

—Jaséle, the extraordinary behavior of your daughter has given me hope.

—So tell me, will I soon receive notification of your wedding?

—*Yes, Jaséle!* ... I think so —said Elizabeth while she hugged Jaséle, with a deep emotion and sense of gratitude.

—I'm really, really happy for you, Elizabeth.

—Thank you, Jaséle. Thank you so dearly. And if I may be so bold, I would like to call you my friend.

—*Well of course!* ... Most definitely, yes! —said Jaséle.

—Jaséle, you cannot imagine how much this means to me.

—Elizabeth, although I don't know where we are going to live in Germany, «*mi casa es tu casa*» my home will always be your home! ... You have an open invitation to come and visit us, anytime! —said Jaséle.

—Speaking of visits, I also wish you to come and visit with us in England; especially the heroine of the day, your precious young Hannah —said Elizabeth.

Elizabeth was not only grateful for all Jaséle had done for her, but she was surprised at what she had learned about Jaséle, and thought:

—«*My behavior towards Jaséle, Laura and Lucy has been despicable. There is simply no excuse. I was not brought up to fall this low. And yet, Jaséle's behavior has been exemplary and entirely consistent with that of a princess. Now I understand her nobility, and I'm certain that through her veins runs the purest Royal Blue blood!*»

That evening they enjoyed a magnificent gala dinner. Jürgen and Alessandro outdid themselves. Having experienced the storm at sea together, the passengers were much attuned to one another. Like young lovers swearing eternal devotion, they swore they would be best of friends forever. Never mind that in the end, this could just be an illusion, a hope. What matters is that at that precise moment, the feeling of camaraderie and shared emotions, left a beautiful and strong imprint on every single one of them, for the rest of their lives.

Athena arrived majestically to the huge Port of Hamburg. Captain Olaf, his officers, the Boatswain, Chief Cook Alessandro and Chief steward Jürgen wearing impeccable white uniforms and gloves, stood in line at the edge of the disembarking gangway. The captain shook hands with each one of the passengers and wished them a safe trip towards their final destination. The last ones to leave were Wolfgang, Hannah and Jaséle. When Hannah stood before large Captain Olaf, in a voice that boomed, he said:

—«*Moment mal, mein Fräuleinchen!*» One moment, my dear young lady!

Hannah was wearing a charming sailor's outfit and hat. The captain bent down, pinned a medal on her dress and said:

—For your bravery at sea, we give you this medal and make you an honorary member of Athena's crew.

Then the boatswain blew his bosun whistle and made a ceremonial *"General Call"* with two long beeps. Immediately, Chief Officer *Axel Østergård* called:

—Attention!

FOR YOUR BRAVERY AT SEA, WE GIVE YOU THIS MEDAL AND MAKE YOU AN HONORARY MEMBER OF ATHENA'S CREW.

All the officers gave Hannah a military salute. Then Chief Officer Axel took her in his arms, kissed her on the cheek and said:

—«*Vielen Dank mein tapferes Prinzesschen!*» Thank you, my brave little princess!

When Jaséle was leaving and much to her surprise, to Wolfgang's and especially to Hannah's, Captain Olaf said out loud for all to hear:

—My dear Mrs. Loewe, next time you should know we don't take any stowaways on board ... *Ho-ho-ho!*

—But Captain, I don't understand —said Jaséle while blushing.

—Your child will have a sailor's blood in him. *Ha-ha-ha! ... Ho-ho-ho!* —said Captain Olaf.

All joined in the chorus and laughed merrily. Elizabeth hugged Jaséle, kissed her and with tears in her eyes, she said:

—Soon we will come to Germany, to see you. *I promise!*

Still, Jaséle couldn't figure out how they learned she was pregnant. What she didn't know is, the cook was suspicious right from the start, because of her strange and strict diet. When she asked the captain how he found out, he pointed towards Alessandro. Everyone laughed. Alessandro once again like a good Italian, at last said:

—«*Avrai un bel bambino!*» You will have a beautiful baby!

CHAPTER 22

DÜSSELDORF, THE CAPITAL OF NORTH RHINE WESTPHALIA, located on the banks of the river Rhine, is a vibrant city and possibly the most cosmopolitan of all of Germany. This city has been able to combine its long historical past with the modern world. And it has been ranked as one of the best ones to live in; so much so that about seventeen percent of their population are foreigners, including one of the largest communities of Japanese citizens, in all of Europe. As one might expect, such multiculturalism would help the Loewes to integrate themselves into the spirit of the city. Thus, making them feel welcome and eventually, at home.

One can easily appreciate the modern character of the city, when looking at the myriad of advanced architectural buildings. For example, let us take the Düsseldorf International Airport with its line of people mover, the SkyTrain, which links automobile transport and bullet trains alike. The city also hosts some of the largest corporations in industries such as telecommunications, advertising, media and finance in Germany. And it is by far, the fashion center of the country.

We must not overlook this seemingly small detail because fashion played a critical role in Hannah, influencing and giving impetus to her own eclectic style, just about from the get-go.

Culturally, the city offers a vast universe of activities which allows a highly discriminating population to express or consume all kinds of artistic venues; from the many theaters, museums, fairs and nightlife, to the influences a large student population entails. Düsseldorf, has been a major contributor to modern music such as Avant-garde, punk, techno and electronic. There are also a great number of bars, cafés and music clubs. Those located in *Ratingen Straße* and *Kurze Strasse* are frequented by locals, students, artists and bohemians, alike.

Fate could not have picked a better modern-day-jungle to offer Hannah so vast a territory to explore, throughout her teen years and early youth.

Nothing is perfect in life; otherwise, it would be boring and Düsseldorf, was no exception. Of all the wonderful aspects of the city, its quasi-year-round-spring weather was neither extremely hot nor humid, as it is in Colombia. But even Wolfgang, a native of this city, missed *La Guajira,* especially during the winter, not to mention how Hannah and Jaséle felt about it too.

The Loewes rented a comfortable three bedroom apartment on *Karolingerstrasse,* in the Bilk district, which is within a short distance walk from *Karolingerplatz* tram station, where they could find transportation to all of the city. Bilk, has a large student population living nearby and many of them attend the Heinrich Heine University.

Across the street from the Loewe's apartment building, there was a small canal. On each side of the canal, there was a line of thick trees; inviting people to go out for a walk.

—*«Hannah, mein Schatz, lass uns einen kleinen Spaziergang machen!»* Hannah, let's go out for a walk, sweetheart. —Her dad used to say, holding hands with her while she was still a child.

One would have thought that once the Loewes were settled in, Hannah would adapt to her new regimented school lifestyle but this was simply impossible. She was too much of a free spirit and considering that during the winter, the insides of many buildings were dark, gloomy and sometimes even depressing in comparison with the sunny *Guajira,* in the early years, she found it difficult to bear. To complicate matters even further, we can add the long days of intense cold, gray skies, rain, trees without leaves and above all, no birds.

—Mom, why are there no birds in the winter? —Young Hannah asked.

—It is exceptionally cold outside, my dear —said Jaséle.

—So, where are they? Did they all die?

—*Good Lord, no!* I guess the smaller ones are just taking cover from the unforgiving cold weather. But most other birds travel south in search of warmth.

—*What?* Is it hot in the south?

—Sure it is. Remember, in the south we have Africa and it is hotter there.

—*Africa!* ... Why don't we go to Africa too?

—*Oh, my sweetheart* ... I am not too crazy about going to Africa. But maybe when you're older you can visit.

No! This was not the ideal environment to motivate Hannah to be a better student. It certainly was not lack of intelligence. She was an intelligent student, who managed her study time wisely and this made a lot of sense to her because then, she could use up all the free time she could get, in her wanderings throughout the city. Still, as energetic a she was, during those glorious days of spring, she often felt trapped in school.

She managed to get good grades in school, in part because both Wolfgang and Jaséle and even she, realized she needed

THE MEDIENHAFEN AT DER NEUE ZOLLHOF IN DÜSSELDORF. DO YOU LIKE IT, HANNI?

to continue on to the university and get a career. Despite all of this, sometimes Hannah felt like she really needed to explore and be in the middle of the hustle and bustle of city life. And on this score, this city had so much to offer her.

She was not a loner either. On the contrary, she was already showing signs of leadership, when she carefully selected her own clique of friends. Like Hannah, her friends were nonconformists. You could say they marched to the beat of a different drum. Although the educational system in Germany is strict, sometimes they would skip school to go out gallivanting on a spree throughout the city, but being careful enough not to arouse suspicion of truancy.

Political activism was more interesting to her. She was always willing to volunteer for any protests, except when these were sponsored by groups from the extreme right. In those cases she would protest with the other side, if only to mock and enrage these right-wing groups. At times these demonstrations would get out of hand, ending up in violence.

Once the police arrested her while demonstrating in the city of Hannover because of plans the *Niedersachsen,* or government of Lower Saxony, had, to allow the construction of a nuclear power plant. Not only did she believe it was scandalous enough that Germany, bought some of its electric power from neighboring countries, which used nuclear power generation. But to build nuclear plants on German soil, that was totally out of the question ... *No way!*

Her political views were taking an increasingly liberal bias with a strong inclination and sympathy towards leftist movements. Although, as of late she was more interested in the new European anarchist movement. Interestingly, these inclinations didn't come from Wolfgang or Jaséle, who were apolitical. And as it is to be expected, having lived in the natural world of *La Guajira,* it was only logical that Hannah would join the environmental protection group, Greenpeace.

CHAPTER 23

MARIA WAS NERVOUS, BECAUSE SHE WOULD SOON MEET Robert's parents, and she wanted to give them the best impression possible. Although Robert never asked her if she wanted to be his girlfriend, this was understood. Since the first moment when they went out on a date to the football game, everyone at school suspected they were now going steady. Astonishingly, the question most kids were asking one another was: How could a girl as attractive as Maria choose such a ho-hum and nerdy guy like him?

Robert, following Chelsea's recommendation, invited her to have dinner at their place, the following week, after the game. Maria, most flattered, accepted the invitation with pleasure. It was six o'clock. Robert would pick her up possibly at six past thirty. Her friend Sandy was with her and seeing her so restless, she said:

—*Oh, my Gosh!* ... Maria, like you're so making me nervous. *I mean, like totally!* So why don't you, like chill, girl?

—*Oh, Sandy!* I don't know why I'm feeling this way. This has never happened to me before —said Maria while she walked nervously from side to side across her bedroom.

—*But yeah* ... like, you silly girl ... you're only going out to dinner. I mean it's not, like you're getting married! *As if* ...

—Tell me, Sandy, do you know anything about Robert's mom?

—I'm, like sorry, my friend. But I don't know much. Steve told me her name is, like Chelsea. *Yeah!* And he thinks she has got a cool personality. She is, like always joking with the kids and with their friends and all. *Yeah* ... It's, like awesome! —said Sandy.

—Are you serious? And what about his dad? What can you tell me about him? —asked Maria.

—*Oh, girl,* you know ... he's like, totally harmless!

—Sandy, what do you mean by that?

—Anyways, like, I know him. *Yeah, fer shur* —said Sandy.

—How so?

—Sometimes Steve and I, like go to the store and we talk to Robert and then, like Mr. Fred always welcomes us and all ...

—What else? —asked Maria.

—Fred is a bit, like gnarly, you know. But like I think he's, like kinda cool ... you know —said Sandy.

—Robert told me he's got two younger brothers. What can you tell me about them? —Maria asked.

—*Oh, girl* ... like, I don't know much either. It's like, Kevin is in middle school and Kael is like, in elementary or so —said Sandy.

Maria and her family lived on the second floor of a two-story apartment rental building. She stopped in front of her bedroom's window, which overlooked the street, to see if she could see Robert approaching. Then she turned around and facing Sandy, she said:

—You know, Sandy ... I think Robert's mother is extremely important in his life and this is probably the reason why I'm feeling so nervous today.

—What do you, like mean, Maria?

"KNOCK KNOCK KNOCK!"

—Well, you know ... mothers can be particularly protective of their sons.

—*Most definitely!* ... You know, like, *Oh yeah!* ... you're right, girl ... *totally!* —said Sandy.

Suddenly, the doorbell rang, *Ding-dong!* Maria's dad opened the door and greeted Robert. Everyone knew he would come looking for Maria to go to dinner at his parents' home. More often than not, Maria's father would tease her, but she was not in a good mood. So he decided it was best to leave it alone. Robert had wavy dark blond hair and light eyes. He wore a light yellow Oxford-cotton-long-sleeved shirt, a navy blue blazer jacket, a pair of khaki pants with cuffs, brown belt, brown leather boat shoes and thick white cotton socks. Robert entered the room and said:

—Hello, Mr. Garcia. How are you doing, sir?

—Hello, Robertico! Come in please.

—I've come to ... —but before Robert could finish speaking Mr. Garcia interrupted him and said:

—*Yes, yes, yes!* ... We know you're going out with Maricarmen. And you know ... she looks awfully pretty today. I think she wants to impress you ... *Ha-ha-ha!*

Robert didn't know what to make of, nor how to respond to such direct and indiscreet comment from Maria's father.

He only blushed and smirked while trying to appear friendly.

—*Ha-ha!*—Robert murmured.

—Maricarmen! ... Robert is here —Mr. Garcia shouted.

Sandy was the first one to come out of Maria's room and said:

—*Yay, Robert* ... Maria will be out in a minute. So, like how are you doing?

—Hi Sandy ... I feel pretty good. And how's Steve?

—*Yeah* ... Steve's cool and, like we are going to the movies later on ... *totally awesome!*

Mrs. Garcia came out of the kitchen into the living room. She was curious to meet young Robert, and indeed, it was only fair that Robert felt the same curiosity about her. Many people say that if a man likes the mother of his potential partner, this augurs good fortune for the couple. While most young ladies vainly try not to look like their mothers, over time, many end up being just like them. Though perhaps not so much on their physical appearance, most certainly so, in their temperament. And this occurs even though the saying goes like: *"Daddy's girl and Mama's boy"*.

Mrs. Garcia was as tall as Maria, possibly above the average height, for a typical Mexican woman. She had an excellent complexion, slender and a fantastic shapely figure. But what was most striking about her, was her hair. It was totally silver-gray, bright and slightly wavy. She wore it long and loose, falling over her shoulders front and back, and slightly pulled to one side and back. Mrs. Garcia's hair enhanced her fine facial features, which in itself, created an attractive contrast with the brown colour of her skin, evidently tanned by being out in the sun, so darn much. It is quite a pity Robert did not noticed Mrs. Garcia's hands, which were thin, with long fingers, a bit bony and without nail polish. To an astute observer, these hands are in effect always indicative of an intellectual.

It was evident that Mrs. Garcia's hair was prematurely gray, because she was a relatively young and vigorous woman. It is possible this was the result of a genetic predisposition, rather than due to stress or aging.

She was wearing blue jeans, not tight but worn out. She had a pair of simple Indian style and open-leather-sandals, such as those used by Gandhi. She also wore a large light and blue man's long sleeve shirt, with the sleeves rolled up to her elbows and tied with a knot at the waist. A small pair of square and modern-and-stylish Italian designer's tortoise-shell reading glasses completed the picture of an intelligent, complex, reserved and passionate woman. Strictly speaking, someone with whom one does not, should not, or could not play around.

To the sophisticated eye of a man-of-the-world, Mrs. Garcia could well be a modern beaux arts artist working in an atelier in Paris, decidedly attractive, sexy and why not say so ... highly sensual.

Although Robert was a wholesome young man and obviously without much worldly life experience, when he saw Mrs. Garcia, he reacted instinctively with a feeling, which possibly originated from the depths of his gut, and he thought:

—*«Oh, My Goodness! Mrs. Garcia is spectacular. And now I have no doubt as to which side of the family, my beautiful Maria took after!»*

Maria's father introduced them but without him making use of his, at times, sardonic sense of humor. Not with his wife. With her, he simply dared not, and said:

—*Ah!* ... Robert, may I introduce you to Mrs. Garcia, my wife.

Mrs. Garcia extended her hand. It was soft but firm and not flabby nor sweaty. With a strong handshake, she squeezed Robert's hand and said:

—*At last!* ... I'm so glad to meet you, Robert.

—The pleasure is all mine, Mrs. Garcia —said Robert, but feeling pretty nervous, because he knew he was being scanned up and down.

—I am sorry for being so direct, Robert, but ...

—Don't trouble yourself, ma'am. How may I be of help? —said Robert, displaying the gallantry of a peacock. However, he was totally unprepared for her comeback.

—I see my daughter has chosen well. I like you. But I think you look a little pale. Perhaps you haven't been out in the sun much ... haven't you?

—I ... I ... I ... —Robert was dumbstruck and stammered.

—*Ha-ha-ha!* ... Easy lad, I was just kidding with you —said Mrs. Garcia.

—*Ah!* ... I see ... *Ha-ha-ha!* —Robert laughed, feeling somewhat relieved.

—Robert, Maria told me you guys are going out to dinner with your parents.

—Yes, ma'am, that is correct. Initially we invited her to have dinner at home but at the last minute, my mother changed her mind, and she decided we should all go out to a restaurant, instead.

—Your mother is right. In her case, I would do the same.

—*Oh,* but I haven't even told Maria of our change in plans yet —said Robert.

—Don't worry, Robert. I don't think it'll be a problem.

—*Excellent!* ... I'm glad —said Robert rather nervously.

—I believe Maria is extremely interested and positively nervous herself, about meeting your mother.

—Is that so? ... *Wow!* ... I wonder why that is?

—Robert, what's your mom's name? —Maria's mother asked.

—Chelsea ... Yes ... her name is Chelsea Brown, ma'am.

—*Ah,* look ... I think Maria is coming out now —said Mrs. Garcia.

Maria entered the living room. When Robert saw her, his jaw simply dropped. She was her mother's embodiment but more so. That is ... new, revamped and most certainly, improved! Mr. Garcia with his usual quick-witted honesty, said:

—You see, Robertico. Don't you think Maricarmen is looking awfully pretty today?

—*Oh, Dad!* Don't be foolish —said Maria annoyed at her dad's indiscretions.

—But it's true, my *niña*. Let's see ... what say you, Robertico? —asked Mr. Garcia.

—Mr. Garcia, I have to say, in this case, I think yours is a great understatement. Your daughter is ... well she is ... yes, she is looking *Gorgeous!*

—Thank you, Robert. You're most kind —said Maria while blushing at Robert's unabashed and heartfelt compliment.

Maria wore fire red lipstick, which matched her glam glossy finger and toe nails. Her makeup exalted her seductive black Moorish eyes. Her long shiny black hair, arranged in a thick and long French braid, hung over her right shoulder, enhancing her solitary pearl earrings. She wore an attractive knee length, sleeveless off-white linen summer dress, with red pastel colour flower prints, tight around her torso, loose around her hips, daring low back cut and halter top, which complemented her outstanding shapely figure. She wore a pair of canvas floral print peep-toe sling-back cork platform espadrille-wedge-shoes, which matched her dress and accentuated her engaging legs.

She was also carrying a small and dainty soft-white-leather seashell purse. Maria had definitely a smart and cosmopolitan stylish look but not necessarily, an ostentatious one.

Perhaps Maria's outfit was more appropriate for a walk on New York's Central Park, in the summer, than for their small and quaint little town of Charming Meadows, in Oklahoma. But it was still to be seen whether Robert's mother, Chelsea, would approve of it. Although, there was no question in Robert's mind, Maria was dressed to kill, she was entirely on a league of her own, and she would most certainly turn heads as she walked on by.... *Wow!*

—Maria, I hope you don't mind but there has been a change in plans —said Robert.

—A change in plans, Robert? ... What do you mean?

—Yes ... you see, my mom convinced Dad for us to eat out at Norman's Grill, on Wallace Street.

—*Oh really, Robert?* I have no problem with that —said Maria.

Sandy saw Maria and winked at her, as if to say things would go much better, than what she had expected.

—Well then, Maria and Sandy should we go? —asked Robert.

—*Yeah, fer shur!* —said Sandy.

—Robert, I guess I'm ready as I'll ever be —smiled Maria.

—Goodbye Mr. and Mrs. Garcia —said Robert on his way out.

—Goodbye, Mom and Dad —said Maria.

—See you later Mr. and Mrs. Garcia —said Sandy.

—Goodbye and come back to visit soon —said Maria's mother.

—Bye, bye *chicos* and have fun! —said Maria's father.

Fred and Chelsea were waiting in the car. They saw Robert, Maria and Sandy come out of the apartment building. And upon seeing Maria approaching, he quip:

—*Oh, my Goodness!* ... I think our son is getting way over his head.

—Fred, I think you're right. She is quite stunning ... *Wow!*

When the kids got closer to the car, Fred yelled at Sandy:

—Hi Sandy ... Say, do you need a ride?

Sandy approached the SUV's window on the passenger's side and said:

—Hello Mr. and Mrs. Brown.

—Sandy, call me Chelsea. You make me feel way too old calling me, *"Mrs. Brown"*—replied Chelsea.

—Thank you, Mr. Brown, but, like I'm meeting Steve two blocks from here and then, yeah, like we'll go to the movies. You know, totally—said Sandy.

—Well Okay then ... Sandy, please give Steve our regards —said Fred.

Meanwhile Maria and Robert had entered the car and were sitting on the back seat.

—Are you kids ready? —asked Fred.

—Yes, Dad, we're ready—said Robert.

Fred started the engine and while driving to the restaurant, Robert introduced them to Maria. Fred told Maria he knew her dad, who went to his shop often. Chelsea said nothing, and she let the pleasant aura of her husband, guide the conversation.

Norman's Grill was one of the best restaurants in Charming Meadows, and it was moderately-to-highly priced. And because Maria had never eaten there, this could prove to be a nice little experience for her. Norman's Grill was the kind of restaurant villagers mostly visited on special occasions. And it seems meeting Maria, was a special occasion.

Although, Maria participated in Fred's small talk, in reality, she was paying a lot more attention to Chelsea, and because she had not said a word, this made her feel nervous. Fifteen minutes later they arrived at the restaurant, and Fred stopped the car in the front entrance, letting the valet service park the car. Robert jumped out of the SUV and went around quickly to open Maria's door. Fred, though more slowly, did likewise with Chelsea. They had dinner reservations for seven-thirty. And although the restaurant was full, the Maître d' received them and told them their table was ready, so they could be seated immediately.

Norman's Grill was elegant and cozy. It had red brick walls, large white French windows with top arches, light pickled wood furniture, lots of plants, and two levels with a balcony on the second floor, from which you could see a huge island bar downstairs and white wrought iron tables for four and booths with high backrests, which offered more privacy. That evening, there was a singer with an acoustic guitar for entertainment, which completed the restaurant's atmosphere. They sat in a booth, with the men facing the aisle. They promptly ordered some *hors d'oeuvres* and drinks.

—Tell me, Maria, do you like school? —asked Chelsea.

—Mrs. Brown, I have studied at various schools and this one seems quite good —said Maria.

—Maria, please call me Chelsea, Okay?

—*Ha-ha!* ... Well alright then, Chelsea it is.

—I know you are a still a sophomore, but have you given some thought as to what you would like to study next?

—My parents would like me to study engineering or perhaps even medicine.

—It seems to me engineering is a solid career. Medicine, on the other hand, takes a long time —said Fred.

—And what do you prefer, Maria? —Chelsea asked again.

—Personally, I prefer the humanities, you know, something out of the School of Arts and Sciences —said Maria.

—Maria, do you like music? —asked Chelsea.

—Yes, I love music but not for a career. I don't play an instrument and besides, I certainly have no ear for music.

—Did you know Robert plays the saxophone?

—*Oh, Mom!* ... Maria, that's not entirely true. I'm just starting to learn the instrument and it is not easy —said Robert.

—So I guess you're into Jazz, Robert. Aren't you? —asked Maria.

—Yes, yes, I like it, Maria. But you can blame my mother for it.

—*Oh, Robert!* ... That's not fair. Perhaps I just pushed you a little ... *Ha-ha-ha!*

—Look, Maria ... as far as the Brown's family is concerned, my wife is the one who wears the pants around this household ... *Ho-ho-ho!* —said Fred.

Dinner went off without a hitch. Gradually, Chelsea and Maria felt more comfortable with each other, and they talked animatedly. The men took a back seat and were only involved in conversation, when they were spoken to. They had all finished their meal and it was now time to order dessert, but Chelsea came up with another idea and said:

—Maria, would you like for us to have dessert at home?

—*Oh!* That sounds like fun. But am I not imposing on you all? —asked Maria.

—Nonsense, Maria! —said Chelsea.

—And don't you have a problem with that, Mr. Brown? —asked Maria.

—Maria, just like my wife prefers to be called by her name because it makes her feel younger, please call me Fred, 'cause in truth, I'm a lot younger than she is. *Ha-ha-ha!*

—*Gosh, Fred!* Are you crazy? Maria, don't mind him because he is just being plain silly —said Chelsea.

—*Ha-ha-ha!* ... Well Fred. So like, are you OK if we have dessert at your place? —Maria asked again.

—*Maria, absolutely yes!* Now, remember I told you, in our house, she is the boss —said Fred, laughing, making faces and pointing fingers at Chelsea.

—And what do you say, Robert? —asked Maria.

—It'll be fun and besides, my mom is an excellent cook —said Robert.

—Well then, it's settled —said Chelsea.

—Well Okay then but first, I have to call my parents and tell them we'll be a little late —said Maria.

—Maria you can use my phone if you wish —said Chelsea.

—Yes, thank you, Chelsea. I will.

—Moreover, why don't you accompany me to the ladies room and call from over there?

—Yes, for sure ... why not? —said Maria.

—So, we'll go and powder our noses and make ourselves beautiful —said Chelsea.

—And what about them? —asked Maria.

—The boys will stay here and pay the bill —said Chelsea.

—Sorry, Robert.... We'll come back soon, Okay? —said Maria.

—*Oh,* no worries, Maria. There's no hurry —said Robert.

—Come, Maria ... don't spoil them. They need to make themselves useful for something. *Ha-ha-ha!* —said Chelsea.

—*Oh my God!* Chelsea, you're terrible ... *Ha-ha-ha!* —said Maria.

—And you haven't seen nothing yet! —said Fred in jest.

—All right, let's go! —said Maria.

Robert was pleased. Chelsea showed signs she liked Maria a lot. When they left for the restroom, Fred asked for the check. Robert took the opportunity to ask his father's opinion.

—Dad, do you think mother liked Maria?

—Son, I think so. I haven't seen your mother so enthusiastic with someone, in quite some time.

Meanwhile, Maria spoke with her father and asked him for permission and was told they had no problem with her staying a little longer. But her father wanted to know if the Browns were bringing her back home, afterwards. And she assured him they would, in fact, do so. When she handed the phone back, Chelsea hugged her and said:

—You know, Maria. I think you're incredibly beautiful and with that outfit, you look simply divine!

—Thank you, Chelsea. In truth I was scared 'cause I couldn't imagine what you were like.

—And what is your verdict, Maria?

—*Oh, Wow!* ... I think you're wonderful and witty. And now I understand why Robert is the way he is!

Maria's last compliment closed *"the sale"*, so to speak. Chelsea and Maria ended up being good friends and who knew, perhaps in a few years they could be much more.

The rest of the evening was a success as well. They talked, they listened to music, and they all laughed when Robert started making noise with his saxophone. Maria met Kevin and Kael.

Between one thing and another, she learned, in his heyday, Fred was quite the dancer, and he asked Maria:

—Maria, do you like dancing?

—*Oh yes!* ... In fact, I love it, totally!

—And tell me, Maria. Do you know how to dance? —asked Fred.

—My dear Fred, I haven't met a single Latina who couldn't dance!

—*Bravo!* Then I'll put on some dance music. Fred, how about some mambo? —asked Chelsea.

—Mambo? Well yes, indeed, my dear. Good choice —said Fred.

—Mambo? *Ha-ha-ha!* ... What is that? —asked Maria.

—Maria, it's an old Latin dance which today, I believe they call it *Salsa!* —said Fred.

—*Oh Wow, Fred!* And you know how to dance salsa? —asked Maria.

Fred didn't answer her question but instead, clowning around, he extended his hand out to Maria, and asked:

—Milady, would you do me the honor of the next dance?

—Monsieur, I would be delighted!

It was unclear who was more excited about Maria, if Fred or Chelsea, but the fact remains everyone had a great time. Around twelve o'clock at midnight, they drove Maria back to her place, and asked her to come back to visit them soon.

CHAPTER 24

FOR HANNAH, GROWING UP IN DÜSSELDORF, PROVIDED HER an exciting life full of adventures. After completing her primary school education, her parents enrolled her in a *Gymnasium,* which is like a high school or vocational school, called the *Lessing-Gymnasium,* located on *Ellerstrasse.* The school was a little over a mile from home. This allowed Hannah to ride her bicycle to school, to use her skateboard or simply walk to school. The school offered four different curricula or study programs. Although she went straight into the Gymnasium, which is a prerequisite for continuing on to the university, *Lessing* was the first and possibly one of the few schools in the city of Düsseldorf, which offered a Sports-oriented curriculum.

With Miranda as her last name, but mostly because she was different from her peers; too independent and proud, she frequently found herself entangled in quarrels, intrigues and even violence. This was the price she would have to pay, to ensure her place and respect amongst the students.

Having inherited Jasèle's physical beauty and the strength and endurance of her father, Hannah had an aura of wild and seductive independence, which confused and attracted her fellow male students. These attributes created envy and jealousy amongst the most popular girls in school, some of which were truly beautiful, in their own right.

Slander can have a harmful effect on the character of a person, and Hannah had been the subject of several character assassination attempts, to harm her reputation. But looking on the bright side, lots of gossip will make a person more popular than ever. To be the target of a smear campaign, could make people despise you, but never ... *to ignore you!*

A recurring theme alleged Hannah was an easy girl. They said anybody could sleep with her, just for the asking. And this was especially true, so they claimed, if these suitors were athletes from the soccer team.

Hannah didn't bother to refute these slanderous gossip. And this behavior, in particular, greatly angered Erik. He was one of Hannah's closest friend. But who is this Erik character, and why is he Hannah's closest male confidant? His Hannah story is not long but perhaps it is interesting and more importantly bittersweet. And after all, such truncated love aspirations are most common remnant emotions, in the game of love and war.

Erik Albert Wotan or EAW for short, was born in Sweden... but wait! What could EAW stand for? Could it be *"Extreme Athletic Windsurfer"?* Or perhaps it means *"European Alleged Witticism"?* Say what? ... *Nah!* ... Maybe it simply means *"Embarrassing Alarmist Waitress"*, or perhaps *"Eddy About-face Warmongering"?*

It is quite likely that in each of these nutty acronym definitions, there might be morsels of truth which do represent Erik in some strange way. But seriously, if we look at the meaning of his name, we are more likely to find some deeper meaning about his personality traits. So come on, let's try it.

It seems the name Erik means *"Ever kingly"*. It is possible that in the darkest recesses of his mind, he could imagine himself being king. Oh, but not a sophisticated one from like the Court of Louis XV of France. No! He probably imagined a more glorious and testosterone-laden warrior *Viking König*. His middle name, Albert, gives credence to this notion in spades, since it means *"Strong as a Bear"*. But his last name, Wotan, does round up the picture because it means *"Frenzy, inspiration and rage"*.

Erik's parents had finally divorced, when he turned ten years old. She could not deal with the army life, for Erik's dad was a career lieutenant within the Swedish armed forces, who was not particularly stellar and would probably remain in his post forever. His mom just got fed up with the constant upheavals caused by their ceaseless relocations, from army barracks to army barracks, throughout all of Europe. One day she packed her bags and took off for Helsinki, never to be heard off again, except for the time when her divorce papers were served.

So young EAW stayed with his father and became an army brat. Essentially, he was brought up by tough military rough necks. This experience did wonders for his health, strong physique and competitive spirit, but in his case, it did nothing for his table manners, let alone his gallantry with the ladies.

As luck had it, while stationed in Germany, he wound up in Hannah's gymnasium or high school. And it didn't take long for him to be smitten by Hannah's wild seductiveness. Unfortunately, his less than sophisticated manners didn't woo her in the least. In fact, his approach had quite the opposite effect. Hannah almost bit his head off and told him to get packing.

But being that Erik was used to sustaining serious levels of physical pain, he thought nothing of it and charged on, again. Of course, he was completely unprepared for the psychological pain she would have to inflict on him, to get him off her back.

And although she could have possibly crushed his heart with the one hand and eat a fresh green apple with the other, all at the same time, she did not.

Instead, and through some laborious but well-intentioned efforts, she managed to get through his thick skull and convinced him that he was really not attracted to her, as a woman, but as a little sister. She could be the fragile little sister, which he never had, and therefore, he could protect her from some awful barbarians, imagined or not.

Now this hoax would have to have some kind of safety lock for it to stick. So Hannah deviously paired him up with one her best pals; uppity, elegant and sophisticated Heidi. And in order to justify her underhanded ways, she chuckled as she thought:

—*«Well why the heck not? After all, don't opposites attract?»*

And to be fair, Heidi, who was really of noble descent, could use some rough and tumble play, to bring a dose of earthly reality, into her life. Finally, being that he was a Leo and she an Aquarius ... Oh man, for their sake let's hope that opposites, that is, truly opposites, do attract.

Thus begun, a long and lasting loyal friendship, whereby Hannah's feminine instinct would "guide" Erik's strong male behavior, throughout some mischievous contortions, or should we just outright say it, *"blatant manipulations"*. Of course, we all know that this was done in the name of the common good.

Besides, this turned out to be a win-win situation for the both of them. Erik cleaned up his act pretty good. He could still be disheveled and all, but he did try hard. And to some extent he succeeded in acquiring a more genteel demeanor about him. Additionally, he wound up hanging out with Hannah a lot, and this was, after all, one of his main goals to begin with.

Coming back to the slanderous remarks, she would tell Erik that in a roundabout way, her enemies were doing her a favor.

—*Good lord, Hannah!* ... How can you say that? —said Erik frustrated.

Hannah, trying to calm Erik, said:

—Look Erik ... Karla and Johanna spread these rumors to make me unpopular with all those attractive boys in school.

—*Wonderful!* ... And then ... so what?

—Well, you see ... thinking I'm an easy prey, these guys are emboldened, and they come up to me and *Bang!* ... they spoil me silly!

—*Hannah!* —Erik protested.

—*C'mon, Erik!* ... It's not that bad. Frankly, I love it when this happens right under their noses.

—Are you for real?

—*Yeah, fer shur!* ... Both of them get super angry when they see all the attention I'm getting! ... *Hee-hee-hee!*

—But Hannah, you have to admit some of these flirtatious compliments can be vulgar and outright nasty... No? —Erik complained.

—*Ugh, yeah!* ... At times these guys can be totally stupid —said Hannah.

—Take Stefan, for example —said Erik.

—*Stefan?* ... What about him? —asked Hannah, intrigued.

—He has been telling everyone in school you're so hot for him and just plain madly in love with him, to boot!

—*Meeeee?* ... Are you kidding?

—And that's not even the half of it!

—*No?* And what else did he say? —asked Hannah while getting visibly mad.

—He also told his soccer team buddies, you slept with him.

—*Oh my God!* ... Unbelievable! ... *Is he like totally crazy?*

—Moreover, he was bragging that in bed, you were truly a cold fish. So much so, he would just as soon forget you —said Erik.

ARGH!!! ... WHERE'S THAT SACK OF HORSE MANURE, RIGHT NOW???

HE IS AT PAUL-JANES-STADION SOCCER FIELD, TODAY!!!

Stefan was the classic popular sports-jock for whom a lot of girls would simply die for. Like many other kids in school, he felt strongly attracted to Hannah. But because of his popularity and perhaps his arrogance, he could not take any type of rejection kindly. *And Hannah flat out rejected him!* You see, even though she did not know it yet, Hannah preferred the intellectual type and Stefan, although cute looking, in her eyes he would at most be, a passing fad.

With his pride wounded, he began to make her life miserable. Lately, every time Hannah entered history class, Stefan and his buddies would laugh and whisper lewd remarks at her. She tried to play it cool, but he was starting to get on her nerves in a big way. If Hannah was asked a question in class for which she did not know the answer, he would tell the teacher out loud:

—*Hey, teach* ... take it easy on her!

—And why do you say so, Mr. Stefan? —The teacher would ask.

—Because aborigines in Colombia, don't go to no school!

—*Bwahaha! Ho-ho-ho! Ha-ha-ha!* —Her class would explode in laughter.

After hearing Erik's comments, Hannah's blue-green eyes lit up in fury, and she asked rhetorically:

—*A cold fish!* ... Is that what he said? —asked Hannah.

—*Aha!* —said Erik.

—I'll show him what kind of a cold fish, I am! —cried Hannah.

Heidi, who was also a member of Hannah's clique, was amazed at the lies being told about her friend. She was only listening in.

—*Argh!* ... Where is that sack of horse manure, right now? —Hannah shouted angrily.

—I don't know! ... Why? —asked Erik.

—Apparently, he is at *Paul-Janes-Stadion* soccer field, on

Flinger Broich Street, today —replied Heidi while joining in the conversation.

—What's he doing there today? —asked Erik.

—They're having soccer practice for Sunday's game —added Heidi.

—*Aaah!* ... You're right, Heidi! —said Erik.

—It's Friday, so there should be a few students and fans of the team at the stadium. A nice little crowd will be watching tonight, for sure —said Heidi.

The big question is how did Heidi end up at Hannah's gymnasium, in Düsseldorf? You see, Heidi was born in the Netherlands. Furthermore, she came from an old noble family and not just one with a title claim to aristocracy, for her family was quite wealthy, due to centuries in the Cocoa bean trade with the Americas. We can only speculate that she was being rebellious and wanted to distance herself from the more traditional and perhaps even socially demanding lifestyle, which limited and asphyxiated her creative juices.

Besides, it appears that there was a strong Haute Couture fashion streak, within some members of her family. Her uncle, for example, had delved into the industry and had some modest successes at Turin's runway shows, in Italy.

—Klara van Harpen! I think you wanting to move to Germany is preposterous! —said her mother.

—*But mamaa!* I want to make a name for myself—said Heidi.

—Oh, shush, Klara! You are talking nonsense. You have obligations here!

—My life here is boring. I can't stand going to another gala ball anymore. Besides, uncle Thorsen made a name for himself. He is a well-known designer.

—Your uncle Thorsen is nothing of the sort. He is a blackguard and a drunkard who is always chasing after young women. How he ended up in our family is beside me: such contemptible behavior.

—Well I don't care. I like him and I will follow in his footsteps —said Heidi.

—What? Are you going to chase young women too? —Mocked, her mother.

—Mother! ... That is not funny. Besides, my mind is already set, so I am moving to Germany.

—That brings me to the next question. How will you support yourself? I mean you are not even of age yet.

—*Oh, c'mon, mom!* You know we have the van Harpen Trust Fund. Do you forget I already started collecting a hefty annual sum? I won't be as pressed for money and you know it!

—*Oh gosh,* that is such an unfortunate state of affairs. You know, I opposed your father on such family trust. But your dad, who is a softie, wouldn't budge on this one. Oh well. You will keep in touch with your poor, old and graying mamaa, won't you?

—Yes, mother. I will. And do not worry your silly little head —said Heidi, sighing and almost giving up on her.

As we mentioned earlier, Düsseldorf is Germany's fashion center. Therefore, we can clearly see why she wound up there. We can safely speculate that Heidi would make a go for it; first as a runway model, for she had the perfect body for it. And later on, as she learned the ropes of this volatile industry, she could become a designer herself.

Heidi was neither the effusive nor the passionate type. On the contrary, she was the truly mental and sophisticated one who was, more often than not, rather blasé about the human emotional experience. At times you had to wonder if she had any pulse beat at all.

She was immediately taken in by Hannah's eclectic fashion style, which was predominantly glam punk, industrial grunge, modern Berlin Avant-guard and sometimes, even strictly conservative, if not outright formal preppy British collegial.

So Heidi and Hannah developed a strong connection, fueled by their mutual love interest in fashion.

Although, Heidi Klara van Harpen was not a sports jock and might even look too delicate, she could definitely carry her on. She was particularly good at skateboarding. And when it came to deep blue sailing, she felt that she was on a league of her own; having sailed on the North Sea, during the summer. Curiously enough, neither Hannah nor Heidi knew of this common interest, amongst the two.

When it came to the dating scene, Heidi was more of a recluse. She could not stand middle class morality and corny mannerisms. Her icy ways would turn off even the most oversexed and passionate guy. Of course, it would very much help the guy's effort, if he were not too bright to know the difference. And if there was someone who fitted the bill to a "T", it was Erik.

However, despite that Heidi thought Erik's table manners were deplorable, if not outright crass, she did started dating him. But one has to wonder if her feelings towards him were more like those expressed for a lovable puppy, than for an actual boyfriend. On the positive side, Erik would keep her entertained and sometimes even emotionally charged, too.

CHAPTER 25

GYMNASIUMS CAN BE RATHER STRICT ABOUT THEIR STUDENTS' overall behavior. Any deviation could trigger a suspension and in extreme cases, expulsion from school. However and unfortunately, the rural schools in her native Colombia, were constantly subjected to serious, and a times, deadly violence. And although Hannah had studied with private governess *Frau Moosbrugger,* which prevented her from being in the direct line of fire, she could remember stories from cousins and friends, about their stressful school experiences. For its part, the atmosphere of her current school in Germany, was quite tame and in no way comparable to the levels of violence she had seen in *La Guajira*.

Hannah's passions could run extremely high, so it was always a struggle for her to keep those emotions in check and not to let them blow over.

Erik was now concerned for her, because he had seen that look before, and he was worried she was going to get into big trouble.

—Hannah ... What are you planning to do? —asked Erik.

—I'm going to pay Stefan a visit, right now!

—Hannah, I'm worried about you! ... I know you're going to get in trouble at school.

—*Oh, c'mon Erik!* ... I don't see why! —said Hannah defiantly.

—Hannah, I know that look. Could you please forget about it? Will you? —Erik begged her.

—Look Erik ... It's after school now. Besides the soccer field does not belong to the school —she replied coldly.

—Yes, but ...

—*But nothing!* ... The stadium is several blocks away from school. And as far as I know, it's on public property. So there, I hope you're satisfied!

—Yes, but, but ... —said Erik.

—*Erik, that's enough!* ... Are you done now? —Hannah interrupted him again, impatiently.

—All right, Hannah ... Whatever you say —said Erik throwing in the towel.

—*Heidi and Erik!* ... Can we move out now? —Hannah demanded impatiently.

Hannah was wearing a casual and loose designer's black and white striped deep V-neck all-cotton T-shirt with mid-size-length sleeves. She also had a short white pleaded tennis skirt, which was partially covered by her T-shirt. Underneath the skirt she had a pair of sexy-black-nylon-short-see-through-tights, about six inches above the knee. Over the T-shirt she had a black leather hip-punk and silver studded leather bag. A brand new pair of fire-red Chuck Taylor's All Star Converse unisex canvas sneakers, matched her bright red glam lipstick and finger nails. A beautiful cream African bone disc necklace, accentuated Hannah's long neck. She wore a pair of white Hollywood Wayfarers sunglasses, and over her red leather wrist guard, you could see a beat-up old black-face Rolex Submariner watch, which her father gave her for her fifteen birthday, hoping she would not give up on scuba diving. When not flying over the pavement and sidewalks, she would tie and carry her slick skateboard, on her back.

Due to the long summer days, Hannah had been in the sunlight a lot and her hair was now a lighter blonde, which she wore long, in a powder-puff airy-fairy-frizzy with tight curls.

With a shapely slender build plus medium sized breast, at age seventeen, Hannah had an imposing figure, which often turned heads; especially when skateboarding along the city's sidewalks, hair flying, smiling, giggling and waving at strangers, to be sure.

Hannah had an Element skateboard with Tensor trucks and Spitfire wheels. Due to his strong physique, Erik had a Zero skateboard plus Fury Trucks and Bones wheels. Heidi, on the other hand, could skate on just about anything with wheels on them and this, even though she didn't looked the part, at all. Currently, she was using a Hello Kitty design skateboard, made by Girl Skateboards.

Hannah's clique were not the best nor the fanciest freestyle skateboarders. However, they were pretty decent and at times, nervy and brash street skaters who had earned their

HANNAH AND

HER CREW

GUYS! GUYS! GUYS! ... I SAID
I WOULD TAKE CARE OF EVERYTHING!
SO, C'MON ... LET'S GO ALREADY!!!
RAINA
FREDERICK

marks, with lots of bumps, cuts, scrapes and bruises. Hannah enjoyed leading her crew, when racing throughout the streets of Düsseldorf, in a reckless gaggle. And they all knew when she was in the mood for it, they had better don their knee pads, elbow pads, gloves and helmets for they were in for a rough ride. When Hannah put on her scandalously bright Nutcase helmet, gloves and sunglasses they just knew she was now mad as hell and all bent out of shape!

While they were rolling fast, zigzagging and skillfully avoiding running over pedestrians on their way to the soccer field, Erik was frantically calling Raina and Frederick on his cell phone, so they would come and help, in case of a fight. Frederick said he couldn't make it because he was busy at work, but Raina told him she would meet them on the soccer field.

Hannah was furious, *Grrr...!* and ready for a fight, but she didn't exactly know what to do. Even though Stefan was an athlete, she wanted to go up to him a break his lip, *Sock!* no matter what the consequences. She wasn't afraid of getting a broken lip herself. But she needed to do something more dramatic, something to humiliate him in front of his teammates and if at all possible, his fan club: Karla and Johanna. She tried to stay totally focused and thought:

—«*I will go up to him and will let him have it. Stefan, this cold fish is going to kick your butt! ... So you'll never mess with a Wayúu again!*»

When they reached the stadium, Raina joined them. It was a bright and clear afternoon summer day. With Hannah in front of this motley crew, the four of them were walking defiantly and ready for anything. They entered the soccer field from the northwest corner. On the west side one could see the roof-covered main bleachers, but they were empty because this section of the field remained closed during practice.

Towards the far southeast corner they could see the soccer players grouped on the field, near the wall. And on the open-air bright yellow-plastic-seat bleachers, there were a couple dozen students, some fans and a few bystanders. They walked diagonally through the length of the field towards a small group of soccer players, on Stefan's team.

When Hannah's crew reached midfield, the players, students and fans noticed them, for they were a scene to behold. Hannah looked like a caricature, right out of a Hollywood B-movie.

Erik was a strong six-foot-two-inch tall Nordic young man with a thick red beard and long hair in a ponytail. He wore a black T-shirt with a prominent "*skull*" anarchy sign in front and the picture of an AK-47 assault rifle on his back. He wore a pair of long khaki cargo pants and black combat boots; but, with no socks. He had a white Japanese-motif bandana tied around his head and with an intimidating look, he was holding his florescent-green skateboard over his shoulders, with both hands at the tips, as if holding a sword.

Heidi wore an unbuttoned long sleeved silver-sequin-matador jacket, which glittered bright in the sunlight. A tight black leather miniskirt with silver spikes, high heel sneakers, heavy makeup, short black spiked hair, a vintage black top hat, stylish black Gucci sunglasses and an expensive Dolce & Gabbana zebra handbag, which hung from her right shoulder while resting her skateboard on her left shoulder. With a pale complexion and long fair legs with black fishnets, she looked more like a runway model than anything else.

Raina with her lush, long and wavy bright-red-fiery-hair, freckles and blue eyes, was wearing a pair of United Colors of Benetton ragged ultra small jean shorts over fishnets, with long black suede musketeer high heels boots, which revealed her beautiful long legs, a short sailor's half-sleeve red striped shirt and a straw cowboy hat. She walked defiantly alongside Erik.

All of a sudden, they heard a loud whistle calling, *Fweeet!* so Hannah and her friends turned around and saw Frederick, dashing towards them. Surprised at him, for showing up at all, they stopped and waited for him.

While Frederick was running he was loosening his Oxford necktie, unbuttoning his collard, taking off his dark-navy-blue pin stripe jacket, showing off his Wall Street stylish suspenders, because he wore a suit at work. He unbuttoned his white shirt's sleeves and rolled them up to his elbows. Frederick, who remind us of Sinatra's Las Vegas Rat-Pack with Fedora and all, looked more like a suave Italian gigolo, than a young German man. He was not nearly as tall as Erik. He had a nicely styled medium length wavy black hair and a heavy five o'clock shadow beard, which looked like he had not shaven in several days. He caught up with the group and while panting and trying to catch his breath, he asked:

—*Goodness Gracious, Guys!* ... What's going on here?

—Stefan insulted Hannah, badly! —said Raina.

—This better be good!

—Why is that, Frederick? —asked Raina.

—Because I had to lie to get out from work!

—*Wow!* ... No way, Frederick! —said Erik.

—Tell me, Hannah ... —continued Frederick.

—*Good grief!* ... What do you want now, Frederick? —asked Hannah, visibly annoyed.

—Are we going to get our butts kicked tonight?

Hannah, pretending she had everything under control, replied:

—*No, Frederick!* ... Don't worry about a thing! ... OK?

—*Oh c'mon, Hannah* ... I mean, really! —said Erik.

—*Shush, Erik!* —said Heidi while shutting him up.

—I said I would handle this.... *Alone!* ... Just sit back, relax and enjoy the show.... OK? —Flat out, said Hannah.

—That's exactly what I was afraid of —said Erik.

—*Baaah!* ... And now what, Erik? —asked Raina.

—Frederick, you're right. We're gonna get beaten up badly tonight ... *Heh-heh!* ... —said Erik maliciously.

Fiery Raina jumped in and shouted excitedly:

—*So what?* ... We'll show those jocks we're not afraid of them! ... *Get it?*

—I'm ready, but just as long as I don't get my nail polish ruined —said Heidi while examining her hands.

Hannah was now completely crossed and shouted:

—*Guys! Guys! Guys!* ... I said I would take care of everything! ... *So, c'mon ... let's go already!*

How did Raina wind up in Hannah's crew? That is quite the mystery, because being that both were strong women,

you could think they would end up jostling for power. But no, that didn't happen. Raina turned out to be a powerful ally, and powerful she was. You see, if left to her own devices, this fiery red-head was a ruthless predator with a very, very short fuse.

And what made it all the worse was that Raina was exceedingly beautiful, with her captivating clear blue eyes and soft-ivory-like-skin; yeah, that's right. You could easily be dupe in thinking she was as gentle as a newborn fluffy kitten, a little doll, if you will. But then, if you'd mess with her, *Oh yeah!* Not good. She would chew you out, spit you out and step on you furiously with her nasty stiletto boots, without even batting an eyelash or breaking a sweat. You should have read the warning signpost on the cage: *Don't feed the beast!* Sometimes one has to wonder at some of nature's twisted sense of humor.

Raina Gisela Brandt was a truly Germanic gal who came to us, from a stable upper middle class family background from Berlin. She was physical, hot tempered and smart. By-the-way she was not only a lush fiery red-head when she was born, but Scorpio was her sun sign too. Oh yes, did we mentioned she collected and discarded men, like other women collect jewelry? *Aha!* ... Yeah, that's right.

Raina means *"Queen and wise guardian"*. Gisela, in turn means *"Noble offspring"*. But let not her first and middle name pull the wool over your eyes, for it is her last name the one that does her honors: *"Fire or land cleared by fire!"* Yeah, that's her alright.

However, all was not bad with this one. She was just the "in your face" type, which in a way, made her quite honest. She despised the weaseling or conniving manipulative ways and was quick to point this out to her female friends and acquaintances.

Raina and Hannah became friends through their love for skateboarding. She had seen Hannah on her board and was intrigued by Hannah's quasi male riding style. Since she could have no less than to beat all the men she skated with, or at least die in the effort. She was comforted by the thought of a fellow amazon woman. And since she knew the town like the palm of her hand, it was she the one who showed Hannah all the cool, illegal and at times dangerous places to ride on. So yes, they became buddies.

So when we say she collected men, what we mean is that many, seemingly strong, but actually weak young tykes from the financial district, felt exceedingly attracted towards her. Perhaps there is some truth in the stereotype which says that weak men are attracted to strong and independent women. And this, in spite that there are some lone cowboys, who are too stupid to know some mares are not to be tamed, and who have to learn their lessons the hard way, through broken bones and nasty falls, before they wise up and let go.

For Raina, getting dressed to kill, with a seductive and risqué black cocktail outfit, to hit the happy-hour club scene downtown, where the suits typically hung out, was common place. This would guarantee her top billing, i.e. champagne, elegant and awfully expensive dinners, lots of attention and if she was in the mood for it, maybe even some wild dancing, before turning her suitors away, never giving them the time of day, let alone her phone number.

But if the poor sap happened to be a Yank or even a Brit, she would take some wicked and delightful pleasure in expunging them dry. For she detested the so called chivalrous white-knight-in-shining-armor common attitudes, telegraphed by these simpleton blokes, which were supposed to win her sweet and innocent heart, just for the asking. *Hah!* Instead, she would lure them into her poisonous trap and give them her nasty *"Thor-Teuton Welcome to my World, treat!"*

Some bartenders, who knew her and her evil ways well, would get a total kick out of it all. And they would be particularly appreciative, when the dame would throw

some crumbs at them, with her added shameless, luscious and fire-red lipstick smile, and an illicit eye-wink, to top it all off. *Oh yeah...* anyway you cut it, she was smoking hot!

Lastly, Raina and Frederick were in an on-and-off relationship. But this to her meant a nice change of pace from some the less than creative specimens she would typically find along the way. And besides, she was intoxicated by his cynicism; perhaps a fellow soul mate? *Nah!* He was just a fun distraction, a light divertimento to break up the monotony a little, that's all.

On the other hand and although still quite young, Frederick Enrico Strauss was a complex individual. His general demeanor sent off a multitude of conflicting messages, which made it difficult to reconcile into a neat little package.

His seemly contradictory messages were plain to see. On the one hand, his dress code was quite conservative; partly due to a part-time job he held at a venture capital firm in downtown Düsseldorf, requiring him to wear suit and tie. On the other, he deliberately chose to join Hannah's crew because he could identify with some of the eccentricities, quirks, if not odd-ball behavior from all members of this group.

However, his reasons for joining the group were not entirely altruistic. He was attracted to fiery Raina and joining the clique, would allow him to spend more time with her and perhaps woo her in. And this is precisely what happened, for they ended up dating each other, in an open and non-committal kind of way.

And here we come to the crux of the matter. You see, on the surface, Frederick would seem to be a team player, supportive, that is. But this would only be so, if it suited him; if there was some kind of personal advantage. He was, after all, a pragmatist who viewed the world like a zero-sum-game, a.k.a. my gain is your loss and your gain is my loss.

His suave charming nature and articulate speech abilities would disarm a lot of people and women in particular. Most people would think of him as the lovable purring kitten, which appears to be caressing one's legs giving out oodles of affection, when in truth it is simply marking his territory. Frederick, like a cat of sorts, was exceedingly independent and deep down inside, somewhat cold and to some extent, quite emotionless. However his wit, flippancy and overall poignant humour more than offset his less than stellar qualities.

He admired Hannah's idealism but didn't share in it, at all. Life had taught him that he needed to be cunning, smart and show some grit. You could almost say he admired her like one admires the beauty of a wild and exotic tropical bird. However, being that human emotions are never black-or-white, there were instances when he seemed to show empathy for his fellow human beings; not many, but some, and enough to give us some cause for hope.

Frederick did frequent some bars in the downtown business district, usually hanging out with some of his work buddies. He loved cracking jokes and generally speaking, being the center of attention. And although there were ample one-night-stand-women to choose from, he did not. To him, picking up a girl, just for the asking, or worse yet, being picked up without having a say so, was not his style. You see, he thought there was no sense of challenge in it, not a true hunt and prey game.

Were he did come into his own, was on the dance floor. But not the modern clubs were they played endless unidentifiable simple beats and house music. Instead, he truly enjoyed the old and cool style of ballroom dancing. Not dancing in a studio per se, but in small quaint and specialty cafés.

He thought that while dancing with a lady, he could really feel and tell whether or not there was any chemistry amongst the two. Rubbing hips, caressing hands, interlocking legs and passionate breathing are all part of the dance ritual, which in some cases takes on a sublime and intense character unto its own right. Such is the case when dancing the sensually and extremely suggestive tango.

It was precisely dancing to tango that he met the one older lady, which captured his heart. She was magnificent and completely carnal in her execution, such that it would arouse him, making his heart race. Unfortunately for him, she was happily and devoutly married to the owner of the place; a classy, fetching and suave Argentinian man who was a magnificent dancer himself.

CHAPTER 26

ONE COULD HAVE THOUGHT THEY WERE GOING TO HAVE A good fight but this was going to be a slaughter, instead. Hannah's crew was far from being able to take on Stefan and his physically fit soccer teammates. Specifically because the latter, as athletes, were a tough bunch and obviously, as we said earlier, they were in excellent physical condition. Besides, Hannah and her friends were outnumbered.

The uniform in Stefan's team was: white flannel T-shirts with striking vertical red stripes, red sleeves and red shorts.

Stefan was a handsome, strong and tall young man with short curly black hair, intense blue eyes and an attractive mouth with all but perfect teeth and full lips, like those of a model. He would make girls weak-at-the-knees and sigh, when he displayed his large seductive smile. He was standing on the field, next to the railing on the bleacher's front row, talking to Karla and Johanna. With his back to the soccer field, he was not aware Hannah was coming straight towards him. When she saw Hannah and her friends, menacingly coming over, Johanna, with an ironic attitude, told Stefan:

—Stefan ... I didn't think *"your"* Hannah was into soccer!

—*What?* Johanna, what the heck are you talking about? —asked Stefan surprised.

Johanna, trying to add fuel to the fire, continued:

—*Well, yeah!* ... Isn't it she and her confused friends coming over here?

Stefan turned around right away. He saw them coming when they were no more than fifty feet away, and said:

—*«Mein Gott!» Oh, my God!*

Now everyone was watching Hannah and her friends. When they got closer, the soccer players surrounded them, creating a circle around them, and then they followed them towards Stefan.

He was getting nervous and his face was turning pale. The other students on the bleachers got closer to the railing to see what was going on. They started pointing fingers at Hannah and also at Stefan, and they began to whisper, giggle and laugh.

Hannah walked straight up to him, planted herself in front of him, and then she dropped her skateboard and helmet on the grass. Being that Stefan was taller than her, she placed her hands on her hips and defiantly looked up at him to say or even better yet, to yell something nasty at him. But before she could utter a word, Stefan beat her to the punch, and said out loud:

—*«Guten Tag Hannah!» Hello, Hannah!*

Hannah, did not miss a beat. With an overt sexual attitude, she licked her upper teeth. With her right hand, she grabbed her sunglasses and lowered them to the tip of her nose. She looked straight into Stefan's eyes and insinuating herself, she smiled provocatively. With a strong and sensual voice, so most people could hear her speak, she said:

—*HELLOOO ... SUGAAAH!*

Erik, Heidi, Raina and Frederick as well as everybody else, where looking at one another and wondering: *What the heck is going on here?* ... Some of them thought she was going to strike him on the spot, but instead she was being blatantly suggestive. Pretty much as if she was throwing herself at him. Was this even possible? ... Do we even know this Hannah?

Hannah held out her arms to shoulder height, she placed the palms of her hand facing each other and separated about a foot and a half. It is obvious she was trying to convey the image of something long. She lowered her head and gazed down at Stefan's crotch. Then she raised her head up slowly, detailing his hips, his abdomen, his pectoral muscles, his lips and at last she was back up, looking into his eyes. With a mocking gesture, feigning servility and a sharp girly voice, she continued:

—*Oh, baby!* ... After everything you gave me the other night ... *aren't you even going to kiss me?*

The crowd's silence was deafening. You could have heard the buzzing of a fly. Given this unexpected behavior, Stefan was paralyzed. But Hannah was undaunted and highly charged, to say the least, and she continued right on.

—Baby, I know I've been like, a cold fish and all, but I really, really want to make it up to you, baby ... *like totally!*

Hannah waited in vain for Stefan to react and say something. So she carried on and said:

—*Oh c'mon, baby!* ... Darling, am I not your favorite little fish?

Stefan knew he needed to do damage control quickly, to save face amongst his teammates and fellow students alike. Gathering all the aplomb he could muster at the time and seeing two of his *compadres,* which were standing barely a few feet away from him, with a clenched fist and thumbs up, he opened his mouth, put his tongue out sideways and biting it, he winked mockingly at them as if saying:

STEFAN, I DIDN'T THINK "YOUR" HANNAH WAS INTO SOCCER!!!

STEFAN

—«*You see, I have her eating right out of the palm of my hand!*»

Playing along Hannah's game, he said:

—«*Aber natürlich, Liebes!*» But of course! ... *Oh yes, my love!*

Hannah, acting as if she was the happiest bunny rabbit in the whole world, she applauded, *Clap! Clap! Clap!* several times and responded immediately:

—*Oooh yeah! Yesss! ... Oh goody, goody, goody good baby!*

Hannah stepped forward to grab hold of Stefan. She reached with her left hand over his right shoulder, clung to his neck, rose herself on her toes, bent her right leg and lifted her foot up: conjuring up outrageous image clichés. She looked as if she was going to kiss him on the cheek. But instead, she stuck her tongue out and slowly licked him from his chin, up to his right eye.

It now seemed as if time had frozen. Erik gasped and his mouth dropped wide open. Johanna was so furious it just about seemed like her eyeballs were going to pop out and explode. Everyone was watching in total disbelieve at what they were seeing. Stefan was at a total loss and did not move an inch. Hannah, in complete control of the situation, asked him:

—*Sugar, baby!* ... Do you know what I want most from you, right now?

Stefan still in shock, muttered:

—*Aaaah* ... what? ...

Hannah was still hanging of off Stefan's neck. She forced her right hand into his crotch. She grabbed it, squeezed hard and while holding it tightly and not letting go, she cried out loud:

—I want this huge thing, my love! ... And I want it, *NOW!*

She paused for a moment; still, she was clamped on to him. Meanwhile, Stefan could not move or risk an injury. Hannah feigned surprise and then started laughing uncontrollably:

—*Bwahaha! ... Ha-ha-ha! ... Ho-ho-ho! ...*

Then she said:

—«*Ach, das ist doch nichts.*» *Oh, but this is too small!* ... This is not what I remember. What happened, baby?

People were now in total shock. Some had nervous giggles while others were outright laughing. Stefan was not only speechless, but he was simply frozen in place. Nonetheless, she was not through with him yet. Not by a long shot.

Hannah let go of Stefan and stepped back. She took her right hand and placed it over on her left hip. Then she took her left hand and placed it over on her right hip. She grabbed her T-shirt with both hands and slowly pulled it up to undress herself and while doing it, she said:

—*Oh, my sweet, Stefan!* ... I'm so hot for you right now! Why don't you show your buddies what kind of a cold fish, I really am?

In an instant she took her T-shirt off, letting it fall on the ground; hence, revealing an elegant black embroidered see through brassiere. She reached for her back, pried open the clasp and all of the sudden, she took it off. Hannah's breasts were proportionate, firm and beautiful.

People just stopped laughing. However, no one could have imagined the intense emotions raging and reining in on her. In a moment of blind fury, she thought:

—«*Although, I've never been with a man before, I'm ready for anything!* ... *I don't care!* ... *Let's see if this idiot has the nerve to do what he said he did, to me!*»

Continuing with the charade, Hannah said:

—*Good grief, Stefan!* ... I cannot stand it any longer! ... Please make love to me and make me *scream!*

She reached for her skirt's zipper to take it off as well. But Stefan, with tears in his eyes, totally ashamed of himself, embarrassed and waving his hands in order to stop her, said:

—«*Bitte, bitte Hannah. Nein, bitte nicht mehr!*» Please, please, Hannah! ... No more, please no more —he begged her.

Next, Hannah changed her demeanor completely. Leaving all her theatrics' aside and with a dead serious look, she questioned Stefan:

—So, then.... You never really slept with me, right?

Stefan looked down and admitting his guilt, he said quietly:

—No, no, no ...

—I CANNOT HEAR YOU, STEFAN! ... WHAT DID YOU SAY? —Hannah yelled at him for everyone to hear.

—NO! ... I DIDN'T DO IT, HANNAH. AND YOU KNOW IT! —said Stefan out loud, at last.

Upon hearing Stefan admitting he had lied to everyone, Hannah stopped. With a grave look, she took her T-shirt and slowly put it back on. She threw her bra to Erik. She picked up her skateboard and strapped it on her back. She removed her sunglasses and staring at Stefan up close; she pressed her finger onto his chest and screamed to his face:

—Don't you ever mess with a *Wayúu* again! ... *You hear?* ... *NOT, EVER!*

Feeling vindicated because Stefan had admitted his guilt, and because she had managed to humiliate him in front of all his friends, Hannah turned around and addressing her crew, she said:

—*Hey gang!* ... I'm in a mood to celebrate. Let's go down to *Kurzestrasse* and go crazy tonight ... *Ha-ha-ha-ha!*

As Hannah and her friends were leaving, the crowd who had surrounded them in a circle, opened up to let them through. No one said a word, on their way out the soccer field; neither Hannah's friends, who were still in shock, nor anybody else in the stadium, because they were still amazed.

She appeared to be totally cool, but she was actually trembling inside, for she knew there would be hell to pay for her little outburst.

CHAPTER 27

HANNAH AND HER CREW TOOK THE TRAM TOWARDS THE center of town. Erik, who knew Hannah was now heartbroken, began clowning around to lighten things up and try to dissipate the heavy atmosphere. Raina and Heidi told her how proud they were for having confronted the chump and given the jerk a lesson, he would soon not forget. However, none of these efforts worked, because she was still feeling quite guilty.

It was about eight o'clock in the evening, when they arrived at Lulu's bar and restaurant. They sat outside on the quaint little picnic tables, where they had a clear view of the water's edge on the Rhine River, because Hannah was in no mood to enter the bar. She wanted to hang out with her friends. They ordered a round of *Alts*, which is a popular type of beer in Düsseldorf. Hannah had tears in her eyes. All along Frederick had not said a word. Hannah, curious to know his mind, asked him:

—Frederick, what do you think of all of this?

He took a moment to think about it and then he answered. It appeared he was going to say something profound. Therefore, everyone waited anxiously for his reply. At last, he just dropped it and *Bang!* ...

—You know, Hannah ... I think your breasts are amazing!

Hannah, pretending to be outraged, but barely being able to contain her laughter, exploded and shouted:

—Frederick ... You're a nasty old pig!

Raina and Heidi immediately joined the chorus.

—«*Ja, ja, ja Du bist ein Ferkel!*» Yes, yes, yes swine, swine, swine, Frederick!

Hannah explained she now felt sorry for poor Stefan. However, she was terribly worried that once they learned of it in school, they would kick her out. She feared this would really disappoint her parents.

Frederick jumped into the conversation and told her not to worry too much about it, because he had her covered. They all looked at him in disbelief and asked: *How was this possible?* Next, he proceeded to explain and said:

—You guys know Brigitte, the new school's headmaster, right?

—Yes, we know her. So what? —asked Raina.

—Although she is more than forty years old, she's devastatingly attractive! ... Don't you think so, Erik? —asked Frederick.

Erik's eyes lit up, he smiled and said:

—«*Ja, sie ist sehr attraktiv!*» *Yeah, for sure!* She's outright sexy!

—She is not only attractive, but she's downright hot and conspicuously married, to boot —continued Frederick.

—*No way!* ... Really? —asked Erik.

—It seems her husband spends most of his time working abroad —said Frederick.

—*OK, Frederick* ... And what has that got to do with me? ... *Huh?* —asked Hannah.

703 Graf-Adolf-Platz
HANNAH AND HER CREW ON THE TRAM TOWARDS THE CENTER OF TOWN

—Hannah, calm down ... *Cool it, buddy!* —said Frederick.

—Frederick, could you get straight to the point? —said Raina impatiently this time.

—Well ... let's just say Brigitte and I know each other rather well!

—*Gee, Frederick!* ... No way, pal ... I mean, you? —said Erik showing his amazement and enthusiasm.

—And if you don't believe me, I've got photos to prove it! —said Frederick defiantly.

—*Oh c'mon, Frederick!* ... That's a blatant lie! —said Heidi.

—*Oh, yeah?* ... You don't believe me? I'll show you I'm not lying —said Frederick.

He reached into one of the inside pockets of his jacket. Then he looked into another, and he kept searching every single one, as if looking for something. At last, Frederick said:

—*Shebang, yeah!* ... I found it! Here it is. Come take a look —said Frederick, pleased with his find.

Frederick pulled out a small photo of Brigitte and himself together, in what was obviously a highly compromising position. Erik snatched it from his hands and started ogling it.

—*Gee whiz, Frederick* —said Erik surprised.

—*Easy, buddy!* ... Take a look and tell me. What do ya think? ... Pretty cool, no? ... *Hee-hee!*

—*Frederick, that's fantastic, man!* ... So like, is it really you? —asked Erik.

Heidi got infuriated with Erik and smacked him over the head with her purse. She yanked the photo away from him, tore it up and threw it into the wind. Next, she scolded Erik and cried:

—*«Schwein!» Pig, pig, pig Erik!* ... You're a pervert, a pervert, and a big pervert!

Heidi in disgust and enraged, turned towards Hannah, and said:

—Hannah, did you see this? I mean, why waste time with men? They are all the same ... a bunch of perverts!

—*Shush Heidi, cool it!* ... Take it easy, please —said Frederick while trying to placate Heidi.

Frederick made a long pause and when everyone was paying attention again, he continued:

—Hey, listen up guys ... I could ask Brigitte to forget this whole incident and maybe, just maybe this time ...

—Maybe what, Frederick? —asked Hannah annoyed.

Looking straight into her eyes, he said:

—*You, fool!* ... Maybe they won't kick your butt and throw you out of school! —cried Frederick.

—*Whoaa!* ... That's like the bomb, Frederick! —said Erik.

—*Bwahaha!* ... *Ha-ha-ha!* ... Hey, thank you, thank you, Erik! —said Frederick, bowing and bobbing his head.

—*Heee haw!* ... Now, this here's my man, Frederick. *He's, Da man!* ... *Ha-ha-ha!* —said Erik laughing excitedly.

—So, my little dear Hannah. You owe me big time, OK? —said Frederick, putting on airs of triumph.

Suddenly, Hannah perked up and like a live wire she threw herself over the table. She grabbed Frederick by the ears, pulled him towards her and gave him a big kiss, smearing her bright red glam lipstick all over his face. Then she shoved him back hard on to his seat, and yelled at him:

—Frederick, I love you! ... *But you're still a big nasty old pig!*

Seeing Hannah's mood change, now everyone was happy, they felt relieved and they all started laughing.

—*Bwahaha! ... Ha-ha-ha! ... Ho-ho-ho! ...*

Erik was ecstatic because of Hannah's change in fortunes. He thought it was high time to cut loose and get down to some insane serious partying. So then he asked:

—Hey people, hear me out! Why don't we head on up to Pub Solicitor's and continue our party over there?

—*Solicitor's?* Are you crazy? That place is for old fogies with a lot of bread and what's more, a bunch of snobs —said Frederick.

—*I got it!* ... Let's go to Club Sensation White because I have a mad desire to dance! —said Raina excitedly.

—*Yes!!!* ... You see, that's what I'm talking about, Raina ... *Now you're talking, baby!* —said Frederick.

Frederick paid the bill and when everybody was getting ready to leave, he put his arm around Raina's waist, yank her hard towards him and squeezing her tightly, he said:

—Raina, my fiery Red Queen ... Tonight, I want to marry you, baby!

Raina slapped him, *Slap slap slap!* several times, in jest. She shoved him off and said:

—«*Schwein, schwein!*» Swine, swine, swine Frederick! ... *Ha-ha-ha! ...*

I GOT IT!!! ... LET'S GO TO CLUB SENSATION WHITE BECAUSE I HAVE A MAD DESIRE TO DANCE!!!

YES, RAINA!!! … NOW YOU'RE TALKING, BABY!!!

Raina laughed, grabbed Frederick's hand again, pulled him towards her, hugged him, kissed him and while holding hands together, they left. Meanwhile, Erik took a good look at Heidi and said:

—*Heidi, my darling* ... I guess tonight it's you and me, baby!

—*Oh, God!* ... But don't you dare break me a single fingernail, *Okay?* —said Heidi.

Hannah, taunting them, asked:

—Hey guys, wait up! ... So what about me? Who will dance with me tonight?

—*My dear Ice Queen,* after the little stunt you pull on poor old Stefan, nobody will ever mess with you, again. Not ever! —quipped Erik.

A few days later, Frederick and Brigitte lay in bed after having made love all night. Frederick lit a cigarette. They had been talking about "the soccer field incident", which is what everybody else was calling it these days. Brigitte was curious, because she had read Hannah's student profile and was confused, as to who it actually was, this energetic and unpredictable creature.

—Tell me, Frederick ... who exactly is this Hannah?

Frederick took another long cigarette drag, inhaled, waited a moment, reflected and then while exhaling, he said:

—Sometimes I think Hannah is a wild man inside a gorgeous woman's body.

—*Huh?* ... You must be joking, right? —said Brigitte.

—Maybe she just came from Mars!

—*Oh,* Frederick, what do you ever mean?

—Or perhaps she's some kind of Joan of Arc, whose sole purpose in life is to break men's hearts ... for the fun of it!

—*Oh, no!* ... Heaven's forbid! —cried Brigitte.

—But whatever she is, I hope she'll soon find her match, for the sake of us men ... you know, the weaker sex!

CHAPTER 28

SEVERAL YEARS HAD GONE BY SINCE MARIA AND ROBERT had graduated from high school. He was on his second year of college at Oklahoma State University, in the city of Stillwater. He had not been able to decide, which career he would follow. On the one hand, his father wanted him to study business administration and on the other, Chelsea wanted him to explore a career in the Humanities, in the School of Arts and Sciences. Robert solved the dilemma by studying both careers at the same time. Fortunately, many of the credit hours for core subjects he would need to take only once, in order to get a degree in both fields of study.

Meanwhile, Maria del Carmen moved to Oklahoma City. She was studying at Oklahoma City Community College. She decided to pursue a computer science career. And because she had no scholarship, she would have to earn some money to pay her way through college, as she went along. A comp-sci career allowed her to begin working, almost immediately, as a computer programmer during the day, and attend school at night. Most importantly, she would be able to take some online courses from home, via her computer and this, would allow her time to juggle her busy schedule.

The city of Stillwater, and Oklahoma City, are about fifty miles apart. This is barely an hour and a half distance by car. Maria rented a small apartment, and Robert visited her almost every weekend. On some occasions, she would visit him in Stillwater, but this was somewhat complicated, because she had to stay in the dorm with him. And they had to time it with Robert's roommate, so when he was away on any given weekend, Maria could then come and visit him.

One afternoon, when both of them were visiting their parents at Charming Meadows, they decided to go to Big Al's soda fountain. Perhaps it was destiny, perhaps it was just a coincidence, or maybe Robert was being sneaky, but they ended up sitting in the same exact booth where they had sat before, when Maria had invited Robert to the football game, so long ago. Mr. Al, the business owner, stood behind the counter near the booth where they were sitting, trying to sniff out what these two, now old timers, were up to. Next, Robert asked Maria:

—Maria, do you remember our first date?

—Of course I remember, you silly! Why do you ask?

—Specifically, do you remember when you told me about your surname's origin?

—Are you referring to Aragón? —asked Maria.

—*Exactly!* ... You said someday you'd like to visit Spain, in search of your family roots. Do you remember that?

—How could I ever forget, you silly boy? That was the day I fell in love with you. Say, Robert, why do you ask?

—Maria, would you like us to travel to Spain?

—*Of course I would!* Are you kidding me? But you know we have no money for that.

—Maria, that's not entirely true.

—I don't get it, Robert. Where would we find the money? —asked Maria.

Robert told her he had been discussing this idea with his parents. Chelsea thought this was a superb idea, from the outset. She even suggested they could spend a few days in Boston, visiting relatives. Although Fred didn't say no, it took quite an effort to convince him. Finally, Robert's parents agreed and what's more, they would pay for most of the total cost of the trip. Now all that was left to do was to coordinate the school holidays for Maria and Robert; also, to time it with Maria's work vacation. The plan, he said, was to spend two weeks visiting the northern region of Spain, but yes, Chelsea demanded a three-day stay in the city of London.

—So then, tell me, Maria. Are we going to Spain?

—Robert, you have no idea how happy you've made me!

—*Wow!* ... Maria, that's so cool, baby.

—Darling, I don't think you could make me any happier!

—Maria, do you wanna bet?

—Bet what, honey?

—That I can make you happier?

—Robert, impossible! ... A trip to Spain? That's like a dream come true. I mean, it's just incredible!

Well, if Maria thought a trip to Spain, was already over the top, she was easily going to fall flat on her butt, because Robert had another little surprise in store for her. Robert pulled out a dark-navy-blue velvet lined square little box. He placed it on the same exact table were he almost dropped his chocolate milkshake, long ago. He open it up, turned it around and while displaying a traditional, yet gorgeous diamond engagement ring, pretending he was totally cool and speaking in a casual manner, he asked Maria:

—Maria del Carmen Garcia Aragón ... *Will you marry me?*

Maria, without being able to control the sudden jolt of adrenalin flooding and rushing all throughout her veins, started trembling, she was most definitely weak at the knees, her heart almost stopped, her cheeks flushed, and she felt like they were burning hot, her pupils were, like totally dilated, and they were huge. She threw herself over the table, embraced

Robert and in a wild fit of emotion, she started kissing him in ecstasy. Terribly happy, and with tears in her eyes, she cried out for everyone to hear:

—*Oh my God, Robert!* ... You were right! ... *Yes yes yes!* ... *Forever, yesss!*

Mr. Al couldn't help to hear the whole conversation. Well, actually he was eavesdropping in on it, and he was surely not disappointed. This could be gossip material for quite some time to come. But in all honesty, he was exceedingly happy with this young couple's vows. He came out into the dining area. He locked the door, turned the "closed" sign on, lowered the blinds so people walking-by on the outside, couldn't peep into the place. He went back to the counter and pulled out a fairly expensive bottle of champagne. He got some wine glasses and headed back to Maria and Robert's table. He placed the wine glasses on the table, opened the bottle, *Pop!* ... and sure enough some foam squirted out spraying Robert and Maria on the face. They all laughed it out, and Mr. Al poured the champagne and while toasting, he said:

—Robert, you have now turned into a man. Isn't it high time you stopped drinking chocolate milkshakes with extra malt? ... *Now, may I kiss the bride?*

CHAPTER 29

IT WAS SEVERAL WEEKS SINCE THE STORM HAD PASSED, OR should we say *"the soccer field incident"*, once more? And now the all time gossiping had pretty much abated. Frederick had managed to pull it off with Brigitte, and Hannah escaped, almost unscathed, those serious consequences she had feared the most. For a while she stayed low and it all seemed to work itself out. Stefan had licked his wounds and was now more popular than ever. Not only with Johanna and Karla but with all the girls in school who wanted to comfort him from the outrageous behavior of that girl, or rather that Colombian wench called ... Hannah!

However, Stefan kept replaying the soccer field incident in his head, over and over again. Not only was he confused, but it seems he was more obsessed than ever with Hannah. He didn't know if he loved her, desired her, despised her, or whether he respected her at all.

Stefan needed closure to end his desperation caused by this incident. But he bided his time, was patient and waited.

One day, when classes for the day had ended and just before leaving school, he approached Hannah. She was not alone. Moreover, she was almost never alone anymore because her crew was closer than ever before. On this occasion Erik and Raina were with her. Stefan greeted everyone and said:

—«*Bitte, Hannah*» Excuse me, Hannah. Could I talk to you for a moment?

Immediately, Erik and Raina took a defensive stance, and perhaps you could even say they were outright hostile. But Hannah told them she was cool, and she would catch up with them later on. She turned towards Stefan and said:

—OK Stefan, I'll bite. What do you have in mind?

Stefan, who was holding a rather worn out skateboard in his hand, asked her:

—Would you like to ride with me to South Park? That is, on our skateboards, of course?

—*Hmmm!* ... To South Park, you say?

—We could be there in twenty minutes. What do you say? Do you want to race me? —asked Stefan again.

Hannah wasn't about to pass up Stefan's challenge; especially because he sounded genuinely friendly. And then again, Stefan was trying hard to put on the charm, and so he shone his bright-seductive-and-fetching smile. Besides, Hannah was already feeling quite playful too. Furthermore, it looked like this could be fun. So she said:

—*Whoa, twenty minutes!* What are you, Stefan? ... A little old lady on a wheelchair? ... *Ha-ha-ha!*

—*Yikes, Hannah!* I just wanted to make it easy on you.

—Easy, Stefan? *Haw!* ... I'll be there in ten minutes. Let's see if you can catch me!

—Catch you? Hannah, are you kidding me? *I'll smoke you!*

—*Well, c'mon already!* ... What are you waiting for? *Oh, man* ... I haven't got all day ... you know??? —said Hannah.

HANNAH KNEW SHE WAS NO MATCH FOR STEFAN
BUT THIS SURE DIDN'T DETER HER, AT ALL!!!

Both Hannah and Stefan were wearing worn out or rather ragged jeans with holes in them and pretty dirty and wasted sneakers, too. Hannah took out her "*Prince Andrew*", that is, her bright-glossy Union Jack Nutcase helmet. Moreover, her knee pads, elbow pads and a pair of black short-finger leather gloves, from her backpack. She put them on. She rolled her watch's face below her wrist and strapped her backpack on. She swung her head from left to right, waving her hair, holding it, fastening with a couple of elastic hair-ties into a ponytail, and then she put her helmet on. Lastly, she put on her sunglasses.

Erik was shaking his head because he didn't approve of what Hannah was getting into. On the contrary, fiery Raina, smirking, salivating and feeling aroused herself, thought this whole scene was suggestive and sweet, if not out right sexy.

Stefan had no gadgets except for a pair of bright yellow parachute goggles, his skateboard and an outstanding cut physique. Erik, who was by now visibly concerned, got close to Stefan, grabbed him by the arm and whispered into his ear:

—«*Bitte Stefan*» Say, Stefan ... *Hey, bro!* ... You know Hannah is nuts ... don't you?

Stefan put his other hand on top of Erik's and whispered back.

—«*Ja, Kumpel, ich weiß!*» Yeah brother, everybody knows that!

—Stefan, please be careful with her, OK? —said Erik.

—Don't worry, Erik. Besides, it's me the one who should be scared!

—What do you mean, Stefan? —asked Erik.

—Did you already forget the little incident? *Ha-ha-ha!*

—*Yeah!* ... you're right, bro ... *Ha-ha-ha!* —said Erik.

If you take *Ellerstrasse* east to *Kruppstrasse* and then south to South Park, the distance will be a little less than three quarters of a mile or about one kilometer.

Hannah and Stefan were now standing outside the school building on the north sidewalk of *Ellerstrasse.* They had to cross the street, but Hannah was not about to skate to the street corner crossing ... *Noooo!* ... Instead, like a crazed daredevil, she jumped on her skateboard and took off without even looking at the two-lane incoming traffic. She knew she was no match for Stefan, but this sure didn't dissuade her, at all. As usual, Hannah was going for broke, as if her whole life depended on it.

Hannah's sudden behavior took Stefan by surprise. No sooner had Erik warned him to keep an eye out for Hannah, than she was already getting into trouble. Stefan had no time to react but only to shout at her:

—«*Hannah Nein!*» Hannah ... *No, No, No, Noooo!*

Hannah reached the other side of the street like a thunderbolt. She was all rush and wanted to signal Stefan, in no uncertain terms, she was a street-skater, and she wasn't going to take no bull from him. She was now coming in fast onto the sidewalk, on the other side of the street. She crouched and then she hit the nose of her board hard and jumped with her arms fully extended to maintain her balance. She was now up in the air, *Woosh!* ... Lifting her back foot, popping the board and flipping it in mid-air, she nailed a flawless reverse *Nollie with a flip! ... Whoa! ... Yesss!* ... She landed on her skateboard, *Klank!* ... She was carrying a strong momentum, and as US Civil War Admiral David Farragut said so himself, *"Damn the torpedoes, full speed ahead!"* [3] ... Next, she began to pedal furiously, *Zip zip zip!* ... to gain more speed and distance. In other words, she wanted to leave Stefan in the dust.

Stefan ran across the street with his skateboard on hand. A bus was coming in fast, and it looked like it was going to run Stefan over, so it blew its horn, *Hooonk! Hooonk!* ... Stefan barely managed to reach the other side of the street without being run over. He threw his skateboard forward, chased it and jumped on it, *Klank!* ... and then he ran as fast as he could, in Hannah's pursuit.

Hannah was about thirty yards ahead of him. She had no time for being cute nor looking pretty, and was pedaling like a bat out of hell. Specifically, she wasn't running but rather flying, *Whoosh!* ... on her skateboard.

She slowed down to make a sharp right turn, *Screech!* ... on to *Höhenstrasse*, a small side street with rows of two-to-three story apartment buildings on both sides. This side street ends on to *Linienstrasse,* which is another small street, which runs directly into *Kruppstrasse*. By taking this detour, she shaved off a little over two hundred feet to their destination.

Stefan was gaining in on Hannah but to say it was easy, in spite of him being a runner, it was not. They soon came on to *Kruppstrasse* and Hannah made a right turn, *Vreeeeeew!* ... without losing too much speed. They were now heading south on a fairly long straight away. Stefan got closer to Hannah, but she was zigzagging, *Zip zip zip!* ... cutting him off because she was determined not to let him get through.

He panicked because he could see that within a hundred yards, they were coming on to the major and busy intersection of *Kruppstrasse* and *Oberbilker Allee,* and he had no idea if Hannah was going to run the red light; thus, putting herself in mortal danger.

Stefan started taking long strides, *Kata-kata-kata!* ... pushing awfully hard. His and her skateboards were now side-by-side. He held Hannah by her hips, in order for them to maintain their balance. And almost losing it and crashing onto the pavement, he pushed on and *Woosh!* ... he overtook Hannah, *Whoaa!* ... *Yeah!* ...

When Stefan was fifty yards away from the intersection, he jumped off his board and continued running forward, because he was carrying a lot of momentum, and he was desperately trying to avoid falling down and crashing onto the sidewalk. When he did finally stopped, he turned around quickly and

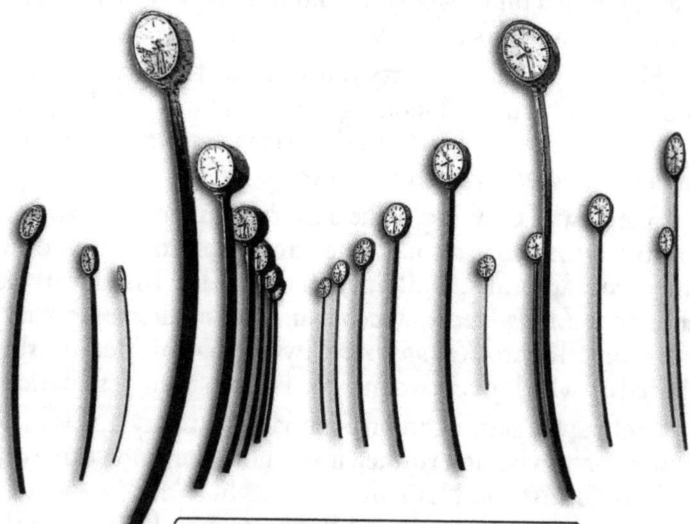

FROM KLAUS RINKE'S TIME FIELD SCULPTURE

Plop! He stood up, he settled in on firm footing, he opened his arms and with all his might while making a stupendous effort, he grabbed Hannah by the waist and *Whaam!* ... He caught her and spun around in a full circle, just in the nick of time, lest she continued on to *Oberbilker Allee* avenue and crossed it, without looking nor stopping. And that is precisely what she intended to do!

Hannah was now caught in Stefan's powerful bear hug, with her feet off the ground. With her clenched fists, panting, agitated, breathing heavily because she was out of air, she was pounding Stefan on the chest, *Pow, sock, splat!* ... and kicking him too, *Kick, knack, knock!* ... And all the while she was shouting, kicking and screaming:

—«*Töffel!*» *You brute!* ... What are you doing to me?

—«*Bitte Hannah!*» Please, Hannah ... *Calm down!*

—*Oh no, no, no, no!* ... Let me go, you beast! ... I could've run the light!

Stefan was also breathing heavily and while trying to catch his breath, he said:

—*Hannah!* ... I'm trying to save your life!

—That's just a bunch of lies, lies, lies Stefan! ... Let me go, now! —cried Hannah.

Luckily for Stefan, Hannah's skateboard was not lost but instead it overturned and ended up in the parking lot of an Audi car dealership, on the corner of *Kruppstrasse* and *Oberbilker Allee.* On the other hand, his board got stuck inside a nearby bus stop. Stefan let go of Hannah, turned around and went back to get his skateboard.

As soon as Hannah was freed from his embrace, and while he wasn't looking, she ran for her skateboard, picked it up by the wheels, ran across the street and threw it forward onto the sidewalk, jumped on it, *Klank!* ... And once again she was dashing like a speed demon, *Vroom!* ... Fortunately for Stefan, this sidewalk section was a two hundred yard straight away, which ran directly into the park, with no more intersections.

They would have to go underneath the *Volksgarten* railway station overpass and the entrance to South Park would be immediately on their left.

Stefan ran after her. And because he was so competitive, he wasn't going to let her win this race so easily; still, she was running ahead of him, but she was pretty much out of breath and about to collapse.

They crossed underneath the dark and rusty train overpass. She made an abrupt sharp left turn, cutting off an incoming car, approaching from the opposite direction.

The car blew its horn, *Beep, beep, beeeep!* ... and the driver had to hit the brakes hard, *Screeeech!* ... coming to a sudden stop. She crossed the street, made smiling faces at the driver, waved her hands goodbye with a military salute and entered the park at roaring speed, like a ball on fire.

She got onto one of the smaller asphalt trails and yelled at pedestrians to get out of her way, *Move out! ... Coming through! ... Watch out!* ... so they would clear the path because otherwise, she would simply run them over.

She continued rolling swiftly for another fifty yards until she reached the park's "Time Field Sculpture", which was located on the right hand side of the trail. This sculpture has about two and a half dozen large clock faces, similar to London's Big Ben, mounted on the tips of thirty-foot-high pylons and arranged in a grid; thus, giving the impression of a garden of giant time tulips.

Hannah veered off to the left on to a large patch of grass and went flying off her skateboard, falling and tumbling, *Flip! Flop! Flam!* ... She was sweaty, completely out of breath and laughing hysterically. *—Ahh-ha-ha! ... Bwahaha!—*She got up and spread her legs apart wide, bent at the waist, with her hands on her knees and breathing heavily. She was trying to suck lots of air into her burning lungs ... *Wuuuoooiii!*

Stefan caught up to her a few moments later, but he did not fall down. He was breathing hard but not as heavily as Hannah.

—«*Oh, mein Gott, Hannah!*» *Oh my God, Hannah!* You're truly crazy. I don't know how you did it, but you beat me —said Stefan.

—«*Habe ich dir ja gleich gesagt!*» I told you I would beat you! ... Didn't I?

No sooner had she caught her breath and although still breathing heavily, than Hannah was on the move again. With her skateboard strapped on her back, she reached and grabbed Stefan's hand. She pulled hard on it and demanded forcefully:

—*C'mon, you lazy bum!* ... Let's go into the park, now!

—*But, Hannah!* ... Now, what?

Stefan had no choice but to follow her. They walked until they reached the edge of the lake. They found an empty green bench, next to a small worn-out-wooden-pier made up of sun bleached planks. There was a beautiful shade-producing acacia tree overhanging the bench and inviting any passer by to sit, relax, contemplate, meditate and enjoy the view. Hannah, exhausted and drenched in sweat, dropped herself on it, *Plop!* ... She stretched her legs and said:

—*Hheyuuhhhh, Stefan!* ... I cannot move another muscle!

—Hannah, me neither.

—*C'mon, Stefan!* ... Go ahead and sit down. Don't be afraid 'cause I don't bite!

—Are you sure about that?

—*Good grief, Stefan!* —cried Hannah.

—Alright, alright ... alright, Hannah!

He sat on the edge of the bench, trying to keep some distance between them. Then, while searching for the right words, Hannah jumped in ahead of him, and asked:

—*Ah!* ... I feel better now. But tell me, Stefan, what did you want to talk to me about?

—Hannah ...

—Yeah...?

—I want to apologize for spreading those lies I told about you, in school.

—*Aha!*

—I know it was stupid of me. I'm truly sorry.

Stefan paused for a moment. Maybe he was waiting for Hannah to give him some kind of signal of approval, but she did not. He was emotionally confused, anxious and mostly looking forward to some kind of closure to his plight. But wearing his heart on his sleeve, he continued:

—But every single day, since the soccer field incident, I've been replaying that scene in my head, over and over again!

He paused yet again, because he was unsure of what to say next. Nevertheless, he opened his heart to her and confessed:

—Hannah ... I'm madly in love with you!

She made no comments. They were silent for about thirty seconds, but to them this seemed like hours. In the heat of a humid and breezeless afternoon, seeing that Hannah was not reacting to his words, he started backpedaling and tried to save the situation and said:

—Hannah, do you think you can forgive me and perhaps we could become friends?

Impetuously, she jumped up and threw herself on Stefan. She put her arms around him forcefully, and began kissing and slobbering him wildly. Just like it had happened many times before, Stefan was now surprised, frazzled, confused and exhausted. With his nerves destroyed, he didn't know what to think. But without putting up any resistance, he closed his eyes and gave in to Hannah's passionate kisses. Finally, sated, exhilarated, with a loud mischievous and bordering on a mocking laughter, Hannah stopped and cried:

—*Stefan, you're a fool!* ... Of course, I love you!

—But, how? ... I mean what? —asked Stefan, bewildered.

—*Absolutely!*

—But Hannah, I don't understand!

—Tell me ... what girl in her right mind would be so stupid, as to not love you? —cried Hannah.

—Hannah, what do you mean?

—You are handsome, strong, tall, and I suspect a good man at heart, Stefan. *But ...*

—*Oh, no! ... Here it comes!* ... But what, Hannah?

—Look Stefan, even though it now seems you're entranced, fascinated, intoxicated and perhaps even owned by me, the truth is ... I'm not the right girl for you!

Stefan was now entangled in Hannah's web, a whirlwind of emotions, which took him out of his senses, pulling him in every which way, all at the same time.

—But Hannah ... I don't understand. But, but please, tell me why?

While running her fingers through his hair and gently caressing his face, Hannah said:

—«*Mein schöner Stefan!*» My lovely, Stefan. Please don't despair for we will be the best of friends.

—Are we really?

—*Yes, we will be!* ... But Stefan, I need you to promise me two things.

Stefan, in a total state of catharsis, was barely able to say:

—*Oh, no!* ... What now, Hannah?

—First, I want you to become a great football star and maybe even make it to the German national soccer team.

—*Sure!* ... Why not? I mean that's, like so easy —said Stefan wryly.

Hannah, who was now excited and emotionally charged, continued:

—And secondly, no matter who you're with or how happy you might be, you'll never forget me! OK, Stefan?

But before Stefan could say anything, she got up and said:

—*C'mon, Stefan* ... don't pay any attention to me, because as you already know, *I'm crazy!*

—Hannah, I don't believe that! —Stefan protested.

—Sweetie, don't argue with me. Just take my hand, walk with me and take me home, please?

After suffering the ups and downs of this huge emotional roller coaster, Stefan couldn't see the subtle but deep wound in Hannah's heart. And in fact, how could he have known? Although he was one of the reasons for Hannah's distress, he was not even the most important one of them all.

Instead, to her he was like a beautiful tree in an idyllic landscape. One of many others, which were painted on her broad canvas with diverse, complex, strong and colourful experiences. Hannah's logic defies explanation. And yet, this is exactly what her inner core was made out of. Strictly speaking, this was the essence of her whole inner being.

Even Hannah herself, could not understand it, let alone explain it. It would have been so much easier for her to give in into her powerful and youthful hormones, which ran rampant throughout her bloodstream and all over her body; therefore, making her long completely, without control and without conditions, this athletic Greek Olympian.

Instead, all Stefan would see that day, would be Erik's Ice Queen; emotionally detached and apparently, cheerful and carefree.

CHAPTER 30

STEFAN AND HANNAH WALKED FOR A LONG TIME HOLDING hands together, but they said nothing, while dusk fell. At last, they arrived at the entrance door to Hannah's place. He stood in front of her holding both of her hands and looking down straight into her eyes. Likewise, with her head slightly tilted back, she was peering intently into his. He was about to say something, but she gently put her finger on his lips and said:

—*Hush, Stefan!* ... Don't say anything! ... Let's not ruin this beautiful day.

She kissed him one last time, and then she whispered in his ear.

—I love you, my silly boy.... Now go away and forget any of this really happened.

Hannah turned around, opened the door and in an instant, disappeared at the threshold. It was already dark outside and Stefan stood in front of her door, for a few moments. But strange as it may seem, he felt happy and quite contented. He put his hands in his pockets and began to whistle «*Die Lorelei*», an old German ballad, and then he left for *Karolingerplatz* tram station.

Hannah quickly climbed the stairs up to the first floor and into the living room. She met Kristian, her little six-year-old brother. Upon seeing her, he became happy, excited and immediately he asked her:

—Hannah Hannah Hannah, let's play a video game. Let's play play play, and I will beat you! ... *Ha-ha-ha!*

But Hannah did not have the energy nor the desire to play. Although she did not show it, her heart was in total disarray. Making a great effort to contain all her emotions, she bent down to kiss her little brother's forehead, and said:

—Not now, my dear Kristian.

—And why not?

—Because your big sister is too tired tonight.

—*No, no, no!* ... I want to play, *now!*—Kristian complained.

—Let's play tomorrow ... Yes? I promise!

—Well alright ... but you promised! ... OK, Hannah?—said Kristian while pouting.

As she was going up stairs towards her bedroom, located on the third floor, she caught sight of her mom and dad. They were in the kitchen preparing dinner. Hannah greeted them from the stairs and said:

—Hi, Mom and Dad!

—*Hi, honey!*—said Jaséle.

—*Hey guys!* ... I'm like really tired today.

—Are you? Really?—asked Wolfgang.

—If you don't mind. I'll go upstairs and get some sleep.

—All right, honey. Do you want me to wake you up for dinner?—asked Jaséle.

—No, Mom ... Thank you. Please don't wait for me.

Wolfgang thought Hannah was behaving strangely, because he knew she had a pretty good appetite. Jaséle noticed it immediately. Perhaps it was the feminine instinct in her, but she was sure Hannah needed time alone for herself. Jaséle looked at Wolfgang, as if telling him with her eyes:

—*«Don't ask any more questions!»*

Then, Jaséle, with all the tenderness, which only a truly loving mother can provide, told her daughter:

—All right, honey. I'll leave food in the oven in case you get hungry later.

—*Thanks, Mom!* Good night, Mommy and Daddy —said Hannah.

—Good night, honey! —said Jaséle.

Slowly, one by one
as if plucking grapes
from a bunch...

Hannah entered her room and felt emotionally spent. She dropped her skateboard, backpack, sneakers and without undressing, she threw herself on the bed. Hannah's strong emotions were now not her friends. On the contrary, she felt the angst of having lost a marvelous opportunity. Her mind was galloping after recalling all the day's events. She could smell Stefan's scent on her clothes and what's more, on her skin, let alone the taste of his sweet fresh kisses, in her mouth. She had killed love before it could take flight and blossom. It was a bold and reckless move on her part, for they say love is the strongest force in the universe. Had she rejected love, forever?

She turned on her side and now she could see the streetlights' dim and pale-gray glow, entering through her window and barely illuminating her bedroom.

Slowly, one by one, as if plucking grapes from a bunch, her tears fell silently on her pillow. She remained motionless for what seemed an eternity to her, until Morpheus, the god of dreams, feeling compassion for her, took her into his kingdom to await the morning lights and a bright fresh new dawn.

The End

EPILOGUE

HANNAH'S ADVENTURES BECOME MORE ENTANGLED, WHEN she decides to follow a young Basque Catholic seminarian on a pilgrimage hike of more than five hundred miles, in Spain. They travel *El Camino de Santiago de Compostela* or St. James Way, from Barcelona, to Galicia, walking through the Spanish provinces of Catalonia, Aragón, Navarre, Castile, and Leon.

The outcome of this bizarre love encounter will open new doors to other wild adventures, which will have her gallivanting, all throughout North Africa, and eastbound towards Istanbul.

Mrs. Elizabeth Rose Moore convinces the Loewes to visit London, during the summer. Will Hannah finally meet her prince charming in England? Or will she have something to do with Robert, who is already engaged to marry Maria del Carmen?

These stories and more, will be revealed in the next installment of the novel, in volume two.

ABOUT THE AUTHOR

BALAM WAS BORN IN PANAMA, GREW UP IN VENEZUELA AND HAS lived most of his adult and professional life in the United States. His name comes from the *Popol-Vuh,* the book of myths of the Maya. From early childhood, he developed great curiosity for knowledge, life and adventure. This has motivated him to seek an eclectic range of activities and interests.

At the age of twelve he travelled from Panama, to Canada, and back, by car; hence, arousing his childhood imagination, when he experienced exotic cultures and ancient archeology. He soared the Chilean Andes, flying sailplanes. He is a sailing enthusiast, a dancer, a pilot, and he even had a garage rock band in his teen years; thus, his love for music and most notably: for jazz, glitz and the big city.

His creative juices found several decades of successful corporate expression in his chosen profession: Information Technologies.

Now, his creative interests take him on to literature, taking shape in bilingual fictional writing, of which this novel is, but his first attempt. His writing style has been heavily influenced by English, Classical and Latin American literature. Still, he is decidedly magnetized by complex technologies and its revolutionary impact, on a planetary scale.

CREDITS

LANGUAGE TRANSLATION VERIFICATION

Dutch: Anneke van Hoek
French: Jeanne and Pierre Clateaux
German: Hannah Kirchmeier
Italian: Elyka Abello, Alexandra Brando

ENDNOTES

1. **"SS John A. Holloway,"** WRECKSITE.EU 29 Oct. 2012, Web. 11 Nov. 2012. <http://bit.ly/Ui2WBN>
2. **"Swinging Old Lady,"** Queen Emma Bridge, Curaçao Tourist Board, Web. 11 Nov. 2012. <http://bit.ly/UwFQ0g>
3. **"US Civil War Admiral David Farragut,"** Wikipedia: The Free Encyclopedia. Wikimedia Foundation, Inc. 11 Nov. 2012. Web. 11 Nov. 2012. <http://en.wikipedia.org/wiki/David_Farragut>

BIBLIOGRAPHY

1. **"Union Jack Bicycling Helmet" Book cover image**
    a. Courtesy of © 2012 Nutcase, Inc. 24 Sep. 2012, <http://www.nutcasehelmets.com>.
2. **"Hannah On the Seashore Cliffs with Pegasus" xiv-xv**
    a. Hue, Édouard. Public performance of the Cadre noir. 19 May 2012, Creative Commons BY-SA 3.0, <http://bit.ly/QCWqKS>.
    b. Heron, Stephen. A Mallard duck displays its wing feathers in a pond in Bushy Park, Dublin. 27 Oct. 2012, Creative Commons BY 2.0, <http://bit.ly/U0bsVA>.
    c. Kainickara, Manjith. Up in the air.... 9 Sep. 2010, Creative Commons BY-SA 2.0, <http://bit.ly/UYqNqB>.
    d. Abello, Balam. Model with arms stretched out. 17 Oct. 2012.
3. **"Map of the Caribbean" 18-19**
    a. Purushotham, Ishwar (ipurush). Compass Rose. 4 Oct. 2008, Creative Commons 1.0 Universal (Public Domain), <http://bit.ly/QAdMoL>.
4. **"Power generation Windmill Farm" 21**
    a. Fuzzy901. Windmills near Palm Springs, as shot from the freeway. 24 Aug. 2006, Creative Commons BY-SA 3.0, <http://

bit.ly/tlS4iE>.

5. **"Hanging Casseroles, Pots and Pans" 24**
    a. Jebulon. Collection of copper saucepans in kitchen of Vaux-le-Vicomte Castle. 10 Sep. 2010, Public Domain, <http://bit.ly/Qfvlbz>.
6. **"Flamingos Flying off of La Guajira" 27**
    a. Garg, J.M. Greater Flamingoes (Phoenicopterus roseus) taking off. 31 Aug. 2009, Creative Commons BY 3.0, <http://bit.ly/ss41D2>.
    b. Garg, J.M. Greater Flamingoes (Phoenicopterus roseus) taking off. 31 Aug. 2009, Creative Commons BY 3.0, <http://bit.ly/rvkDtE>.
7. **"La Esmeralda, a Spanish Hacienda-style Home" 34**
    a. Los Angeles. Courtyard at Temple Mansion, City of Industry, California. 4 May 2008, Creative Commons BY-SA 3.0, <http://bit.ly/rCN21U>.
    a. Public Domain Photos.com. The image of a beautiful fountain. 12 Feb. 2012, Public Domain, <http://bit.ly/OETTdm>.
8. **"Wolfgang and Jaséle on their wedding day" 47**
    a. Inaglory, Brocken. Bride and groom at the ruins of Sutro bath. 1 Oct. 2009, Creative Commons BY-SA 3.0, <http://bit.ly/Qz0f2I>.
    b. Frostnova. Ocean Vista. 9 Oct. 2007, Creative Commons BY 2.0, <http://bit.ly/skISRB>.
    c. Marcuswsims. Cabo de La Vela. 5 July 2007, Creative Commons BY 2.0, <http://bit.ly/rSs02W>.
9. **"Wolfgang's dream —Nude Lady Galloping on Horseback with Sword" 52-53**
    a. Allen, Larissa. Friesian Horse. 27 Apr. 2009, Creative Commons BY-SA 3.0, <http://bit.ly/U52RC5>.
    b. Michael (Freehorseriding). A nude young woman riding a brown horse bareback. 17 Sep. 2007, Creative Commons BY-SA 3.0, <http://bit.ly/NWjPWo>.
    c. Courtesy of Joanne (Tigg-stock). Sword fight. Reference stock 20. 21 Sep. 2008, <http://bit.ly/Q9HP6X>.
    d. Rogilbert. Un Katana moderne et son fourreau. 19 Aug. 2007, Public Domain, <http://bit.ly/OBxy0p>.
    e. Nas2. Blooming Canola field (Brassica napus), located in East

Central Saskatchewan. 24 Fe. 2012, Creative Commons 1.0 Universal (Public Domain), <http://bit.ly/Pc0go4>.

f. Poon, Wing-Chi & Kjetil r. Cumulus clouds towering over yellow prairie. 9 Dec. 2007, Creative Commons BY-SA 2.5, <http://bit.ly/TD2u5I>.

10. "Jaséle Laying Naked on her Side" 57

a. Fabiano, Fabien & Colporteur. Nude. Original etching by French artist Fabien Fabiano. 24 May 2006, Creative Commons BY 3.0, <http://bit.ly/Q9I4is>.

11. "Like Waves Crashing Loudly on Shore" 59

a. E. Rosset-Granger & Kilom691. Flotsam, 1853-1934. 28 Dec. 2009, Public Domain, <http://bit.ly/SypGTr>.

12. "Breakfast the Morning after the Wedding" 60

a. Unknown. Ready for the wedding reception to begin, Merthyr, 1894. 27 Sep. 2011, Public Domain, <http://bit.ly/U53awA>.

b. Bencherlite. The Arcade. 5 Nov. 2011, Creative Commons BY-SA 3.0, <http://bit.ly/S830mr>.

13. "Carnivals in Barranquilla" 73

a. Jdvillalobos. Cumbiamba La Pollera Colorada. Gran Parada de Tradición, 2007. 20 Mar. 2008, Public Domain, <http://bit.ly/vUaeQB>.

b. Ruca. Bailarines del Carnaval de Barranquilla. 19 Aug. 2007, Public Domain, <http://bit.ly/s2Mk2T>.

14. "Port of Barranquilla" 98

a. Jdvillalobos. Barranquilla's port. 25 Nov. 2011, Creative Commons BY 3.0, <http://bit.ly/Pjz1eF>.

b. Tabaš, Bratislav. Cumulus Clouds from Montenegro. 15 Jun. 2008, Public Domain, <http://bit.ly/QFDCYf>.

15. "Aluminum Bleachers" 117

a. Allen, Chuck. Liv running the bleachers at HHS. 3 Apr. 2010, Creative Commons BY-SA 2.0, <http://bit.ly/QEiEFL>.

b. Ensign_beedrill. Stadium electric lighting. 5 Jul. 2012, Creative Commons BY-SA 2.0, <http://bit.ly/Qz2ray>.

16. "Panama Canal Crossing" 125

a. Wollstadt, Roger. Panama Canal — Looking Back. 5 Dec. 2012, Creative Commons BY-SA 2.0, <http://bit.ly/RyHzA7>.

17. "Willemstad Bay" 128-129

a. Melendez, Marcos (Mtmelendez). Tourist section of the Willemstad Harbor in Curacao. 23 Jul. 2008, Creative Commons BY-SA 3.0, <http://bit.ly/P5GlJ1 1.0 Universal.

18. "Sleeping Beauty & Robert" 139

a. Farber, Matteo (emmeffe6). Sleeping Beauty. 4 Nov. 2009. Creative Commons BY 2.0, <http://bit.ly/REC0KY>.

19. "Andrew's Hiding Place" 146-148

a. Alfvanbeem. Containers at Antwerp. 31 Aug. 2012, Creative Commons 1.0 Universal (Public Domain), <http://bit.ly/QEj8Md>.

b. Harden, Zachary. Flag of the United Kingdom, Union Flag. 8 Sep. 2008, Public Domain, <http://bit.ly/TKklGu>.

20. "Athena in a Severe Storm" 156-157

a. Beem, Alf van. MSC Daniela – IMO 9399002 – Call sign 3FIA2. 27 Apr. 2012, Creative Commons 1.0 Universal (Public Domain), <http://bit.ly/QAfciM>.

b. Cates, Dean M. Waves break over the Ticonderoga-class guided-missile cruiser USS Bunker Hill (CG 52). 28 Dec. 2011, Public Domain, <http://bit.ly/Q9IuoQ>.

c. Ganguly, Biswarup. A squall passed over Alipore. 17 May 2011, Creative Commons BY 3.0, <http://bit.ly/UFebXB>.

d. Liebgard. The TS Bremen encountered stormy waves for 24-hrs. on its last Atlantic crossing for the Norddeutscher Lloyd. 20 Jan. 2012, Creative Commons BY 3.0, <http://bit.ly/Nl1ukc>.

e. Shimada, Allen & NOOA Photo Library. A common view in the vicinity of the Aleutian Islands. 20 Dec. 2010, Creative Commons BY 2.0, <http://bit.ly/Nl1y3w>.

21. "Athena's Container Yard lit up in the Storm" 170-171

a. Morard, Jean-Gabriel (jgmorard). 090316.044.Chateau. 15 Mar. 2009, Creative Commons BY 2.0, <http://bit.ly/P8pG7U>.

22. "Hannah Receives a Medal for Her Bravery at Sea" 180-181

a. Evans, James R. Capt. Bruce Lindsey, commanding officer aircraft carrier USS Carl Vinson salutes scouts while moored in Port Klang, Malaysia. 26 Jan. 2011, Public Domain, <http://bit.ly/PXihHr>.

b. Ries, Gunnar (Amphibol). Das Dockland, futuristisches Bürogebäude am Kopf des Edgar-Engelhard-Kais in Hamburg-

Altona. 9 Nov. 2006, Creative Commons BY-SA-2.5, <http://bit.ly/Om1tOo>.

c. Pan, Jimmy C. An Italian navy visit, board, search and seizure team member secures the flight deck aboard the Military Sealift Command container and roll-on/roll-off ship USNS LCP. 3 Jun. 2010, Public Domain, <http://bit.ly/U53XgU>.

d. Green, Charles. Okinawa, Japan (November 14, 2006) - Former dock landing ship USS Harpers Ferry (LSD 49) commanding officer Commander Marlin C. Anthony is saluted by his fellow shipmates as he departs the ship. 22 Oct, 2009, Public Domain, <http://bit.ly/UFeAcy>.

e. Piotrus. Tekkoshocon at David L. Lawrence Convention Center (2010). 22 Dec. 2011, Creative Commons BY-SA-3.0, <http://bit.ly/Nl1Ozm>.

f. Brunlich, Gerhard. Coat of arms of Aussersihl, Zürich, Switzerland. 18 Dec. 2007, Public Domain, <http://bit.ly/TD5kaR>.

g. Matlock, Terry. SUBIC BAY, Philippines (Oct. 31, 2011) Sailors pose for a group photo with U.S. Ambassador to the Republic of the Philippines Harry K. Thomas Jr. 3 Nov. 2011, Public Domain, <http://bit.ly/OBAqdF>.

23. "Wolfgang shows Hannah a Modern Building in Dusseldorf" 186-187

a. Perlblau. Medienhafen by Frank O. Gehry in Düsseldorf. 15 May 2006, Creative Commons BY 2.0, <http://bit.ly/NWlkUy>.

24. "Paul Jones Stadion" 208-209

a. Addicks, Johann H. Paul-Janes-Stadion in Düsseldorf-Flingern. 5 Jun. 2009, Creative Commons BY-SA 3.0, <http://bit.ly/Qoz7SC>.

25. "On the Runway" 213

a. Fashion, Lover of. Photo from Spring/Summer 2010 runway show Toronto. Dec. 5, 2009, Public Domain, <http://bit.ly/TVzHbF>

26. "A skateboard truck" 216

a. Tp. A skateboard truck. May 22, 2005, Creative Commons 1.0 Universal, <http://bit.ly/Z2ZfZ>

27. "Hannah's Crew" 218-219

a. Mayorga, René. Tango / Show callejero de tango en peatonal

Lavalle, Buenos Aires Argentina. 13 Mar. 2008, Creative Commons BY-SA 2.0, <http://bit.ly/P5I2WN>.

b. Nutcase, Inc. Nutcase Union Jack Helmet. Courtesy of © 2012 Nutcase, Inc. 24 Sep. 2012, <http://www.nutcasehelmets.com>.

c. PJ Rhymeswithsausage. 2011 Natioinal Beard & Mustache Championships. 8 Oct. 2012, Creative Commons BY-SA 2.0, <http://bit.ly/VBOuG1>

28. "Raina pops an Ollie" 223

a. Gómez, Paula. fk kickflip, campeonato. Dec. 12, 2011, Creative Commons BY-SA-3.0, <http://bit.ly/Zn7aiW>

29. "Raina's red lipstick smile" 226

a. Burrluck, Lucy. Untitled. Apr. 17, 2008, Creative Commons BY 2.0, <http://bit.ly/Rso7GJ>

30. "Johanna, Karla and Stefan on the Soccer Field" 232-233

a. Lissoy. Duck Samford Stadium in Auburn, Alabama. 12 Aug. 2011, Creative Commons BY-SA-3.0, <http://bit.ly/UFeYId>.

b. Goyak, Brian. Lt. j.g. Phillip McCorvey and a member of the local Equatorial Guinea soccer team exchange soccer balls signed by the members of each team. 23 Oct. 2009, Public Domain, <http://bit.ly/ROvkOM>.

31. "Hannah and her crew take the tram in Dusseldorf" 239

a. Saviour1981. Low Floor Tram NF8U at Second Christmas Day. 6 Jan. 2012, Creative Commons BY-SA-3.0, <http://bit.ly/Pc3nfA>.

32. "Club Sensation White" 242-243

a. Skatebiker & Magnus Manske. Sensation White 2007 Fireworks. 24 Apr. 2009, Creative Commons BY-SA 3.0, <http://bit.ly/T4X30x>.

33. "Robert's Engagement Ring" 248

a. Sutphin, Rhett. MGP2079.JPG Engagement Ring. 24 Dec. 2007, Creative Commons BY 2.0, <http://bit.ly/Nl2a9b>.

34. "Stefan on a Skateboard" 251

a. Moe-zie. Photo session of skaters in my city Alexandria, Egypt. 14 Sep. 2010, Public Domain, <http://bit.ly/UFf9TJ>.

35. "Dusseldorf, South Park, Time Fields Sculpture" 254

a. Kan, Ethan. Volksgarten, Düsseldorf, North Rhine-Westphalia, DE. 4 Jul. 2006, Creative Commons BY-SA 2.0, <http://bit.ly/OBAZUT>.

36. **"Hannah and Stefan sitting on a bench in South Park" 259**
    a. Cincooldesigns. Lake. 19 Oct. 2009, Creative Commons BY 2.0, <http://bit.ly/Nl2c0W>.

www.ingramcontent.com/pod-product-compliance
Lightning Source LLC
Chambersburg PA
CBHW062128170626
46813CB00002B/605
* 9 7 8 0 9 8 8 5 8 0 6 0 2 *